Strange as Angels

Voices of the Dead: Book Four

Victoria Raschke

ALSO BY VICTORIA RASCHKE

Who by Water - Voices of the Dead: Book One

Our Lady of the Various Sorrows - Voices of the Dead: Book Two

"A Wand Needs a Witch"
in *The Magical Book of Wands* anthology

Like a Pale Moon - Voices of the Dead: Book Three

for Aleksander & Tiha

ACKNOWLEDGEMENTS

Getting to this final book in Jo's story has been its own tale of adventure with many companions along the way. For bringing the first physical book of the series into the world many thanks are owed to Eli Collier and Gryffin Ink Publishing and to A.J. Scudiere who read the first very bad draft of Who by Water and encouraged me to keep going. Thanks to Beth Terrell for keeping me going on subsequent versions of the first book and Christina Wilburn for her keen eye for detail. Jennifer Goode Stevens has been wonderful to work with as editor and has made me more careful and precise in my language and storytelling. The look of the books has all been the work and love of keifel a. agostini, and I am always grateful that he's my partner—in this particular adventure and life in general.

Though most books are sold online these days, nothing compares to walking into your local bookstore and finding a new gem recommended by a friend and neighbor. Flossie McNabb and her team at Union Ave Books are champions of the written word and writers. Special thanks to Davis Shoulders for working with me on events and many conversations about writing and publishing.

Trusted early readers make Jennifer's job less tedious and offer invaluable insight. Thank you to my colleagues at Griffyn Ink, D.B. Sieders and A.J. Scudiere, and to Su Fertall and Janet Neely for their comments and suggestions on this book and the others in the series. Mystie Thongs has also been an early reader for the series, and I especially appreciate her help in fine-tuning blurbs and marketing copy.

Working at home means I often need to get out of my house to get any writing done, and the folks at Wild Love Bakehouse always make me feel welcome in addition to making the best cafe latte in town. I don't know the exact percentage, but I'm guessing about two thirds of the series were written or edited on its premises. If you find yourself in Knoxville, Tennessee, you should find your way to Wild Love or one of its sister establishments—Old City Java or Pearl on Union.

And always, love and thanks to the friends and family who've read the books; supported me through research, writing, and travel; come to events; and championed the books to others. The list is long, and I've made it my mission to thank them when I see them. Special, heartfelt gratitude goes to Boris Novak, Melody Dobbins, and Summer Albin for having the uncanny ability to offer kind, kind words about my work when I needed it more than they could know.

Lastly, but most importantly, thank you for reading and making this all worthwhile.

A note on Slovenian pronunciation

Slovenian uses a few extra characters.
č is pronounced like the ch in church.
š is pronounced like the sh in shirt.
ž is pronounced like the second g in garage.
Familiar letters are pronounced differently.
e is most often pronounced like a in bay.
i is most often pronounced like the e in be.
j is pronounced like a y.
r without a paired vowel is pronounced like the ir in skirt.

CAST

Jo Wiley - a Voice of the Dead, tea slinger, and the reborn Queen of the Witches

Morana - the Slavic goddess of death and winter, life and rebirth; Queen of the Witches

Dušan Črnigad - Jo's ex, Faron's father, and Črnobog, Black God of Slavic myth

Rok Zorko - a Long-Lived, Jo's friend with benefits and a man of many names and secrets

Vesna Kos - Jo's best friend and business partner, a witch, and the Witchfinder

Igor - an artist, a witch, and Vesna's boyfriend

Faron Črnigad Wiley - Jo's son and the resurrected White God, Belinus

Ivanka Novak - Faron's girlfriend and the oldest of the Novak witch sisters

Veronika Novak - Ivanka's sister and a powerful witch

Ana Novak - the youngest Novak sister

Frédéric Berkane - the chef at Renegade Tea

Reka - the current dishwasher at Renegade Tea

Rebecca Wiley - Jo's Civil-War-era great-grandmother

Goran Kralj - Jo and Vesna's neighbor and a witch

Gregor Bregant - Jo's best friend and chosen big brother

Other assorted deities and ghosts

"All the gods, all the heavens, all the hells, are within you."
Joseph Campbell

CHAPTER 1

Long before Jolene Wiley, the last Voice of the Dead, had ever been born, the gods had made a plan for her. But the memory of a god is like the thread wound onto a spindle. As the twisted fiber winds over itself again and again, the images and experiences of a life blur together. Črnobog, the dark god of Slavic myth, often asked himself if he was watching or if he remembered, Morana kneeling, raging into a gray sky. Her unending scream cracked the ground beneath her, the dust disappearing into the spreading fractures and leaving her alone on hardpan.

Her grief flayed him, laying bare his complicity in casting her into the Nav. Dažbog, the sun god, had loved her—as did Črnobog and many others—but the Sun is a jealous god, and he had not wanted to share her affection.

With Črnobog's keys in hand, Dažbog had forced Morana into the underworld where she would rule over the dead alone. Dažbog wanted to believe she would beg him to come to her—to set her free or to rule by her side. Instead, she had exploded into a rage, withering every leaf and darkening the sky of the Nav.

Her anger also drew the sun god back. The scream had been unceasing, and the other gods begged him to rethink what he had done. Dažbog was still too jealous to let her go, but he had gone to sit with her on the newly barren plain. The black outlines of what had been trees jutted out of the ground in the distance. Beyond them, the throngs of dead waited, too frightened to approach their new queen.

Morana opened her eyes and closed her mouth, pulling her cracked lips together into a grim line. The look she gave Dažbog was enough to make even a god's blood run cold.

Črnobog could see the sun god's dark thoughts turning. Even in her altered circumstances, Morana's self-possession was a reminder of why Dažbog had wanted her dragged to the Nav to begin with. If released, she would return to the world, to her old ways, and Dažbog's jealousy wouldn't bear it. He had no problem cavorting with random nature spirits and the occasional human, but the Sun wanted his lovers enthralled only to him.

"If you aren't going to talk, why bother coming?" Morana stood. The dust clung to her robes, but where it dulled Dažbog's clothes, it added a shimmer to hers. Without speaking again, she walked away from him, heading toward the dead trees on the horizon, claiming the Nav as her own with each footfall.

"I came to ask you, on behalf of the others—" He ran the few steps to catch up to her.

"You needn't have bothered. I've made my own arrangements." She didn't stop or look back to talk to him.

"What do you mean?"

"You underestimated Črnobog."

Dažbog ran another few steps to get in front of her, to face her. "He only gave me the keys. This has nothing else to do with him."

"Who has the keys now? Črnobog played you, and because you're here, I don't have to be."

With her words, an opening back to the living plane appeared. A lush, green forest lay beyond the door. As she crossed the threshold, the leaves on the trees began to twist and turn, transforming into reds and golds. She turned and spoke her last words to a thwarted Dažbog before disappearing through the opening, "The spring will come for you."

As Morana reentered the world, Črnobog's view, his memory, shifted. He watched her as the forest changed around her. Her expression softened as the breeze chilled and the animals of the woods hurried to their dens to hibernate. She was grateful for this reprieve. It was not the world awakening, as it did with the spring. It was not the full ripeness of summer, when the air itself tasted of growth. Morana, once the goddess of life, would come to rule the living only during the autumn and winter, the seasons of death and rest.

She walked out of the forest and into the open valley of the river. Črnobog waited for her in the tall grass at the water's edge with a harvest feast of welcome.

She sat among the reeds and took an apple from the offered basket. The long days of summer ran down her chin, and she wiped the juice away with the back of her hand. Morana smirked and took another bite of the fruit. Her eyes closed as she savored all that she had been separated from. "I knew you would never give anyone exactly what they asked for. Even me." Her laugh was the sound of ice-covered limbs chiming in a breeze. "Dažbog should have known."

"Dažbog will have a long winter to ponder his actions." Črnobog ran a hand over the sparkling dust on the hem of her dark robes. She watched as it crystallized into thousands of tiny gems. "I hope you will remember there is beauty in the darkness."

Morana looked out over the setting sun's light playing on the surface of the river and into the long futures of the gods. Their time was limited. Not in the way the lives of mortals were limited, but by their own inability to weather the changes that would come. Half the year. That was the deal she had struck with Črnobog, and she would have to live with it.

Črnobog took her hand, but there was no warmth in her touch. They had been lovers once, but she didn't trust him and was wise enough to know that other betrayals would come. He had welcomed her with a feast and a place to rest after her journey from the Nav, but as she lay dreaming of evergreen forests and deep snows, he would take the seed of spring from her heart and plant it along the river. Vesna, goddess of the earth's renewal, would emerge to overtake Morana as the seasons turned.

Vesna, this new goddess of the spring, would be the one to welcome Dažbog when he returned, and she would rule the bright half of the year by his side. But she would never love him as Morana had, because she knew he was jealous from the beginning.

Many seasons turned, and Črnobog's long memory held the image of Morana standing in the barje watching the river swell with the first snowmelt. She waited for Vesna as she watched the crocus push their heads through the crusted snow. She and Vesna had made their peace, a dance of sorts, as the seasons changed. Vesna knew life and death were intertwined and that she could not green the earth without Morana's long winter of work. They didn't become adversaries as Črnobog had expected, but sisters.

Mortals, however, understood this dance of life and death less and less as the season cycle rolled on. They cowered in their houses, fearing the long winter and the dying season. They feared Morana's embrace and prayed only to Vesna for their safety. Soon they prayed to new gods brought first from Greece and Rome, then the East. These new deities didn't embrace the cycle of birth and decay but instead promised to vanquish death and the old ways with it. Morana became the hag they feared when they forgot darkness wasn't a punishment but a necessity that allowed the light to burn. The mortals in power turned on those they believed to be in league with devils and witches when their new gods didn't protect them from plague and famine. Črnobog lost his ancient name and became the devil, a symbol of evil.

No matter the state of the world, spring always appeared at the river's edge. And Morana walked into the icy water at winter's end, returning to the dead, her heart heavier each time. Those righteous in the new gods tortured and burned or hanged the women, the men, and even the children they believed still prayed to her. She felt every death and gathered them to her in the Nav, but she could offer them no further comfort.

Dažbog grew envious and spiteful of the new gods. In resignation, he sought out one of the witches known as a Portal, a door to mortal life, and died an old man. His shade went then to Morana to ask her forgiveness. She could only welcome him into the desolation of the Nav with the others.

With Dažbog's death, the work of the green world and the light half of the year fell to Vesna alone. She asked Morana for help, but fewer and fewer people did anything but pray for the perceived safety of spring. They drowned witches and effigies of the goddess of death and winter in an effort to please Vesna and the new gods. They tore down statues of the old deities and dragged them through the streets. Morana's power receded, and she became a ghost story—a demon like Črnobog—to frighten children into saying their prayers and doing their chores.

The throngs of the dead grew, uncomforted in an underworld blanketed with Morana's sorrow, until she could no longer bear their weight. She sought out one of her daughters who had been imprisoned for believing in the old ways, another Portal. Morana offered the condemned woman a quick death and took her place at the stake.

Through the flames, Morana had watched the mortals cheer and laugh as a witch and a heretic burned. She screamed her last vision of the future into the sky as the fire consumed her: A trio of sisters would come and bring the witches out of hiding. Črnobog had taken her words and kept them, another seed to be planted.

Long after Morana's death, he stood alone in the flat, gray light of the Nav. Centuries are nothing to a god, but the world of mortals had completely changed. There were glimmers of a return to faith in the old ways, but his transformation into a god of the darkness was complete. There was a measure of power in being the very embodiment of evil, and he warmed to the role. Every human epoch required a trickster. The same group of mortals who had burned Morana at the stake had made it their work to stamp out belief in magic, in miracles, in him, and in all gods who walked among humans. They created a Council, which became the near-constant irritant called the Board.

He had watched as his fellow gods embraced oblivion until he stood with only a handful of those too stubborn to give in. He kept record of every child born to a family of Voices—those women, descended from the gods, who could make the dead speak—paying special attention to the few still marked as Portals. He wanted those doors closed to the remaining gods should they choose to give in. He tracked every Long-Lived—who like the Voices were the offspring of gods and humans—and had convinced a few to follow him and the other remaining old gods. But there were so few of them left.

A Long-Lived who had been called Linditus, among his many other names, watched over one of the last line of Voices, looking in on each generation to see if a Portal was among them. That last existing line of Voices, the Wileys, had produced a single woman in the most recent generation. Her mother was unstable and violent, and her aunt was resentful of the burden of their legacy. Neither had trained the child, and they had ignored the signs that the girl Jolene—Jo, as she called herself—was more than a Voice. Črnobog asked his ally (and one of the few remaining gods with any power) Achelous—as the ancient god of the waters had been named by the Greeks—to protect her. Achelous had taken his charge further than Črnobog had asked; he hid Jolene Wiley's powers from her with a whisper in her ear the day her father had been killed.

Črnobog had been angered at first, but it had protected her in ways he hadn't foreseen. She was of interest to the Board, who worked so diligently to keep what they deemed the supernatural hidden from the world, but only as a curiosity and not as a threat. The few remaining gods who might have wished to step through her into a mortal life ignored her, other than to believe that her lack of abilities was proof that the Voices were dying out and the old gods would fall in their time.

Jo's secret had given him time to lay his plan.

CHAPTER 2

Jo Wiley lay curled on her side in the mud. She hadn't known a body could contain enough water to cry for days on end. There had been no food, nothing to drink. She breathed because she had to, and she cried because there was nothing else to do. Črnobog, the god of darkness, the father of her only child, had taken everything away from her, including her name. And she had let him.

Rok, who had been her friend and often her lover for almost half her life, had betrayed her at Črnobog's request. He'd pushed her into an unchecked rage to open an abyss in the middle of her apartment, and they had landed in the underworld—where Rok had called her Morana, Queen of the Witches, Goddess of Life and of the Dead. In the days before that, she had lost … she had lost more than she could bear to name, but their names had come anyway, repeating in her head like a litany. She had let herself love Leo, had tried to make things work after he had left the church, but he had been taken from her by his own guilt and a revenant of his past. She had buried too many friends and watched those who remained be scattered to the wind by Dušan, the man Črnobog pretended to be when he walked among humans. His last betrayal, which had been planned from the first moment he had known of her existence, had landed her there in a swamp of her own tears, alone except for his spy.

Rok had stayed away from her at first. Then he'd tried to comfort her, but she was inconsolable. He left again as the marsh around her grew, but she could still feel his presence out beyond where the cattails had begun to sway.

A drop of cold water hit her cheek. Another landed on her eyebrow, followed by an icy bead in her ear. She took a ragged breath and sat up. Marsh sedges had grown up around her, and her body left a bare spot in the undergrowth where she had lain. The sky was gray, but not the flat gray it had been on her arrival. It was turbulent with the dark edges of a thunderhead growing. Off in the distance, a lightning bolt zagged from cloud to cloud, illuminating the underbelly of the approaching storm.

Rok came to her. His footfalls no longer rang in the emptiness but squelched in the soft mud. A spark of anger jolted through her vision, an echo of the lightning, but faded quickly leaving an afterimage on her retina. He didn't smile at her. That would have been too much. He may have gotten played by Dušan, but Rok wasn't a complete fool.

Jo raked her hand over her crown and pushed a matted lock of hair behind her ear before the rain could plaster it to her face. She disturbed a damsel fly in the movement, and it paused in her field of vision—bright blue against the clouds—before disappearing. Her weeks of ugly crying had brought life to what had been the desolate wasteland of the Nav. What was the punishment for that?

Rok stood in front of her and offered her a hand up.

His beard had grown almost to his chest, and his eyes had changed. They had always been a warm brown but had taken on a deeper cast and glinted with flecks of copper. She took his hand and pulled herself up from the muck, naked. Her clothes had rotted into the bog in the days or weeks she had been there.

The breeze chilled her damp skin. The sensation of cold had become so familiar to her. She had been cold to her core since the night her friend Helena had been murdered. Irreverent, mischievous Helena. Jo hoped she had found peace in the Next, or whatever the afterlife turned out to be, and hadn't been thrown down into the Nav with her again. Rok hadn't looked her in the eye yet, and she hadn't found her voice. It was for the best, really. She didn't have anything to say. Or at least not anything nice.

A warm robe settled over her shoulders. Jo turned to find Dušan standing behind her in his full Black God glory. He towered over her, his skin and hair the color of midnight, his eyes star-filled windows to faraway skies. He ran his fingertips over her temple, pushing her damp hair behind her ear again, the tenderness surprising and disarming. Minutes before she would have flailed against him in her anger. Now she waited.

———

Vesna Kos, the sister of Jo Wiley's heart, stood on the rocky coast of the Isle of Man near Castletown. Igor, her lover who could see into the future in his own way, was back at the crofter's cottage they had shared in the months since leaving Ljubljana in the wake of events that had left her Uncle Leo and her mother dead. The wind carried shards of the hard winter to come. Igor would have the tea on and the bread toasted to nestle on a plate of fried eggs. He had been uncommonly good to her, considering she had dragged him from his life and work with no thought of when they could return.

She squinted into the sunrise, waiting for their guests. Two seagulls coasted toward her, dipping and turning in the offshore wind. The morning light reflected on a golden chain that tethered the two birds together. Vesna turned as the gulls blurred past her and landed somewhere in the emerald grass between her and the cottage. Two women, dressed warmly in woolen coats and knee-high boots, appeared from behind a green hillock and waved to her. That they were sisters was obvious; massive red manes and milky white skin gave them the air of tourist board ambassadors for Gaelic lands.

"*Moghrey mie,* Vesna!" Fand, the elder sister, smiled as Vesna approached.

"*Dobro jutro.*" The sisters had taught her a bit of the dead Manx language, and the syllables rolled off Vesna's tongue more easily now. But she remained self-conscious about her pronunciation, so she stuck to her native Slovenian or English. "Igor has breakfast on."

"Good. I'm famished." Lí Ban, the younger sister, pulled her collars up around her ears.

Vesna led the women to the small cottage tucked into a rolling sea of technicolor green. Smoke curled from the chimney against the faint glow from Castletown awakening beyond. The cold had found its way into every gap in her clothes, and she was grateful for the fire Igor had stoked into a comforting crackle in the grate.

Fand and Lí Ban hung their coats on pegs by the door and went to the hearth to warm their hands. Igor scooped Vesna into a hug against his lanky body and landed a kiss near her ear with a whisper. "Are you going to settle this today?"

Vesna nodded, pulled away, and bade their guests join them at the scrubbed farm table for breakfast. Antony mewed at her from under a chair and turned up his black and white face. "Did you feed them?"

"Yes, but not eggs and bacon. I'm sure he and Cleo are more interested in our breakfast than whatever mystery meat is in those cans." Igor intercepted Cleopatra, the orange tabby, as she leapt onto another chair and made aim for the table.

The cats' arrival had been a surprise. Dušan had arranged for Antony and Cleopatra to go to a long-term sitting service when she and Igor had left Ljubljana in the early summer. She had said her goodbyes thinking she would never see them again, but within days of finding and renting the cottage, still following Dušan's directions and holding passports with unfamiliar names, a blonde mountain of a woman had arrived balancing herself with a carrier in each hand.

Lí Ban and Fand laughed as they took their places at the table. Fand spread her napkin in her lap. "I'm sure a little egg couldn't hurt."

"No, but they won't leave you alone if you feed them." Igor deposited Cleopatra on the tidily made bed in the corner and joined them at the table.

Vesna had surprised herself with how quickly she had grown accustomed to the cottage. It did have a few modern conveniences. She wasn't up for no electricity or an outhouse and was happy the place had been connected to power and water and had a serviceable, if tiny, bathroom added in what had to have been a lean-to.

Vesna poured them all tea and dug into the hearty breakfast Igor had put together. It paid to lay in some fuel to get through the increasingly colder days.

"Lí suggested on the way here that this breakfast might be a working meeting." Fand took a bite of toast and looked at Vesna, pointedly.

"I wouldn't presume to keep anything hidden from the two of you." Vesna pushed a lock of dark hair behind her ear. It had taken weeks to get a response to her seaside offerings, and she hadn't wanted to rush into an ask in the early days.

The sisters were nearly all that was left of their pantheon. There were a few others, including Mannan, Fand's husband. He kept to himself, rarely coming ashore to interact with the modern world. But Lí Ban and Fand were the only two who had answered Dušan's invitation to meet Vesna and Igor at the cottage. Dušan had seen the Isle of Man as a mostly neutral location for the British Isle deities. Apparently the deities themselves had not seen it that way, or so Fand had explained on her first visit with her sister in tow.

"I'm guessing you already know what Dušan sent us here for." Vesna set her fork on her plate and looked into Fand's face. The woman's eyes were as green as the grass carpeting the coastline around them and as dangerous as the sea cliffs.

"We do." Fand's gaze didn't waver.

Lí Ban nodded in agreement with her sister but didn't speak.

Igor picked up the empty teapot and returned to the

kitchenette to make more.

Fand watched him at the sink for a moment. "You are lucky to have a consort who doesn't mind serving."

Vesna snorted. Consort? She and Igor had grown closer in the months since they'd left Ljubljana, but she wasn't someone who had a consort.

Fand smiled. "I forget the two of you are mortals."

"This seems like a place where that is easy to forget." Igor leaned against the sink and waited for the water to boil.

Lí Ban nodded again, and Fand continued, "In this I am speaking for only Lí and myself. The others have no interest in dealing with Črnobog."

"I only know what Dušan, Črnobog, has shared with us, but I believe, though he extended the invitation to all of the remaining Tuatha Dé Danann, he will be grateful to any who join him." Vesna resented negotiating on Dušan's behalf, especially considering she didn't have all the facts and pretty much zero idea what she was really asking for.

Lí Ban muffled a laugh with a cough into her closed hand. "He would be. I don't think he really understands what he's asking of us or the others."

At mention of "the others," Vesna's thoughts tumbled out to the unknown whereabouts of their circle of friends from Ljubljana. She had believed them all dispatched on their own missions, or fool's errands. She hadn't heard from anyone else, but she sensed they were having similar luck to hers and Igor's. Being a seer was doing her precious little good in her current circumstances.

"What does Črnobog expect will happen if we, or anyone

else, join him?" Fand finished her eggs and swiped her toast through the last of the yolk pooled on her plate. "Our time has passed."

Vesna shrugged. Dušan—it was still difficult for her to think of him as Črnobog—had given them only the smallest amounts of information, enough to get them to the next place or to the next step in whatever plan he was devising. "He told me once that he wished for a reenchanted world, but he didn't elaborate on how he intended to make that happen."

Standing in his apartment that day was the first time she'd seen him as fully a god and fully as the man her friend had fallen in love with. He'd served wine in soap bubble thin glasses, and the two of them had stood in front of a triptych of photographs he'd taken of Jo in an orchard. Vesna had seen then that Dušan the man had fallen in love as well. She had guessed that hadn't been part of Črnobog the god's plan at all.

"You'll hear from him soon, but I wouldn't start packing. Not today anyway." Lí Ban pushed her plate away. "Thank you for a lovely breakfast. It was more than worth the trip."

Fand indicated her agreement. "Have you been to the witch museum in the town?"

"It closed. Some time ago." The two goddesses' sense of human time passing was amusing, but Vesna would have avoided the museum anyway, had it still existed. She was all too familiar with the one in her hometown of Ribnica, and she had no desire to stroll through another display of witch trials and Witchfinder sins.

"It wasn't like that, it was more about the work and lore

of witches." Lí smiled. "Oops. Sorry. But you were thinking rather loudly."

On the sisters' first visit, there had been an agreement that hospitality on both sides would be offered without strings attached, and that the two women of the Tuatha Dé Danann would not read Vesna's and Igor's minds. They had been true to their word until then, or so Vesna believed. She couldn't blame Lí Ban. Feelings about her family's crimes tended to crowd out any other thought she could have. And now that the title of Witchfinder had fallen to her, it was on her to make amends as best she could.

"It's fine. But you haven't said anything about what I should tell Dušan when he turns up." Vesna looked across the table for some measure of support from Igor.

"We haven't." Fand drained her teacup and set it back on the saucer. "Because we haven't decided."

"Let's finish the tea, then I think we could all use a walk." Igor poured another round before Cleopatra made a second attempt at the table.

CHAPTER 3

Bettine tucked her legs underneath her and skimmed again through the report Alessandro had submitted from Venice. He had been the closest Observer to Ljubljana after Gustaf Lichtenberg's murder and the events that followed, so the task of bringing the Board up to date on the whereabouts of the city's most troublesome supernatural residents had fallen to him.

She had read it thoroughly, many times. There was a certain pleasure in reading about one's own death. Maybe it was the dark heart wish of every Long-Lived to believe that Death waited for them with longing. Whatever the reason, she enjoyed the descriptions Alessandro had procured from the police and other witnesses in Ljubljana. Her body, or rather the body of her fetch, had burned in a fire the local police had said was from a malfunction of the explosives in her suicide bomb. Only mundanes would be more comforted by the lie of a terrorist threatening their city than by the truth that there were things far beyond their understanding.

Though it amused her to read the news of her death, there was something that had not made it into the report that troubled her. Her fetch had watched Jolene Wiley erupt in anger at the death of the weather witch Dušan had placed outside the hotel doors, and an earthquake had shaken the ground underneath them. Bettine had seen it happen through her fetch's eyes and had replayed the scene in her thoughts trying to determine if Jolene's anger and the temblor were related. The ability to cause earthquakes was not a known ability of the Voices. Perhaps it was nothing. And besides, Črnobog had been on the scene, meddling.

Bettine looked out the window of her Paris apartment as the Eiffel Tower came to life with twinkling lights against the dusk. Catching a glance just as it illuminated was a kind of magic. Though she had far more power at her fingertips, she believed this everyday enchantment was all the world really needed.

The Board was meeting the next evening. She and the two other Long-Lived who had taken positions were going to have to reveal their bigger plan. Gustaf Lichtenberg's death may have been neatly covered up in Ljubljana as part of an act of terrorism, but the Board had already seen through that. There had been questions. The fact that her name, or a version of one of the many she'd used over the years, had been released to the public with the statements was a problem. The Board were none too happy about reporters and international police organizations sniffing around her life and affiliations.

She wouldn't be hopping a train to Slovenia anytime soon. Not that she needed to. Dušan Črnigad had scattered her quarry across Europe. He was the only one who had stayed in Ljubljana after the business with her fetch. She was sad to lose that one. Training a fetch to act in such a human manner had taken her years. The one she had now was little more than a housekeeper. Any future interactions with Črnigad and his crew would have to be in person. She didn't doubt her abilities against any modern dabbler. She'd learned her craft from some of the most powerful European witches who had lived, and she'd had a millennium to hone her abilities. Given the success of the Witchfinders and her faction of the Board over the centuries, she might be one of the most powerful magic users alive. She would never admit it out loud to another living being, but she did question what use human magic was against even a tired old god like Črnobog. There were other ways to thwart them though.

She frowned at the report and set it on the table next to the couch. There were a few mortals who were interested in the old gods and their old ways. The fascist ones didn't interest her much. Their gods weren't too interested in them either from what she could tell. But there were others who had taken on the whole resurrection of ancient beliefs with a surprisingly academic fervor. They lent credence and seriousness to a group who had previously been written off as kooks or hounded into secrecy with charges of practicing Satanic rituals and sacrificing babies. She had to hand it to the actual Satanists for pointing out the hypocrisy of the overculture, but their tactics and existence still fanned the flames of belief in the supernatural. The secular Satanists were as troublesome in the end, even though they probably agreed with her about the usefulness of magic.

She had spoken with Otto and Christina the previous day, to discuss how they would maneuver their takeover of the Board. They had hoped to enlist another Long-Lived before a takeover became absolutely necessary, but Dušan

Črnigad's—Črnobog's—actions made it clear they didn't have time to wait him out. She was curious as to why he had chosen to finally act, but his reasoning didn't matter as much as his timing did. If she was right about what she thought he was planning, he was about to plunge the entire world into chaos, beginning with Europe.

CHAPTER 4

Jo pulled the robe around her, admiring the tiny crystalline jewels that lay on the black fabric like frost. The rain began to fall more steadily. Dušan, in his true form as Črnobog, looked up at the roiling sky and turned his palm up. The rain pattered against an invisible pane suspended over their heads. Rok looked as surprised by the small magic as she was.

Every word she thought to utter stuck in her throat. Arguments and disappointments, anger and sorrow. What did she owe either of them? They had schemed together to bring her to this place, but it was too late to rail against them. What was done was done.

"Thanks for the cloak." Four words. It was a start.

"It isn't a gift. I was simply returning what belonged to you." Črnobog reached out to touch her again, but she wrapped her fingers around his wrist to stop him.

"I'm not ready to talk to you." She let go of him, and his arm dropped. Rok stood off to the side, watching. She didn't look at him, but she could easily imagine the expectant look he had on his face. "I want to see my father. And Helena, if she's here."

Črnobog hesitated but answered her. "Helena went into the Next when she attempted to save your priest."

Jo was relieved her troublesome though loved spirit guide had not been thrown into this place again because of her, but she was also selfishly disappointed that there was no one here who was truly her ally. "Leo was never mine." That fact had become clear to her in the long days she had spent literally crying a river into existence. Leo had loved her, but he had never belonged to her any more than she had belonged to him. And it had taken her right to the very end to choose him, so perhaps she had gotten exactly what she deserved. What had the Virgin Mary said to her on that day, when she had encountered her at the crossroads? *That is not the nature of love.* Jo wished she had understood that sooner, but she couldn't go back and change what had happened. If she was to go on existing until time stopped, she would carry the knowledge that they had both tried in their broken ways, however briefly. And she would not make the same mistake again.

"Your father is there, beyond the trees."

Jo looked out at the distant horizon. What had been blackened trunks scratching against the leaden sky with skeletal hands were now trees leafed out in the verdant gloss of high summer. The hardpan of earth beneath them had become a sea of grass, now a strange blue-green in the light of the storm.

Rok finally injected himself into the slow-motion tennis match of their conversation. "You're just going to let her walk off like that?"

"The Nav belongs to her. Nothing here would harm

her." Črnobog smiled, but it was more disconcerting than comforting given his current face. "Or you."

As Jo watched, Rok's eyes glowed with the warmth of the sun but—thankfully, for her retinas—not the intensity. Rok looked at Črnobog with confusion and hurt in his expression, though it was harder to tell with the bright, shiny god eyes thing going on.

"This wasn't part of the bargain."

"No one ever said the gods play fair." The threat of a smile played at the corner of Črnobog's mouth.

If Rok had trusted Dušan, well, he'd gotten what he deserved. Jo could only muster the smallest puddle of sympathy. Besides, she wasn't sure how much of an inconvenience it really was to add semi-divinity to a Long-Lived's resume. She walked away, leaving them to their pissing match, and headed toward the line of trees, looking back only once to make sure they weren't following her. The hem of her cloak dragged behind her and left a trail of swamp tulips and kingcups in her wake.

Would wonders never cease?

Please. Please let them cease.

She followed the river, a school of fish swimming alongside her, a few jumping occasionally for either her amusement or their own. Črnobog's magic followed her, and she stayed dry under the invisible umbrella until she neared what turned out to be an orchard of apple, plum, and cherry trees leafed out, in bloom, and laden with ripe fruit all at the same time. The air buzzed with pollinator wings, and under that, a din of human thoughts and voices hummed. Throngs of the dead had gathered under the trees, out of the rain. Now that she was aware of them, their thoughts crescendoed in her head. Centuries of confusion and loneliness overwhelmed her, and she sank to her knees in the wet grass, still far enough away that no one had noticed her.

A hand touched Jo's shoulder, and the voices stopped. She looked up expecting Črnobog, or whatever Rok had become, but it was a woman. Her face was as familiar as Jo's own, but she didn't have a name to go with it. The woman gathered her long pastel robes in her hands and sank to her knees in the wet grass and soft earth next to Jo.

"It seems to them that you have been gone a very long time." The woman gestured toward the dead milling about and picking fruit in the orchard. "But for me it seems like you were here yesterday."

Jo waited for the woman to continue speaking or to introduce herself, but she didn't. The two knelt there together, the rain thrumming above their heads, but Jo had finally had her fill of silence.

"Who are you?" She attempted to soften her tone, but the words still sounded accusatory.

The woman laughed. "Črnobog is a terrible host. Did he not tell you I was waiting for you?"

"No. He said I would find my father 'beyond the trees.'" Jo stood up and waved her hand at the orchard that had sprung up on the edge of the marsh.

The woman stood up next to Jo, facing the trees. "He's there." She didn't point or indicate where "there" was, but she continued, "He will be ready to see you soon, but not yet."

"You didn't answer my question."

"I didn't. It will be easier to show you."

Jo followed the woman as she walked farther along the river, growing more bemused and perturbed. Being a god, demi-god, or whatever she was, didn't get her any more direct answers than being a Voice of the Dead or a Portal had.

The woman led her farther from the orchard to where the river began to widen and slow. The fish that had been frolicking along beside her joined them and kept up a steady song of splashes and bloops as they leaped and twisted before diving or falling back into the river. Jo would have been happy to sit on the riverbank to watch the full show instead of following Ms. Cryptic Goddess Person to what would surely be another riddle wrapped in an enigma dressed up for her own frustration.

"It's not much farther now." Cryptic Goddess Person paused to chirp at the fish, and they all ended their Cirque du Soleil encore and simultaneously plopped back into the clear water and swam away.

"I was enjoying that."

"They were showing off."

Jo frowned at the back of the woman's head. She would show off, too, if she was a fish who could do a triple axel or whatever that was.

The river narrowed again briefly, and the two women had to hop over or ford a number of smaller brooks and creeks that either joined it or branched off from it. Jo couldn't tell, as the water sometimes seemed to move in two directions at the same time. As she was watching her step to avoid the numerous lizards and frogs who populated the riverbank, Jo didn't notice when the other woman stopped, and she ran into the back of her, almost taking them both down into the wet reeds.

"Sorry." Jo righted herself, straightened her cloak, and gathered another handful of the overly long hem to keep from tripping again, as the Cryptic Goddess Woman turned around to look at her. Her face was beautiful and unmarred by the fine lines one got from living and smiling and squinting against a bright sun's light. To say "her" seemed a bit presumptuous, though, now that Jo really looked at her. The features were both angular and softened, like a child's, and the flowing clothes could either be a gown or toga; there was nothing that marked her companion as woman or man. Made sense. Gods were many things and capable of existing in ways she couldn't wrap her brain around yet. A binary understanding of gender didn't really work with humans, so it probably didn't apply to gods either.

Past the Cryptic Deity Person's shoulders, the thing she'd been brought to see jutted up out of the green of the surrounding landscape. An egg-shaped geode the size of a house erupted from the earth, and the river they'd followed spilled out of one of the dazzling cracks in the surface. Refracted rainbows glinted off quartz, even in the dulled light from the stormy sky. It would have been too bright to look at for long in strong sunlight.

Jo brushed by her companion and walked closer to the Source. That was the word that popped into her head— "Source" with a capital S, maybe underlined and bold for good measure.

CHAPTER 5

Ivanka looked through the grit-frosted glass of the small window of their cottage. The contrast between the darkness inside and the sun-blind brightness outside made her think of old paintings obscured under layers of blackened lacquer. What did that make her? Some put-upon domestic toiling in a dim interior? She could clean the window later. Faron and Ana had gone to the rocky beach to look for shells and the occasional sea creature that would have Ana bubbling about their afternoon over dinner. Ivanka didn't see which way Veronika had struck out but knew she had gone for a walk, looking for the herbs their new teacher had sent her to find.

It was the first time Ivanka had been alone in days. The cottage was too small to offer anything like privacy. She and Faron had taken to evening walks to be away from her sisters long enough to have some physical connection. That was the only thing that made her feel like she hadn't floated off the earth or into the pages of the books of mythology she had devoured as a kid and thoroughly forgotten as an adult. All those hours spent fantasizing about living on a rock-strewn, bone-bleached island in the Aegean had not done much to prepare her for her current reality.

She picked up her hat and the book she was reading—a retelling of the story of the Gorgons that their new teacher, Clotilda, had given her—and stepped outside. There was one gnarled and spent olive tree next to the cottage that offered dappled shade in lieu of ever offering fruit again. She and Faron had moved the table and chairs underneath its branches the afternoon they had arrived, and the arrangement had become their de facto family room.

She needed a drink. It was always hot, except when a wind came from the ocean. Those days were tolerable. The nights were cool, and she had done more of her own exploring when she didn't have to squint even behind sunglasses. She placed the book on the table and walked back inside to rummage in the corner that served as their kitchen. Learning to cook and live with the bare amenities had been an adventure at first. The charm and novelty of life without electricity had long since worn off, and she'd stopped herself from making a calendar of tally marks on the front door on more than one occasion.

Their teacher brought ice when she visited their Greek island of exile—one of the many small miracles the woman performed. Veronika was entranced with her and had become a different person from the bitter avenger barely in control of her anger or her magic. The sadness Ana carried with her after Leo's death had lifted, and her youngest sister had found a sweetness in their enforced simplicity. It was only Ivanka who rankled under Clotilda's tutelage, but she held her unhappiness close and concealed her thoughts from her sisters. She had shared her concerns only with Faron, who had been understanding but unhelpful.

A few cubes floated in the water of the old-fashioned

aluminum ice chest, which meant the bottle of water inside was still cold. Ivanka poured her tin cup half full before holding the chilled metal against her chest. She closed everything up and returned to the driftwood gray table and her book, surprised to see an unannounced guest seated in the shade.

"Ivanka, I thought I might find you alone."

Where Clotilda lived or how she got there was never discussed. The woman had shushed Ana the first time she had asked and had since given anyone who'd been forward enough to inquire what could best be described as a mother's side eye. Ivanka had trouble remembering how they had even gotten there. She remembered taking the train to Zagreb and waiting for Veronika to join them at a boutique hotel Dušan's minion had checked them into. There had been a long car ride through the countryside, where their passports had been taken and replaced with ones with different names and countries of origin. And then they were on the island, living for what seemed like months in a cottage above the sea with nothing but sunlight and rocks and a privy that smelled like rotting seaweed and human funk. And there was Clotilda, the teacher Dušan had introduced them to, who was supposed to continue the lessons started by Goran after Veronika had killed Jo and nearly killed their sister Ana.

"I was alone." Ivanka settled at the table and looked out past Clotilda's intense gaze to where the blue of the sky blended into the blue of the water. She looked away before she again had that sensation of not being able to tell up from down.

"I won't take all of your solitude, but it is long past the time we had a chat." Clotilda gestured toward the book and the olive leaf Ivanka had tucked between the pages to mark her place. "You've almost finished."

"I know gods are real and that some of the stories are true or based in some truth, but the deeper I go, the more I realize that gods are just as imperfect as humans. And that their mistakes cause much more harm."

"Well observed. Anything else?" Clotilda thumbed the corner of the pages.

"Women always seem to end up as monsters."

Clotilda smiled a sad half smile. "Not always."

"Nothing ended well for Medusa." Ivanka pushed the book away. It was hard not to think about trios of sisters: the Gorgons, the Fates, and her family. Things weren't going great for them either. Her parents were dead. Her grandparents disowned them all after their mother and father had been killed. She had no idea what Dušan expected of them—only that he sometimes appeared and took Faron with him for a couple of days. Faron returned more changed. She laid on her cot on the nights he was gone, listening to the waves or her sisters murmuring in their sleep, and wished she could believe anything good was going to come of this adventure.

"You aren't a Gorgon." Clotilda picked up the book and tucked it into her bag. "Or a Moirae. Whatever Dušan may have said. Those jobs are taken."

"That's a relief." Every word that came out of her felt like a smirk, and she hated feeling like she'd reverted to petulant teenager.

"Dušan has been wrong about a lot of things. And I know he is wrong about you and your sisters."

Ivanka perked up at that. "And what does that mean?"

"The three sisters have come as Morana said they would. But they aren't you and Veronika and Ana." Clotilda looked behind her for a moment, as if she expected someone to join them. "We … I believe he was very wrong about that."

"Then who are the three sisters?" Jo had mentioned once how much she hated trying to get information out of supernatural beings, but humans could be equally cagey.

"Vesna Kos, Jolene Wiley, and you. But not like the Fates. More like the Rojenice."

"Rojenice? The old fairy women who come to make their pronouncements over babies?" Ivanka furrowed her brows at Clotilda. That made even less sense to her than Dušan's babbling on had.

"They aren't fairies, or not exactly. But they are truth tellers, predictors. They have always come in threes. I really thought you would put that together on your own." She looked behind her again.

"Are you expecting someone?" Clotilda's fidgeting made Ivanka nervous.

"No. But that doesn't mean he won't show up. Look, there are a few things you need to know before Črnobog pops up again to whisk your lover away." Clotilda took off her wide-brimmed hat and shook her hair out. The dark curls gleamed in the sunlight as she tossed her head.

Ivanka watched as the woman subtly transformed. Her skin glowed, and her eyes sparkled with the same metallic flecks as Faron's and Dušan's. Their new instructor in witchery wasn't human.

"I've tried to be good about not reading your thoughts, but you're thinking very loudly. And no, I'm not human."

"You're a Fate."

"Nicely spotted." Clotilda laughed.

"Clotilda? That isn't one of the sisters' names." Ivanka cocked an eyebrow at her.

"You try being Clotho in the modern world."

"The spinner. Like Ana."

"Ana is many things." Clotilda smiled. "And she may well be many more, but this is not her time."

"Was that the other thing I needed to know, that you were more than a random witch trainer Dušan found for us?"

"No. I think Črnobog has convinced Faron that his plan is going to work, but Črnobog has deluded himself. Gods really shouldn't spend so much time with humans. Makes us weird."

"What plan? You act like he or Faron has offered to clue the rest of us in."

"Don't you think it's odd that he sent you and the others so far away?"

Ivanka hadn't thought about it much past the idea that he was scattering them to protect them from the Board and whatever retaliation they had planned after Jo and Vesna had disturbed the peace of the mundanes in such a brazen fashion.

"Črnobog has ancient, dark powers. Do you really think he couldn't protect your little enclave in Ljubljana from humans, even the Long-Lived?"

Ivanka stood up and walked out into the sunlight, squinting toward the sea. "Okay, so why drag us here then?"

"You're here, Vesna's on some dot of land between Ireland and Great Britain, and Jo is, well, she's also far away. He may have figured out his mistake and made it hard for the three sisters to be in contact, spread so far apart."

"You know where Jo is? Faron asks after her every time Dušan shows his face, but Faron says he won't tell him anything." Ivanka looked back at Clotilda, hidden now in the shade.

"He wouldn't. And yes. She's in the Nav, but you can't tell Faron that. Not yet."

"The Nav?"

"The underworld. What do they teach you all at school?" The Fate laughed and stood to join her in the sun.

Ivanka rolled her eyes, though a better instruction in European mythologies would have been helpful. "You can't ask me to keep that from Faron."

"I would prefer Črnobog not know I revealed myself to you. There are still lessons to be learned."

Faron and Ana came into view, though they were still too far away to hear anything Ivanka and Clotilda said.

"If you do tell him. You'll have to swear him to secrecy. Thankfully, Črnobog can't see his thoughts."

"If Dušan knows we are the three sisters sent to fulfill Morana's prophecy, why would he want us separated?"

"Because the three of you are planners, doers. He doesn't want anyone fomenting rebellion. Not against him, anyway."

Clotilda laughed. "And, it would be better for you to call him Črnobog. That you think of him as merely a man lets you underestimate him. He isn't just a pain in the ass."

"Point taken. So what next?"

"I'm looking at some things. I just wanted you to know that you're right to be suspicious and unhappy here. It isn't a vacation." Clotilda put her hat back on. It shaded her now-very-human-looking face. "Don't tell your sisters yet. Let them enjoy this. Take your exile as time to study and prepare." She waved at Faron and Ana and turned to leave.

"You aren't going to wait for them? Ana will be disappointed." She didn't ask "prepare for what." She knew already that whatever it was wasn't good.

"I didn't come to see Ana today." Clotilda took three steps behind the cottage, brushing Ivanka's bare shoulder with her fingertips as she passed, and was gone as mysteriously as always. At least Ivanka now knew why. When Faron and Ana made it to the cottage, they were looking for Clotilda.

"You know how she is. She comes and goes like the breeze." Ivanka waved her hand in the air in a way that immediately make her think of Jo. What did it mean to be sisters with someone you weren't related to? Especially when that someone was your boyfriend's mom? She really didn't need her life to be any more complicated than it already was.

Ana frowned a little at Clotilda's disappearance but then quickly forgot she had a reason to be sad. She held up her pail filled with soft blue beach glass and other treasures they'd found among the rocks.

"Nice! And what will you do with those?" Every inch of

windowsill was covered in things Ana had already brought up from the beach.

Ana looked up at her and smiled. "What's for dinner?"

Ivanka wished she could be as unconcerned about the future as her baby sister.

CHAPTER 6

Jo crept closer to the Source. Its heartbeat—if that's what she was hearing—thrummed louder and steadier inside her head. She squatted down and ran her hand through the water at the edge of the river they'd been following, expecting it to be icy. It was cold, but soothingly so. She cupped her hands and brought a scoop of the water to her face. She hadn't noticed how dry her throat was until the first sip passed her cracked lips.

After downing several handfuls, she remembered her companion. "Sorry, I was thirsty." Jo dragged the back of her hand over her mouth.

"No wonder."

Jo sat in the grass, hiking her robe up as she scooted toward the water to dangle her feet in. "Are you going to tell me who you are now?"

The Cryptic Deity Person sat next to her, extending their feet off the bank then sliding into the river. "Now is as good a time as any. Please join me."

Their invitation felt like a trick. Jo had had enough of

the river god Achelous's shenanigans to know that she was at a disadvantage in a water deity's realm. She still didn't even know who the hell this person was. But she wanted answers—not just to who this new deity was, but to why she'd been cast there, what it meant, and could she go home? She shrugged the dark robe off into the grass and slipped into the water naked, expecting a shock of cold. The water instead held her suspended at a temperature that made it hard to tell she was wet.

Her companion dove into the current like a seal, and Jo followed, surprised at how easy it was to swim. She only had to think of the direction she wanted to go, and the water carried her along. Her companion swam through one of the channels in the geode, and Jo followed, certain it was a bad idea—images of divers never returning from watery caves swirling in her head—but drawn in by the possibility of figuring it all out. As if that were an achievable goal.

Cryptic Deity Person headed finally for the surface, and Jo followed in the gentle bubbles of their wake, taking a deep breath once her nose and mouth cleared the surface tension of the water. The two of them were, as she expected, in a very different place. A woman stood on the river bank waiting, a grove of gnarled oaks behind her. Her face woke a deep memory inside of Jo.

Jo's companion easily climbed up the bank and offered a hand to Jo. She was lifted from the water and found herself standing on the bank with no effort on her part, dry and warm. God magic; she could smell it on the breeze.

"Your father. As promised."

Jo looked from her companion to the person who greeted

them. It clearly wasn't John, her father who had died—who'd been murdered by her own mother—when she was a child, but the woman was familiar in a way she couldn't explain. She was wrapped in a heavy black cloak similar to the one Dušan had given—had returned—to her, but made of coarser stuff. A crown of dulled and broken crystal points nestled into the chaos of her fine white hair. If Jo hadn't already figured out the woman was a god, the eyes, set into a brown, heavily lined face, would have been a dead giveaway. Their cast was a thousand-yard stare that had turned inward with chestnut depths and a thousand gilded flecks that glimmered with every turn of her head.

"You are confused, understandably so. Vesna's English is rusty. He, she, they all run together."

Jo still stood looking at them. It wasn't a he or she question, it was a what the fuck is going on question.

The older deity offered Jo a muslin garment that looked like a rudimentary nightgown. "For your comfort."

"Thank you." She took the shift and pulled it over her head. It fit loosely, even around her hips, and barely had any weight to it at all. Jo looked up into the two deities' faces as she fiddled with the unnecessary ties at the front. "Are you two going to tell me who you are now?"

The older deity laughed. "Morana, I see you haven't lost your directness."

"Can we stick with Jo?" She ran her hand through the crown of her hair to get the damp tendrils out of her face and looked at the two deities. "I can accept that things have moved beyond my ability to control them. I might even be able to accept that the Nav," she said, waving her hand about to indicate where they were and where she had been, "might be home now. But I'm not going to pretend to be someone I'm not."

"Jo it is then. This is Vesna. But you knew that, correct?" The other being didn't offer to identify herself.

"Vesna, like the goddess Vesna?" Jo thought of her friend Vesna, who looked nothing like the deity in front of her.

"Yes. Your friend was named for me, or maybe more for the season." This Vesna smiled at her.

Jo raised an eyebrow. How in the hell did Vesna Kos's witchfinder father agree to name his late-in-life daughter after a pagan goddess? She shrugged to herself. That wasn't even close to being the weirdest thing in her life. "Okay. And you?" Jo looked up at the older god.

"I am … I was of the first gods, what your scholars now call a proto-deity. So in that way Vesna was right."

"Was?" Jo looked at the woman. "You seem very 'is' to me."

"I faded from the minds of the people a long time ago and found my way here. Some would call it heaven or the Summerlands. I believe you refer to it as the Next."

Jo's eyes widened.

Deity Vesna touched her arm. "I know there are those you would want to see, but we can only be here by the bank until our time to join the dead comes."

Of course. Because even gods have stupid rules. "So, then why bring me here?"

"Because I needed to speak with you alone." The older woman put her hand on Jo's arm, and a warmth flooded to her core.

Jo gave them both a pointed look.

"To us." Vesna added.

"Jo, you must not let Črnobog succeed."

"Really?" Jo clenched her jaw and tried to think carefully through her next words. "Did you allow this? Did you allow for him to manipulate me, to send his spies, to maneuver all this into place so you could pit me against him? And now you want me to fix it?" She felt the same white-hot anger rise in her that had opened up the abyss in her apartment in Ljubljana weeks or months before, dropping Rok and her into the Nav. The anger came alarmingly quickly now, and she didn't like it—or the feeling it left her with.

The old deity was unsurprised by her outburst. "I did not. Morana set this in motion long ago. I have only waited to make certain what was taken from her was returned."

Jo pulled at the front of the nightgown before crossing her arms and tucking her hands into her armpits as if she were cold. "And what was that? Can I leave after you give it back? I would like to find my father and figure out how to go home." A trickle of thoughts drifted through her mind, something about not being able to go home again and not being able to step into the same river twice, and both ideas only fueled her anger. Whatever.

Deity Vesna nodded. "I will take you to John, and I have what was taken."

Jo hadn't expected help from either of them. Vesna's offer killed the next smartass sentence before it fully formed in her mouth.

"Whatever Črnobog thinks he will accomplish will only break the order of things further. You have to convince him of that." The woman reached up into the nest of her hair and produced a single unbroken crystal point. Jo opened her hand to take it, but it disappeared when the god placed it on her palm. Disappeared wasn't the right word. It sank into her palm like something in a dream.

The older god nodded and smiled at her, the curve of her mouth in her dried-apple face registering somewhere between indulgence and amusement. That half-smile pulled up an image, another dream or deep memory, of lying on a river bank eating apples.

Jo shook off the thought and made her way to the edge of the river before diving into the deep current without saying goodbye. She headed back the way they had come. Deity Vesna was soon beside her, and the two of them swam side by side back to the newly greened Nav, Črnobog's waiting room of the dead.

Jo's cloak was still waiting there on the bank, now thrown over her father's arm just like he used to carry his coat. He didn't look particularly happy to see her.

CHAPTER 7

Vesna Kos waited as close to the edge of the sea cliff as she was willing to stand. The wind attempted to creep into every gap it could find in her heavy coat, but she crossed her arms tightly in front of her and peered into the endless gray sky trying to spot a sea bird. The goddess Fand had agreed to meet her for a lengthier talk after their day exploring Castletown as tourists. Igor was ready to wash his hands of the whole business and return to Ljubljana; Vesna didn't blame him. She would happily take on the Board and whatever army they could muster if it meant she could sleep in her own bed.

A gull soared past. Before she could turn to see where it had landed, Fand appeared, walking toward Vesna's perch on the cliff, red hair blowing wildly.

"Let's get out of this wind."

Or at least that's what Vesna thought the goddess had said. The ocean-driven air currents snatched every other word. She nodded, and the two of them walked toward the cottage. Its whitewashed walls jutted up like bones planted in the greenest grass Vesna had ever seen. The low, thatched roof almost met the turf on the side facing the ocean. Wisps of smoke appeared at the top of the chimney before being rushed away by the turbulent air. Igor had banked the fire before walking to Castletown to catch a bus into Douglas. There was a bigger grocery there that he liked to wander. She suspected he just needed to get away from the tiny space they shared and be alone with his thoughts. Inside, he had left the tinny radio on, and an ethereal cover of an old Cure song tried to be heard above the wind whistling outside. Vesna tapped the button on the top to turn it off, silencing the refrain of just like a dream, before shucking her coat.

Fand followed her into the cottage and hung her heavy wool coat on the peg by the door. As she did every time she'd come into their temporary home, she headed straight for the open fire grate and warmed her hands over the glowing coals.

"Do you have more of that tea?" Fand turned to face Vesna and to warm her backside.

"The one we had at breakfast? Yes." Vesna busied herself in the kitchen. It had become Igor's domain in their time there. He needed the creative outlet more than she did.

Fand joined her in the kitchenette but tried to stay out of her way while still peering over her shoulder. Apparently a human making tea was incredibly interesting to a goddess who spent most of her time lounging in the ocean with her sea beast husband. The song on the radio had delivered its earworm of angels dancing in the ocean, just like her guest.

"You understand what Črnobog is asking is impossible, yes?" Fand put her hand over the steam as it erupted from the electric kettle spout, then quickly pulled it away again.

"Is it? He wants, or at least I think he wants, to destroy the power of the Board by bringing everything behind the Veil into the light. Gods, witches, demons, all of it." Vesna poured the boiling water over the Twinings Earl Grey Igor had picked up in Douglas. The smell of bergamot made her miss the teahouse and her life. At this point, she was past caring about Dušan's plans other than when she could go home.

Cleopatra wound her way around her ankles and mewed up at her. If anyone approached the refrigerator, it was surely a sign she was going to be fed.

"Not now, Cleo. You've had breakfast." Vesna carried the pot and cups to the hard-scrubbed table and offered Fand a seat. "The Board is overrun with murderers. It can't be a bad thing to rid the world of them." The image of Gustaf Lichtenburg, the Observer previously assigned to Ljubljana, sitting on the couch in Bettine's hotel room with his head lolling on his broken neck, came immediately to her mind. Bettine was dead, too, but she still represented all the murderous tendencies the Board had encouraged over its long existence. They'd made it their job, just like the Witchfinders, to put down anything that "didn't belong" in the rational world. Gustaf had been the exception that proved the rule. He had cared about Jo, had tried to warn them all about the Board, even if that warning had come too late.

Fand settled into her chair but watched the pot as if her attention would make the tea brew faster. Maybe it would. Vesna had stopped guessing at what the gods were and weren't capable of.

"The world has moved too far beyond the time when people were willing to entertain things there aren't ready explanations for." Fand looked at the pot, then at Vesna, expectantly.

Vesna pulled the basket that held the spent leaves out of the pot and carried it to the sink over her cup, before coming back to the table to pour. "I guess, but he seems to believe it will cause some great reenchantment, or something."

"It's a noble thought. I would be happy to have back the existence we had when the groves were honored." The goddess looked wistfully out the window. "I mean, I miss the land and not having to pick plastic bits out of my hair."

"So, you'll support him?"

"No. Not after talking more with Lí Ban and Mannan. As much as I want to believe it will work, I think it will only bring sorrow. The world has moved on." Fand sipped her tea and smiled at the cup. "I will miss this when you and Igor leave."

"Dušan hasn't made any noise about us leaving, but Igor is ready to go back. Me too." Vesna hurried to add, "But I will miss this, meeting with you and Lí Ban."

Fand laughed. "You don't need to pretend on my account. This isn't where your heart is. And you should call him Črnobog. You shouldn't forget that he is a god, however much he pretends not to be."

"Maybe. Do you think we are tied to the places we are from? Is that the only place that can really be home?" Vesna had lain in bed at night listening to the wind, wondering about the people who had built the cottage and had lived there in the centuries it had existed. She wondered if she could ever feel at home there, if she couldn't return to Ljubljana.

"I used to. I used to believe that only those born on these islands had leave to believe in the Tuatha Dé Danann, and that if a person died away from the home of their birth they would never find rest." Fand's eyes took on a faraway cast, looking back through a span of existence Vesna couldn't even imagine.

"You don't believe that anymore?"

Fand came back to the moment between them. "I'm not as certain. You've seen the photo the astronauts took of the Earth? This rock isn't even pea-sized in the soup of the universe. That someone could be called to another spot on this speck and feel that is where they belong no longer surprises me. Whether or not the land accepts them?" She shrugged. "That depends on their reason for coming and how they act when they get there."

"And maybe that's why I think Črnobog will fail if he attempts this great reveal. Humans have science. They have had time to figure out the vastness of the universe and the way the smallest pieces of matter make up everything. That's a magic that once only the gods knew. But why would humans need us, now that they have a glimpse of that knowledge?" Fand finished the tea in her cup and reached for the pot.

Vesna leaned back in her chair, holding her teacup and turning Fand's words over in her mind. "I don't think I can stop him from trying." Science hadn't explained everything, and she was taking a less and less materialistic view of the world given her recent experiences. But she was surprised to learn that Fand thought more of human reason than she did.

"I don't think you're the person who is supposed to." Fand paused. "Or at least not by yourself."

"Jo? But I don't know where she is."

"Črnobog does, but he won't have control over her for much longer. She'll find you soon. Our Black God thinks he has more sway than he does. What's left of the Tuatha Dé Danann will not be the only ones who oppose him, but he will be his own undoing."

"Why doesn't that surprise me?" Vesna set her cup down. Fand was holding something back.

Fand laughed again. "You are a smart woman. You could be a better witch though. Lí Ban and I won't follow Črnobog into folly, but we will offer you a boon."

"Offer? I take it there are some strings attached?"

"See, you are a smart woman. Or you've had enough dealings with the gods to know we drive a hard bargain."

"And what do you want from me?" Vesna picked up her cup again and leaned back in the chair to look at Fand and take a sip of tea, only to find her cup was empty.

"Nothing too horrible, but we can discuss that later. For now, you have a book? One given to you by your mother?" Fand took Vesna's cup and filled it.

"How did you… Of course." Vesna pushed up from the table and went to the case of her father's things she'd brought with her to the island. On top of his papers was a splintered box with a worn leather book inside. She'd thumbed through the thin volume many evenings but had never been brave enough to attempt any of the spells or incantations her grandfather had so painstakingly recorded. Igor didn't practice magic and had no interest in starting. He had only said she would be smart to light a black candle for the goddess Morana before she tried anything. She had studiously ignored the vial of glittering magic she had stolen from Bettine's hotel room, as revisiting the night of her mother's death didn't do much for her mood or Igor's.

Fand joined her in the cramped space by the bed and took the box from Vesna's hands. The goddess handled it like a holy relic, and in her hands it took on a new aura of importance.

"You are lucky to have such a thing. So many were destroyed on purpose or in ignorance." Fand opened the box carefully and took out the soft leather-covered volume. There was a faint outline of something that had once been embossed on the covers. Vesna imagined it had been intertwined vines.

"It was thorns." Fand looked sheepish. "You were thinking very loudly." Fand picked up the vial and tilted it; the liquid shimmered as it sloshed back and forth. "That's interesting."

CHAPTER 8

Frédéric Berkane, Fred to his friends, stood in the kitchen of the Kensington flat he had shared with his "daughter" for the past few months. Only a god, or someone with more money than a human could ethically accumulate, could afford to live in the neighborhood they'd been set up in. Both he and Reka had expected to feel alien in London. And London being what it was, no one had paid them any notice. Reka had been unhappy at first to be his pretend daughter, and it had changed the playfulness of their work relationship into something awkward and formal.

Reka's family, like his, was gone. She'd come to wash dishes at Renegade Tea when she'd finished a training program for disadvantaged youth. He'd found Renegade Tea when he'd untethered himself from a life that didn't feel like his anymore. His wife and daughter had been killed in a car accident on a visit home to Algiers, and he'd decided he didn't want to spend another day in his head sitting at a drafting table. He had begun to think of the teahouse Jo and Vesna had created as a place of sanctuary. And it had been, before the bottom had been ripped out by Dušan Črnigad.

It took some time for him to wrap his brain around who, or what, Črnigad was. It wasn't every day that a god came into your place of employment and ordered a bowl of soup. He had taken an immediate dislike to the man the god pretended to be, and Fred liked Dušan even less now—despite the nice apartment and the fact that he had honored the request not to be sent to Algiers when scattering their strange little family to the winds.

Dušan had nodded imperceptibly at Fred's refusal to go home, with Reka in tow. The remnants of distant family were still there, but so were the ghosts of his wife and daughter. They were ghosts not in the way that Jo, his employer and friend, could manifest them, but instead the source of a sickening sense of loss that sank into his belly when he thought of returning. Perhaps dealing with such things would be necessary someday, but it would be his choice when, if, that happened. Dušan had sent him and Reka instead, as father and daughter, to London to this palatial flat in a city where many were happy to afford a bedsit. The father and daughter arrangement had been Dušan's petty revenge, or so Fred believed, but it had made a few moments along the way easier to navigate—once Reka realized he had no intention of chaperoning her. She was an adult, and he had come to view her as a friend and colleague. Once that had been sorted, they had almost enjoyed their time in London, pretending it was a vacation interrupted with the occasional task sent to them by courier. That was how they discussed it between them, at least—as a vacation. He couldn't speak for Reka, but that wasn't exactly the truth for him.

This most recent task had left him puzzled, but he was up early to carry it out. He left Reka—who had refused to give up the name she had chosen for herself, no matter what her real or fake passports said—sleeping and headed out into the early morning of Kensington. The street was on the cusp of coming to life for the day with the muffled sounds of a few early morning exercise enthusiasts and a milk delivery truck, something he was surprised to find still existed. He'd guessed with enough money it was possible to live in whatever time period you wanted. He crossed the street and headed toward the Earl's Court tube station. He'd entertained walking to the museum, but after checking the map on his phone he realized it was more of hike than he'd anticipated.

The tube wasn't a crush of people yet. He'd learned within the first few days of their stay to avoid it at peak times. Commuters didn't have much patience or sympathy for hesitation, and he couldn't blame them. They all wanted to get the morning trip behind them and begin their day or, in the evening, wanted nothing more than to be home. He and Reka had found new smartphones with local numbers waiting for them on the marble countertop in the fully stocked kitchen. He couldn't decide if the white headphones made him blend in better or made him look like an idiot, but he appreciated the cocoon of sound they offered once he'd gotten his bearings. Ljubljana had spoiled him for the quiet life.

The Piccadilly Line would take him to Holborn, and a short walk would find him at the gate of Sir John Soane's Museum. There he was to meet a woman with dark hair in a dark gray coat. It would have been nice to have a name, as every third woman on the tube was wearing a dark gray coat. It was London in early November, and even the days without rain were dampened by clouds that didn't seem to know they weren't meant to linger between the buildings once the sun was up. David Bowie filled his ears with "Modern Love" as he rode the long escalators up to street level. He frowned at the thought of love. Neither he nor Reka had found much in the way of companionship as the weeks had turned into months. He thought, she being so young, that she would venture out to find people her own age, but she had instead found the Kensington Central Library and a conversational English class "to work on her accent." She read and ventured out occasionally to museums and tourist sites, but she didn't leave the neighborhood for long.

Perhaps he should have been more of a chaperon, or even father figure, and urged her to go out, but he didn't venture out much, either, beyond haunting museums and reading his way through the same library. They didn't have a return date to race against to see things they might want to see, and instead of making them leisurely it made them reluctant. A set departure date was the thing about a real vacation that made the days precious. Dušan had never offered them one.

Fred emerged onto the street in front of the station and paused to get his bearings. Maybe he'd read too many novels, or maybe there was something to the idea that there were two Londons stacked on top of each other. The London of the Tube and the endless miles of Victorian sewer tunnels and lost rivers was the more real of the two to him. Stepping back out into the cacophony of the London of double-decker buses and black cabs, which were apparently rarely black anymore, left him feeling like a secretive, magical London would be preferable.

His steps carried him to the closed wrought-iron gate at the front of the museum. A small group of white American tourists milled about chatting, their broad vowels on loud display. He didn't know enough about American accents to place where they were from. He had watched Jo guess customers' origins correctly many times in the shop, despite the fact she'd left home as a teenager. One of the women noticed him and started to smile before her face went flat and she looked away from him to mumble something to her companion.

Fred had agreed to meet Dušan's emissary at this place. She was late, though not horribly so. The American's reaction to him made him more keenly aware of his presence as a brown man waiting in front of a landmark. He pulled out the fancy smartphone and scrolled through the morning's news. He could dwell on her reaction or he could ignore it. A light tap on his shoulder pulled him away from a story about the American elections.

"Frédéric?"

A dark-haired woman in a charcoal coat looked at him expectantly. She had sun-burnished, olive skin and the deepest eyes he'd ever seen. He pulled his earbuds out and nodded at her.

She stuck her hand out to greet him. "Minnie."

"My friends, um … you can call me Fred." Her handshake was firm and quick.

"Fred. I like it." She smiled at him and clapped the pockets of her coat for emphasis. "Have you had breakfast?"

He shrugged. He'd thought he was just meeting her here to collect something and be off again. Most of Dušan's requests had consisted of picking up a package and transferring it to another location, or of sliding letters into specific post boxes.

"Well. I'm starving, and there is a great little pub not far that does a mean fry-up." She threaded her gloved hand under his arm and rested it in the crook of his elbow before leading him away from the gate toward breakfast.

One of the Americans whispered "She must be somebody" as the two of them passed. Fred smiled, happy to have the spotlight shifted away from himself. He was as curious as the tourists about who this woman could be, and about what Dušan wanted of him now.

———

Ivanka crouched to wash her hands in the sea. A miniature crab clung to a pebble, trying not to get swept out with the gently lapping waves. She scooped it up and set it on the beach just out of reach of the water and watched it scuttle away from her, its tiny pincers aloft.

"You're welcome." She stood, wiping her hands on her pants.

"Who are you talking to?" Faron's voice surprised her.

She'd gotten up early and headed to the beach alone. Clotilda's lesson from the day of their first real conversation replayed in her thoughts as she walked along the edge of the tide. Her sisters had grown in their powers. Veronika had mastered new concoctions and had coaxed a small herb garden into existence around the cottage. Ana had become as comfortable in the space between dimensions—the In-Between, she called it—as she was in this world and talked to her spirit guide openly, unconcerned that none of them could see or hear Breda. Ivanka was a little jealous Ana had someone to talk to who seemed to listen so well. Why couldn't all witches have spirit guides?

Ivanka's own abilities were stuck where they had begun. Occasionally she would get a jolt walking under the gnarled olive tree that flanked their glorified beach hut, but it was only good for predicting when Clotilda would show up. Ivanka was always surprised by Dušan, and that pissed her off. Clotilda, in her infinite Fate wisdom, had pronounced her improved anyway. Apparently it was an accomplishment to predict any god's arrival.

Despite Clotilda's praise, Ivanka's inability to guess when Dušan would appear and then leave with Faron was still a failure to her. She'd come down to the edge of the sea to try to wash off the previous night's dream in which Dušan had disappeared with everyone but her. The cottage, the olive tree, and everything else had vanished with them, leaving her standing on a pile of sun-baked rocks in an expanse of blue, blue water. There hadn't even been room to sit down.

Before Faron's question had startled her, she had decided it was time to leave. Faron could come if he wanted, but she was taking her sisters home.

"I was talking to the crab." She finally turned to look at him. He was still Faron, and decidedly not so. Unlike Clotilda and Dušan, he couldn't completely hide what he was yet. It was mostly the eyes and those metallic flecks that were a dead giveaway a person was more than human.

Faron gave her a half grin. "Everything is packed. A boat should come by in a couple hours."

"How?" Faron had promised not to read her thoughts. As intimate as their relationship was, she deserved her privacy and he respected that. "How did you … Did you …?"

"I promised, and I didn't. It's just time for us to go."

This was Faron. She trusted him. She loved him. But in that moment she was a little afraid of him, and from his air of sadness, he knew it.

———

Bettine stood with Christina and Otto at the head of the long wooden table the Board had met at since the time of Charlemagne. Though the Board was diametrically opposed to the use of magic in the mundane world, the table had long been held together by judicious use of the dark arts, and the wood had taken on an inner light because of it.

All the chairs were filled. The Board was in charge of Europe and a few far-flung places that still belonged to the various crowns or nations thereof. Other places in the world had developed their own systems. Over the centuries the face of Europe changed with the waves of humans who came and left. She and Otto and Christina had come from far-flung corners, each sick of the world in their own way. Otto was tired of watching the men he loved die as his long life dragged on. Deep in his cups one night, he confessed he was too much of a coward to take his own life. Despite the centuries, he still believed the act of self-murder would land him in hell with a demon of his own to torture him. If Bettine were a kinder person, she probably would have done the humane thing and had him killed, but he was still of too much use to her.

Christina was less predictable. The centuries had taken their toll in a different manner. As a child she had sent her own mother to death as an accused witch in the cleansing of Torsåker. Bettine admired Christina's fervor, but it meant keeping the secret of her own sorcery very close, lest Christina point the accusing finger at her. The mere mention of magic lit a fire in Christina's eyes that even Bettine found overzealous.

But Christina knew her secret now. Almost every chair held a dead member of the Board, though they looked to be sleeping. It was quite calm after the row that had ensued over the vote Bettine and the other two had asked for. The tall man from Latvia—Bettine didn't bother to learn their names, as none of them lived long enough to matter much— had risen and accused her of being in league with the demons they sought to protect the world from. He wasn't completely wrong; she was happy to make the enemy of her enemy a comrade.

The others had joined him in his accusations like a ring of fire encircling the ancient table. When Christina and Otto didn't join the chorus of recriminations, the accusations spread to them. She had called Christina and Otto to her side and slammed a small glass vial on the table, crushing it under her palm before shielding the other two Long-Lived with her arms. As the invisible contents of the vial swept down the length of the table, the elders—a laughable term in this case—of the Board slumped in their chairs. Only one had been sick first, and the smell of vomited breakfast hung in the air.

Christina backed away from her, her eyes wide with fear and hatred. "You! You are one of them." She spat on the ground at Bettine's feet.

"I am not." She looked to Otto who stood back, waiting. He would not choose sides until he was certain it was the winner he was picking. "It is sometimes necessary to take on the weapons of the enemy to defeat them."

"You murdered them all. That was never the plan." Christina hissed the words at her.

It hadn't been the plan. The plan had always been to convince them the time had come to completely rid the world of withering deities, monsters, and magic users so they could disband the Board and slink back to their corners, living without the interference of an organization that had grown slack in its decline. The Long-Lived generally kept to themselves these days, unless they were the pets of those rotting gods. Bettine found that prospect far more disgusting than using the tools of witches.

And now Christina's anger had further changed Bettine's plan. Perhaps it was better for the Long-Lived to follow the Board, and the twilight gods, and all the rest into the darkness. Herself included. Being on a suicide mission would gird her to the horrors to come.

As Bettine walked closer to Christina, Christina's impossibly wide eyes dilated further and she shrank into the corner of the room, praying loudly in an archaic Swedish dialect. That magic wasn't going to help her either. Bettine caught the taller woman by the throat and pulled her face close to hers. "Oh, Christina, thank you. I see now." Bettine whispered her own prayer of sorts and felt Christina's trachea collapse under her fingers. The woman gasped for air before her lips blued and her head sagged, still supported by Bettine's outstretched grasp.

Otto crossed himself in her peripheral vision. She dropped Christina on the floor and turned on him. "If you help me, I will slay you last, sparing you the tremors of your soul."

He crossed himself again and swallowed hard before nodding in agreement.

Bettine turned and walked to the head of the table again before slamming her fist down hard on the wood. Blue sparks shot from under her hand, and a crack ripped through the table cleaving it roughly in two and scattering the bodies slumped over it. The faint smell of smoke filled the room before flames bloomed along the broken edges of the table top. Bettine ushered Otto out of the room, closing the door behind them without looking back.

"There are only two of us, against so many." Otto finally spoke when they were out on the street. He looked up as the first plume of black smoke escaped from the windows.

"We are more than two. All of the Observers are still in place and now answer only to us." She walked down the narrow lane, built when Paris still grew like an infection from the banks of the Seine. They left the area as the fire brigade arrived with their hoses and ladders, and gawkers began to gather in the street. Maybe a humanity not beholden to superstition and cowed by fear of the unknown could do more than this lot had accomplished.

CHAPTER 9

Jo's father handed her the heavy cloak Dušan had returned to her. She draped it over her shoulders and fastened the intricate jet closure at her throat. It was clearly made for someone much taller than she, as the frosted velvet pooled around her in the wet grass.

She had expected a hug from her father once she was dressed, but he didn't move to do so. He hadn't said a word and acted as if he were waiting for her to explain the situation they found themselves in.

Jo stumbled over the words, but she introduced him to Deity Vesna. Her father and the god nodded at each other. It was all very formal, and very weird.

"Do you two already know each other?" Jo looked from Deity Vesna's unlined face to her father's pale, bruised one.

Her father nodded again and finally spoke. "I didn't expect to see you here so soon."

Jo laughed. How did she explain to him that this was her third trip since his shade had been swallowed up by a hovering demon cloud of eyes and wings? "If it's any consolation, I didn't die to get here." Or at least she didn't think so.

"I'm not sure if that's better or worse."

She wasn't sure about that either, but it was a philosophical debate she could have with herself later. Fuck his formality and distance. She quickly closed the gap between the two of them and threw her arms around his shoulders. After a staggered step back, he put his arms around her and squeezed her back.

"Jay, what have you done?" He whispered the words into her damp hair, and the sadness in them made her stomach leaden.

With that and him calling her by his childhood nickname for her, her heart tightened in her chest too. She took a deep breath before speaking.

"I wish I understood it all, but I don't." Her breath caught again, and, despite wanting to wail against her father's shoulder, she kept her composure.

He continued to hold her and ran his rough hand over the back of her hair. "I'm so sorry. If I had truly understood, maybe I could have warned you. But I didn't know, not until I was here."

Jo pulled away from him. "Know what?"

"That we were all playing a part in some bigger game." He sighed and let her go. His arms dropped heavily to his sides, defeated.

Jo had forgotten Deity Vesna was still standing there until the god spoke. "You two have much to say to each other. I'll excuse myself but will return soon."

Jo nodded. Her own sadness had been layered with a wariness akin to walking through underbrush knowing there were snakes, the harmless ones that would only surprise you as well as the hazardous ones that could do much worse.

She sank to the damp grass and pulled her father down next to her. "Spill. I know there is more to this story, but first why didn't you tell me the truth about Mother when you came to me in Ljubljana?" Jo had watched her mother walk into the Next only moments after learning that her father's accidental death had been anything but, and she'd carried the weight of that knowledge right down into the dust of the Nav.

"Would it have helped you to know your mother was a murderer?" His face had taken on a tightness around his eyes that she instantly associated with the stern lectures he'd given when she'd been late to come in from the woods around their house. As an adult with her own child, she'd realized he hadn't been angry at her when he couldn't find her. He'd been afraid.

"Helped is a funny word. I mean, would it have explained all the crap I went through with her? Probably not as a kid. But I think it would have explained her better to me as an adult, so I didn't carry around so much of younger me's brokenness." It wasn't just her mother's rages that had cracked her open though. His death had been the first blow.

"I'm not a shrink, Jay. I didn't have the words. Did your aunt tell you?"

"Mom told me herself before she died. She thought you would come to claim her, and she would be able to apologize. But it was Rebecca, Great Great Great Gramma Death, who came." Jo could still see the blue-lit screen door her mother had passed through to enter the Next as if her mind had taken a particularly clear photograph of it and was happy to show it off given any chance at all.

Her father hung his head for a moment. "I'm glad Rebecca was there."

"You know Rebecca? Of course you do, you met Death. But, wait. If you met her, why you didn't go into the Next?"

"When Rebecca came that day she opened a door I could have walked through, but I didn't want to leave you." He looked at her, and she saw it again, the pain and the sorrow he'd been carrying around since his death, maybe before.

"Mother was pretty awful after." Jo ran her fingertips over the scar on her cheek. It was the only one she still had after her demi-god magic healing powers had corrected everything else. She knew there was something to it, but she hadn't exactly figured out all the human rules, let alone the god ones.

"It wasn't your mother I worried about. I watched a man come up out of the river and swagger his way over to you. He bent down to whisper in your ear and then stood over you, looking too pleased with himself for my comfort."

"You didn't think to maybe show up and mention that to me at some point? I mean some point before I was on the back side of forty?" She stared at him in disbelief. He'd told her when he'd first come to her in Ljubljana that he'd stayed to protect her. Not filling her in on watery supernatural dudes hovering around her seemed contrary to that statement, especially given her interactions with one water deity in particular.

"You couldn't hear me or see me. I tried for years, but whatever he said to you changed you."

She heard that whisper in her ear. *Don't let them in.* The thought of it sent shivers down her arm, and she recognized the voice. All those years she'd chalked it up to her mind trying to protect her from the reality of his death. Since finding out what she really was, she'd wondered if it had been her father warning her about what she would become. Nope.

"Fucking Achelous." She wanted to spit. "He's been part of this since the beginning." And how many times had he lied to her since she'd met him that first time in the flooded basement of the City Museum?

"I think you'll find it hasn't been any river god pulling the strings." Her father looked over her shoulder. "I think you'll find the architect is headed this way."

Jo followed her father's gaze and saw Dušan, still in his Black God getup, walking toward them. She might have imagined it, but she would have sworn there was a smile playing in the corners of his mouth.

"I see you two found each other." He sat down next to them in the damp grass as casually as a seven-foot-something ancient Slavic god could.

"Could you maybe reel that in and just be Dušan for a minute or two?" She waved her hand at him to indicate his whole Black God look. His eyes were especially difficult to look away from, and she definitely did not want him thinking she was happy to get lost in those fathoms of stars.

"Not possible. I am a god in a realm of the gods." He did smile then, and the full effect of it on his god face was truly disconcerting.

"Gotcha." She found a loose lock of hair on his temple to focus on when she had to look him.

"I came to tell you I was leaving for a short while. Vesna will see after your needs, and I will return soon." He was on his feet again before she could figure out how he'd managed to stand.

She stood up in front of him and made the mistake of looking into those damned eyes when he looked down at her. "You aren't leaving without me and without making sure he can go into the Next." She pulled her father up to stand with her.

"There will be plenty of time for that when I get back."

A tiny voice in the back of her head said she should be afraid, but a much louder one in her ears was screaming, Fuck it, what else have you got to lose? That voice propelled her right up to Črnobog, to glare at him, starry eyes and all. An unexpectedly authoritative voice came out of her. "I said, you will help usher my father into the Next, and you will take me with you."

That disconcerting smile reappeared, but now it was more irritating than scary. "You aren't ready to have this argument with me." Then the asshole disappeared.

Jo wheeled around on her father, who backed a few steps away from her.

"What?"

"Your eyes."

Jo blinked. Her lashes were a little sticky from keeping the tears at bay. "What about them?"

"They're black."

———

Fred slid into a booth facing Minnie. He kept catching himself staring at her. The server had to ask him twice what he wanted.

"Sorry. Just a coffee and some toast." His stomach had been unsettled since Minnie had introduced herself.

"That's not much of a breakfast. Are you sure?" Minnie looked from him to the server and back at him as if the young man should step in and convince him to order more food.

"I'm good," to her and, "Thank you," to the server who walked away shaking his head just enough for Fred to notice.

"Well, I'm famished. I'm sorry I dragged you here if you weren't hungry." Minnie had ordered a full English with fried bread and all the trimmings. She smiled at him, showing very white but character-building, imperfect teeth.

"I can definitely use the coffee." He smiled back, unable to say or do much else.

"While we wait, I can fill you in."

Yes. There had been a reason for getting up so early and making his way to Holborn.

"There is an item in the Soane collection your friend Črnobog would like. I have been able to procure it, and you and Reka are to take it to him in Ljubljana."

Before Fred could find words to string together beyond he isn't my friend, she continued.

"I'm not happy about this, but I owe him a favor, and, well, you've met him." She gave him a conspiratorial smile that pulled her plump lips taut.

His stomach turned over, and he chided himself for acting like a teenage boy, since that was the last time he had remembered anyone having such an effect on him.

"I have met him. But I don't know what all of these errands and tasks are in aid of." He didn't believe they were in aid of anything good, but he didn't want to speak against a man, a god, who appeared to be her friend.

"I don't agree with him. I want you to know that." She looked up at him again, but she didn't smile this time.

"Why is it important for me to know that? You don't know anything about me."

She reached across the table and took his hand. Her gaze stilled him, and he got lost again in dark eyes. His thoughts went to a trip he had taken to Tebessa with his family as a teenager. They had walked the Roman ruins, and in the temple he had run his fingertips over the edge of a mosaic, the small tiles warmed by the sun. He'd imagined the ancient people who had come to rule over the Berbers, not even the first colonizers and certainly not the last. The temple to Minerva had been a short side trip before heading on to his aunt and uncle's house in Tunis. He'd felt the reverence those people had had for the place, for the god they believe dwelled within. Then he'd forgotten the trip, until Minnie had taken his hand.

Minnie.

He looked up from her hand to her face again, and the

smile she gave him was accompanied by a golden flash in the burnished depth of her eyes. His first instinct was to pull his hand away. He'd had enough of meddlesome gods, but other senses overrode the impulse. They had just met and barely conversed, but he wanted to trust her, wanted to keep her warm hand there covering his.

"Hello, again." She spoke in English, but he heard a whisper of all the other languages she held in her past, as if several voices had said the words in chorus.

"What has Črnobog asked me to do that the Roman Goddess of Wisdom could not do on her own?" He held her hand in his but leaned away, surveying the position he found himself in.

"You are right. I could do all of this myself and had in fact planned to travel to meet Črnobog in Ljubljana the day after tomorrow. He said I should instead send the artifact with you and your daughter Reka." She unclasped his hand to produce a small package from the well-made leather bag at her side.

"I would hate for you to miss the opportunity to travel to Ljubljana. The holiday lights will be on soon, and the New Year's markets will be open." The thought made him miss the smells of chestnut vendors along the river and the mixture of spices the holiday season brought to the specials at the teahouse.

"You long to be home." A thought flashed through her eyes. "But there is nothing in Črnobog's message that would prevent me from accompanying you."

"Are you certain that was not the man's plan from the beginning?" Fred had no trust in Dušan Črnigad. Anything associated with him that seemed like it could be a good thing was suspect, even the opportunity to spend more time with Minnie.

"Črnobog doesn't really want what he thinks he wants. I have told him as much, but he won't listen." She looked up as the server brought their breakfast, a platter of food for her and some very dry-looking toast for him. "But I owe him and will support him. To a point."

"What does he want?" Some variation of that question had been swirling in Fred's thoughts since they'd left Ljubljana.

She cut a bite-sized piece of blood sausage and persuaded a few beans to join it on the back of her fork before taking a satisfied bite. "Mmm. He thinks he wants war. He wants to put an end to this modern ruse of pretending the supernatural doesn't exist." She curated another bite before continuing. "That is a fool's gambit."

"So why attempt it, if it's going to fail?" Fred tried to scrape cold butter across the toast and wished he'd ordered at least an egg.

"He wants to be venerated. Loved." She took a sip of coffee and looked at him.

"There are those who go into the forest and seek the old rites. They put flyers up at the teahouse all the time." He undid the gingham printed lid of the miniature jar of mixed-fruits jam and spread it over the shards of butter.

"Črnobog isn't exactly an old god. I mean old to you. But ..." Her words trailed off before she took a bite of mushroom and closed her eyes.

Her expression made him want to cook for her. Anything

they produced at work would be better than the blandness of beige on her plate. He reminded himself there were more pressing things. "What do you mean, not an old god?"

"Črnobog is … how do I describe this? He's a pastiche of sorts. Oh, there are traces of the ancient deities modern scholars refer to as proto Indo-European and bits of the Slavic trickster lost to the ages, but as you see him now? That's mostly the doing of monks belittling the religions that came before. The Black God has never been worshipped; he's been the devil and the nightmare. But like the rest of us, some part of him remembers what it felt like to have fire in the temples." Her eyes glittered with what he was sure was her own memory of such times.

CHAPTER 10

Dušan Črnigad, Črnobog to his friends and enemies, walked along the banks of the Ljubljanica. The plane trees had long since lost their leaves, but their dark seed pods still clung to the branches, making them look as if they'd been decorated for the season. Groups of students, families, and couples wrapped in coats and scarves caused him to wander in his path as he headed to his gallery and apartment.

The chestnut vendors were doing a brisk business along the river, and the scent of the roasted nuts brought a slight smile that made him feel more at ease in his human disguise. The lights had all been strung to celebrate the New Year. The wires and dark shapes they made contrasted against the buildings and underlit sky that was never truly dark because of the glow of the city. He had the briefest thought that it would be nice for Jo and the others to be home in time to enjoy the beginning of the season when the lights were first turned on, but he remembered himself and quickened his steps.

He followed the river on to Zajčeva, turned onto the short, cobbled street, and pushed the thick wooden doors open to reveal the darkened courtyard. He was greeted by the faint impressions of the hundreds of people who had passed through that particular portal and a whisper of vanilla. He didn't dwell on whether the scent came from the place memory of Jo or the bakery, but he was reminded how attuned to her presence—and absence—he had become, especially in his human form.

A figure stood up from the bottom of the stairwell that led up to the flats above the teahouse and shops. He wasn't surprised to find anyone there. He had expected it. With a thought, warm, orange light flooded the courtyard.

"It took you long enough. My butt is cold." Gregor Bregant stood in front of him with his arms crossed and his hands tucked into his armpits for warmth.

"You needn't have bothered meeting me. I do have keys." Črnigad had no desire to make an enemy of Jo's friend. He'd called him back to Ljubljana first, with his partner, Janez, to help ease the others' return. A god could do many things, but he preferred to leave mundane logistics to someone else.

"I didn't come to let you in. But I'm guessing you knew that." Gregor smirked at him.

Gregor didn't have any extraordinary abilities but was more than adept at keeping his thoughts quiet. It was impressive for a mundane.

"Just so." Črnigad continued walking toward the gallery. "Frédéric and Reka will arrive tomorrow or the next day. I expect the others not to be too far behind."

"Does that include Jo?"

"No. I suspect it will be longer before she is back." Dušan turned the key in the lock and walked into the gallery. The lights, hidden in the recess of the ledge at the top of the walls, flickered on from front to back.

Gregor had walked to the threshold but hesitated. It made Dušan think of the human stories of vampires needing to be invited in. Maybe Gregor thought in some reversed way that he had to be beckoned inside his lair. "Why will she be delayed?"

Dušan looked at the man outside his door. There was a slight step into the gallery which put the two of them eye to eye. That was probably the only aspect of their acquaintance that was on the level. "You saw her before she left. She needs time."

Gregor stepped up inside and looked down at him. "Bullshit." He didn't raise his voice or change tone, but Dušan could see the restraint required not to. "Jo is—"

"—'stronger than that? Made of sterner stuff? You don't really know her?' Where were you going with this?" Dušan might regret mocking Gregor's concern, but he pressed on.

"I never understood what she saw in you. I wonder now if you just used whatever powers you have to compel her. I find it hard to believe she would choose such an asshole of her own accord."

Dušan laughed. "Have you met any of her other lovers?"

Gregor lost the rein of his thoughts if not his body. A different man might have punched him.

"I won't be the only one who wants to know where she is.

If you think Vesna isn't going to come down on you like a load of bricks, god or not, you are kidding yourself." Gregor turned and walked out the door. He stopped briefly in the courtyard to throw a ring of keys onto the floor of the gallery at Dušan's feet. "To the flats, for Fred and Reka. Fred is going to give you hell too."

Gregor disappeared through the archway of the courtyard door, and Dušan picked up the keys. He would probably have to make things right between him and Gregor but it didn't matter at the moment. He had other things to do.

The faintest scent of mold hung in the air, most likely brought on by the unusual level of humidity over the blistering summer months. Humans were doing an excellent job of destroying the material world almost as thoroughly as they had destroyed the enchanted one. He put the keys on the lower ledge that ran around the walls of the gallery and held framed and matted photographs still in place from the last exhibition months before. There were a few gaps. The assistant he had hired, and paid handsomely, had done her job and gotten the sold pieces to the new owners.

He pulled his phone from the pocket of his peacoat and called her.

Zala's voicemail told him she was otherwise engaged, and he left her a message to bring someone by the gallery to address the mold. He thanked her again for tending to business in his absence and rang off before tucking the phone back into his coat pocket. He walked to the end of the gallery to stand in front of the last photograph, placed on the ledge near the painted white reception desk with a guest book and a stack of glossy brochures Zala had insisted on having printed.

He took the photograph down and held it at arm's length. It was a new print from an old negative. The degradation of the original added a patina to the newly printed image that made it even harder to discern the subject. Given the other photographs on display, it was easily mistaken for an oddly framed landscape. It was instead the last photo he had taken of Jo, a closely cropped image of her torso pressed against her thighs, her breasts hidden.

She had appeared at his studio, distracted, wearing a long black dress that crossed across the front, held together only by a tied belt. He saw that she was changed and knew why she was there the moment she'd come through the door. He waited for her to tell him what she'd come to share in her own good time.

She had avoided looking directly at him and distracted herself with a stack of contact sheets he'd been making notes on. She picked up the lupe that was acting as a paperweight and turned to sit on the edge of the table, fidgeting with the eyepiece in her hand. While she made small talk, he set up the camera and checked the lighting.

"Do you have a model coming over?" She looked up at his face, waiting for his answer. "I could come back later or tomorrow."

"No. But since you're here and the camera is set up." He made a sweeping gesture toward the couch plopped on the white drop cloth.

She seemed pleasantly surprised despite the two dark half moons that hung below her eyes. "If you'd like."

The lupe went back on the table before she pulled the bow at the front of her dress apart. He joined her at the desk and stopped her hands, taking the ties away from her. When he pulled the dress open, there was nothing underneath, as if she'd anticipated taking photographs and tried to avoid the marks a bra or underwear would have left on the skin.

She responded to his questioning look with a shrug. "I was in a hurry."

He slid the dress down her shoulders so it hung on her arms like a robe. "I'm not."

She had pulled him into her, tucking her hands on either side of his neck and kissed him deeply. She smelled of vanilla and tasted like sadness and resignation. And fear. Her body gave no hint of the turmoil in her thoughts, but that wasn't unlike her.

He pushed her farther up onto the desk and pressed his hips into the V of her thighs. She kept her mouth hungrily engaged with his but pushed his body away to give her enough room to undo the front of his trousers. He wanted to draw out his pleasure and hers. It was the last time he would have her, but he still found himself rushing, pushing her to gasp and writhe in his arms. She didn't fall into him as he expected, but leaned back propping herself on her palms, skidding the contact sheets onto the floor, and looking at him like she was waiting for the right gap to slide her news into.

As he put his clothes back together—she had done a spectacular job of bunching up his undershirt and jacket— she slid off the desk, shucking her arms out of the dress as she went and sat on the sheet-covered couch. He joined her and took her arm to begin to arrange her body. Usually she let him move her about like a child's doll but there was a tension in her limbs. When he had her in the position he wanted, he returned to the camera and looked at her through the viewfinder. It hid the glow of her aura that he could see without the interference of the lens, a crimson halo that radiated from her and tried to drift away in tendrils. A new glow had infused it, making it vibrate closer to the purple end of the spectrum.

Stepping away, he clicked the remote, opening the shutter with a soft snick while giving her instructions to turn a fraction of an inch, this way or that. When he'd taken all he thought he would need to get a good print, she sat up on the couch and stared straight ahead before announcing she was pregnant in a tone a person might use in announcing that they were hungry.

That he had already decided to spend some time in New York and that he was married were only the first two givens as to why it was a bad idea for her to have a child. He wasn't surprised she wanted to keep it, only that she felt like it was inevitable. There wasn't even a fight. An observer would have said they were talking past each other. He had expected her to cry from the moment he said he was still going to leave, but she never sobbed or railed at him. Instead silent tears had welled and fallen. It was worse for him than if she had raged at him for leaving. As often as he had said gods do not fall in love with mortals, those silent tears and her resolve had cut him to the bone. Whatever evils she believed of him, he had carried the regret of those moments with him. But him staying had never been part of the plan.

She had pulled her dress back on and retied a lopsided bow

to the side. Her hands trembled as she did so, and he had still held back from touching her or trying to comfort her in any way. He pressed a great deal of cash into her hand, which she'd looked at with disdain but had taken anyway. She would need things. He didn't walk her out, but he sat for a long time on the couch after she left, imaging he could still feel the warmth of her body underneath him.

That had been a long time ago for Jo and moments for him. He looked at the picture he held of the landscape of her body, skin taut but softly curving over the skeletal architecture of her hip. The last time he had kissed her, maybe months before, leaning against the wall where this photograph had been propped, she had not tasted of sadness. Ever so briefly, she had tasted of longing and, after all this time, that had surprised him.

"Gods do not fall in love." He laid the frame on the desk.

"But men do."

It is very hard to startle a god. Only Death incarnate can do that.

Rebecca Wiley stood leaning in the open doorway, a cascade of strawberry blonde waves spilling from pale freckled temples over the shoulders of a winter white coat of boiled wool. "What are your intentions with the granddaughter of my line, oh, dark lord of Slavic myth?" She straightened up and walked toward him with all the swagger Death was due.

"My intentions are honorable." He sat on the edge of the desk and motioned for Rebecca to join him.

She pulled the desk chair around to face him instead and sat down. "That's new."

"The rules of fair play do not apply in love and war."

"Jo didn't sign up for your war."

They sat in awkward silence for a moment, looking into each other's faces before Rebecca continued.

"Do you love her?"

Rebecca was stunning and so different from Jo. Even in her role as Death, Rebecca still had a brittle, fragile quality. Jo was made of sterner stock. Handsome was the word English speakers used to use to describe a woman who had come into her own with age. Rebecca was ethereal, a creature of air, where Jo was of earth and, more recently, fire.

"Does the darkness love the light?" Mortal or immortal, no one enjoyed having a question answered with a question. Rebecca was no different, and it showed in her face.

"Which are you in this scenario?"

She was good at this game even if she didn't like to play.

"That is a very good question. Perhaps both."

She stood up and straightened the lapels of her coat. "Whatever story you as Črnobog or Dušan or whomever else you pretend to be, choose to comfort yourself with, I have seen how you look at her. You can hide it from everyone else and maybe even yourself."

"But I can't hide from Death."

"Not even you." She got very close to him, close enough that the smell of nicotiana flowers filled his senses.

He didn't flinch from her. Gods, even when pretending to be human, did not do such things. "Is this where you tell me you'll come for me if I hurt her?"

"No. Jo is her own being, with her own agency. But if you cross her again, you will have made more than one enemy." She turned and left, as quietly as Death does.

He had no intention of crossing Jo or enlisting her for this final battle. She would be safe in the Nav until he retrieved her, or he at least liked to tell himself that.

CHAPTER 11

"It's true then." Jo's father stepped closer to peer into her face in that way parents have that let you know you shouldn't try to hide anything.

Jo backed away from him a half step, defensive.

"What's true?"

"He changed you."

Deity Vesna appeared again. Maybe she had walked up to them slowly but neither Jo or her father had noticed. "He didn't. Not really. She was always what she is."

Jo screwed her face up in frustration. "What does that even mean? You and that old-school god you took me to spout all this cryptic nonsense and act like I'm supposed to follow the conversation."

"It isn't meant to be nonsense. Do you really not remember anything?" Deity Vesna looked hurt.

"No." That was a lie. Since waking up in the swamp she'd sobbed into existence, there had been a vague sense of having known this place before and there had been the very clear image of sitting with someone on a river bank, but they were little more than thought shadows and felt like someone else's memories.

Deity Vesna moved toward Jo and got close enough that the two could have easily embraced. The cryptic god person didn't blink but stared into the depths of Jo's apparently black eyes. "I said I would return to you what was taken." She held up her hand at shoulder height, the palm facing out.

Jo instinctively reached up and placed her palm against Deity Vensa's. She watched as their two hands fused together before Vesna's disappeared into hers. Jo jerked back but Vesna caught her wrist with her free hand.

"Don't be afraid." Vesna stepped toward her and into her.

The sensation at first reminded her of when Achelous had possessed her in the basement of the City Museum when she had prayed for anyone listening to save her and her son from the demon that had come for them. It had felt then as if Achelous had put her body on like he was stepping into a pair of pants. This was different. It was like walking into a waterfall, but the water wasn't battering her and splashing away—it was entering her, flowing out to her fingertips. A cascade of images flooded her mind with the sensation, but these remembrances didn't belong to anyone else. They were her recollections from her own very long memory. A few of those reclaimed moments were clearer than others and bubbled to the swirling surface.

The first one she clung to from the torrent was of her lying on her cloak in the tall rushes next to the Ljubljanica just as it escaped the barje to find its way east toward the Sava. A basket of apples overflowed next to her, and she felt a warm hand in hers before turning to look into the face of her companion. Črnobog stared back at her, but instead of seeing the pinpricked velvet depths of galaxies, she saw her own face reflected in his eyes. In that reflection, she was burning. Flames licked up her body, choking out her breath as they consumed the oxygen around her.

Jo gasped as if she were drowning and fell to her knees in the lush grass of the Nav. When she could again take a deep breath, she looked up to find her father staring down at her, the throngs of the dead who had been milling about in the orchards pressing in behind him.

Her father offered her his hand to stand. "Morana, Goddess of Life and of the Dead, we welcome your return to the Nav." He said it with reverence and with a deep sadness that pulled at Jo's core.

She reached out to him but pulled back when she saw her hand. Her skin was the color of bleached bone. Every vessel and capillary was visible and ran blue-green, ruddy red, or burnt umber, the colors of all the rivers that flowed in and out of the Nav. She stood on her own and found she was towering over her father. The hem of the cloak that had previously pooled around her feet brushed against the grass as she turned. She touched the top of her head where it felt heavy and found she had acquired her own crown, similar to the one the ancient deity at the edge of the Next had worn. She ran her fingertips over what felt like crystal points wrapped with cold wire. There was also a fleeting thought that she could have kissed Leo, eye to eye in her current form, layered with the knowledge that some things were never meant to be. That truth stung with a clearer perspective that revealed her own failings in what had happened between them.

She looked out over the gathered crowd, each person framed in different colored auras. Some of the light clung close to the bodies of the dead, and some of these long deceased were burning bright and large. So many were ready to transition into the Next. They had been waiting a very long time for her to release them. Without even considering that she didn't know what she was doing, she uttered a phrase in a language so old it was lost to all but the gods, and a glowing portal opened next to her. Those with the supernova auras were instantly drawn to it and made a hurried exit from the Nav. He father's aura shone with that same intensity in shades of green and sunflower golds, but he stayed until all of those poor souls who had waited, some for centuries, to make the journey had passed through the archway.

He looked up her. That was an unusual sensation, to have her father tilt his head back to talk to her. "You have come into your own, Jay." He started to reach out to embrace her but stopped himself as if he'd suddenly remembered his place.

Jo didn't hesitate in pulling him into a rib-crushing hug. She could see it now. She could see how he had sacrificed his peace in the Next to look over her as a little girl and tangled with a demon who had landed him in the Nav trying to protect Faron and her. He loved her, and he had tried to love her mother. He was imperfect, human, beautiful.

"Thank you." She whispered it over the top of his head, again a very strange feeling to be taller, bigger than the man who had loomed so large in her childhood. He let go first and stood back from her.

"There's no thanking to it. I may not have been the best

father, but I wanted the best for you."

No manner of miraculous demi-god healing of scars could fix everything. Part of Jo's heart would always be broken. It would always carry the indelible marks she had collected over a life of loss, but the shattered pieces that had been wreaking havoc inside her were now held in matrix by a longer vision, one that allowed her to understand why people—including herself—made the decisions they made and to begin to forgive. "You did do the best you could."

The dead who were not ready to leave the contemplative, preparatory embrace of the Nav wandered back off toward the groves and left Jo standing with her father on a sea of grass next to a door pulsing with the blue light of the Next.

"Part of me wishes you would stay, or that I could somehow restore you to live a full life in the world." She wasn't sure she couldn't do that, she only knew it wasn't the right thing to do.

"Even if you could, I'm not interested. I've stuck around longer than I was supposed to anyway." He looked off toward the grove and back at her, resolved. "Take care of yourself. And Faron. You did good there. And don't forget who you are, who you were before this." He gestured at the length of her changed form. "I have to think that still matters."

Jo nodded, aware of the weight of the crown on her head in both the physical and metaphorical senses.

He looked around as if he had forgotten something, gave her an awkward last wave, and disappeared through the archway. It collapsed behind him into a pinpoint and popped out of existence. Jo stood by herself on the riverbank looking out across the water. No one else existed in the living world or in the Nav who would ever call her Jay again, and she said goodbye to that part of her as well as her father. She wasn't alone though. There were more parts of her that she realized had always been there, or that she had known were missing, like a faint ache or the gap left by a pulled tooth that you worry at with your tongue. Deity Vesna and the many spring seasons she had ushered into the world had settled inside her with Morana and all of that dark goddess's centuries of loss— next to Jo and Jolene and Jay and all the pieces that made up her human life. There was beauty and sorrow, creation and destruction, ebb and flow, and all of it was part of her. There was also Rok standing off from her, watching and waiting.

Črnobog had scattered her family to the winds. It was on her now to collect them and get to the bottom of his plotting. The threads of a thousand possible futures spun out from that thought. She could have seen to the end of all of them, but instead she stopped the spinning in her mind. It was better to make decisions because they were right in the moment than to know all of the possibilities. Trying to outsmart fate, outthink Dušan, that was the kind of thing that had landed her there in the first place.

Had she really set all this in motion as that proto-deity had said? If she had, that memory had not yet returned to her. Even if it bobbed its way up from the depths of all she had been given that day, she would squash it back down. The past was important; it framed the present and what would come, but she was no longer going to live in it. She was going to go home, as soon as she figured out how to do that. What she could do, what she would do, was collect the first of her family, first of the many tethers her aunt had said held her and prevented her from following her mother into the darkness of her mental illness.

Rok—he would always be Rok to her no matter what names he used or acquired—joined her on the riverbank, still tentative.

He had changed, but she could still sense the human behind the demi-god eyes. He, too, had always carried that piece inside him, an inheritance from the gods who had intermingled with their distant ancestors, and now she guessed those pieces were made manifest and whole. Being a god or demi-god, or whatever the hell she was, really should have made everything clearer. "I guess we're divine now." She laughed as she said it, but Rok frowned at her.

"I don't know what that means yet."

"Are we supposed to?" Jo took his hand in her pale one. His skin was warm and made her think of sun-kissed bodies and the ripeness of high summer. She was sorry for him, but she couldn't forget entirely that he had betrayed her. He had helped Črnobog drag her here but had been unaware of the price he would pay. She could spare him a small part of it by taking him with her back to Ljubljana, and maybe they could figure out all the other stuff from there.

"I'm going home. Would you like to join me?" She didn't ask him where his loyalties lay. She didn't want to know, best not to test her resolve to be kind in the moment.

"Yes." He nodded as he said it, in case there was any doubt about what the word yes meant. She thought of what Mary, Jesus's mom—not hers—had said to her before she'd gone up to her apartment and had the fight with Rok that had brought them here. She had said Rok believed he could only serve one god and she worried what would happen if he were forced to choose. Jo hoped he chose himself.

Those things would sort themselves. She could feel the deep magic of Morana moving through her. Every cell was transformed with the potential. Jo squeezed his hand tighter and thought of home.

CHAPTER 12

Frédéric Berkane stood in front of his now former flat with his former and maybe current coworker Reka and with Minnie—Etruscan goddess of wisdom, medicine, war, art, schools, and commerce. Each of them held a single piece of luggage and, among them, carried several lifetimes of baggage. Fred, as he was affectionately known to his friends, which now included Minnie, had an additional parcel.

The small box tucked into a zippered inside pocket of his bag contained, as Minnie had explained to him, the last piece of the puzzle Dušan had been assembling over the last few months. The small box held a linen-wrapped piece of the Lance of Longinus, which had once been fashioned into the hilt of Charlemagne's conquering sword Joyeuse. According to Minnie, the version of Charlemagne's sword that rested in a glass case in the Louvre was a replica. The Council, before they became the Board that oversaw the peace of the Veil and all those supernatural creatures and magic users forced to live behind it, had decided the sword was too powerful and should be disassembled and its constituent parts scattered. Minerva, in her walk-on role as the Gallic deity of war Brigindo, had taken it upon herself to keep track of where all the pieces had been disappeared to over the years, just in case. She had also managed to put herself in a position of owing Črnobog a favor, hence the reason she had used her goddess magic to "borrow" this particular puzzle piece from the off-public-view collection of the Sir John Soane's Museum and give it to Fred to deliver to Ljubljana.

What none of them knew exactly was what Črnobog intended to do with the sword once he had all the pieces. Fred suspected Minnie had a pretty good idea about it and that she was keeping it to herself. Whether that was to protect him and Reka or to protect Črnigad remained to be seen.

The other thing Fred didn't know, or at least didn't fully understand, was how all these deities who had managed to survive to the current day kept all their pantheons and overlaps and origins straight. He'd asked Minnie to draw out a family tree for him so he could understand it. A similar diagram had come in handy when he was being introduced to his late wife's enormous family in Tunis. Minnie had laughed at the suggestion and commented that she would make an effort for him but doubted that it would be of much help once all the lines of connection were drawn in. She said it would look more like a spirograph doodle than a family tree. He had asked her how she knew what a spirograph was. "There's a lot of overlap in maths and the arts," she had said with a shrug. He imagined a very adult Minnie turning a pink Biro through the holes of a 1970s plastic toy. Then he had imagined other adult things about Minnie and checked himself.

"So what now?" Reka set her well-worn backpack on the ground at her feet to pull open one of its many pockets. She extracted a black and white scarf that she wrapped around her neck.

Minerva offered and Reka allowed her to arrange the scarf. He was always amazed at the artistry fashionable women had with a simple square of cloth.

Fred had assumed they would take the tube to St. Pancras station and board the Eurostar. It was the fastest way to get back to the continent as Minerva had made it clear she did not fly unless other means were impossible.

"We are taking the tube to St. Pancras and then the train to Dover to catch the Calais ferry." Satisfied with Reka's style, Minerva shifted her bag on her shoulder and headed toward the nearest station.

"Why the ferry? Why not the Eurostar?" Fred attempted to say it in a manner of mild surprise. He assumed one did not question the plans of a goddess.

"I don't travel through the Channel Tunnel for the same reason I don't like to take airplanes." Minerva hadn't broken her stride or turned around to look at him.

"Are you claustrophobic?" Reka was apparently less concerned with potentially offending their travel companion.

"No. But I do find it's too easy to be flanked in a metal tube, more so when traveling in one under the ocean." Fred wanted to believe she was being funny, but there was no hint of amusement in her words.

After safely traversing the south of England and the English Channel, the trio made their way to the nearest rental car office outside the train station in Calais. Minnie had decided on the ferry that she'd had enough of other people for the day and had asked Fred if he knew how to drive and was licensed to do so.

Fred was happy to ditch the convoluted schedule of trains that would take them to Ljubljana and presented his passport and Slovenian driver's license to the agent at the rental car desk. After several minutes of clicking keyboards and making copies of his documents, the agent rewarded him with the keys to a Renault Captur. The three of them piled their bags into the boot and hit the road.

The drive through most of France was uneventful. Companionable silence filled the car, and thoughts of what his return to Ljubljana would be like filled Fred's head. He missed his routine and the regular customers. He hadn't realized how much of his life was filled with his connection to the teahouse until he'd had to find other ways to occupy his days. If nothing else, he'd caught up on his reading in London.

Minnie suggested a stop to stretch their legs and get a bite to eat when they got to Haguenau. One of the books Fred had devoured in his reading binge was The Maginot Line. A sandwich and a history detour would be a welcome break from the long drive. They had decided to drive on through rather than stop overnight, and thirteen or so hours in a car, even with people you liked, was a long time.

Fred pulled the car into a traveller plaza, and the three of them gathered provisions for a chilly picnic. He still found himself surprised by the array of goods available at what amounted to fancy petrol stations. Reka took the opportunity to have a quick cigarette in the smoking area before they returned to the warmth of the car and headed north toward

Schoenenbourg and the Maginot Line museum.

The smell of the bread Minnie had purchased made his stomach rumble. He hadn't felt hungry until the petrol station coffee hit his system. They arrived at the museum to find a very closed gate and, after a quick online search on his fancy Dušan-gifted phone, Fred learned the gates would be closed until the week of Christmas. So much for a stroll through the well-constructed but failed fortifications. The provisions still beckoned, and they opted for a less picturesque picnic in a nearby carpark.

Fred half sat, half leaned against the bonnet of the car and took a bite of his bread and cheese. Reka had wandered off a distance for another cigarette. She had tried to quit while they were in London, unsuccessfully. Fred had pointed out that such an uncertain time might not be the best opportunity to give up a habit that calmed her. Minnie leaned next to him, surveying the empty parking spaces and general quiet of the sleepy village. It was warm enough in the sun, but the occasional gust would chill and spur him to finish his lunch more quickly.

With a mouth full of the paste of half-chewed bread and cheese, Fred noticed a dip in the temperature that didn't correlate to any breeze. He felt more than saw Minnie's demeanor change, and his own alertness put all the hairs up on the back of his neck.

Minnie handed him the remains of the sandwich she'd made herself, and as quietly as one could speak without whispering said in his ear, "Get to Reka and run."

The hairs on his arms and all down his back joined the upright sentinels on his neck as he forced himself to stroll to where Reka stood gazing into the middle distance finishing her smoke.

"Can I have one of those?" Fred knew the out of character request would get a reaction from her.

When she looked up into his face, her eyes widened and her gaze dashed about trying to find what had frightened him.

Without Fred's having to say a word to her, she bolted toward the nearest structure, a tiny outbuilding that must have been a maintenance shed. Fred, older but still fit, was on her heels. Having reached the cover of the building, they crouched low and peered out from behind the corner.

Where their companion had been leaning against the Captur, now stood the British-Roman-Etruscan Minerva in all her braided-coiffure and breast-plated glory. A blazingly white toga draped over her body in contrast to the armor, and she held a small round shield in one hand and a pike in the other. Seeing Minnie in her god form was shocking enough; that she was squared off against another deity was more disconcerting. A slender, boyishly built woman equal in height stood about ten feet away. She wore a short-skirted, shift-like tunic with a quiver strapped across her body. The arm that held a bow to her side looked as ready to spring into action as an old-timey Hollywood gunslinger's. It was too far to make out either of the goddesses' expressions, but the body language indicated this was not a friendly meeting of colleagues.

Fred heard a low growl behind him and slowly turned his head. Two large hunting dogs stood shoulder to shoulder, their hackles up and their teeth bared. The growl intensified when the dogs realized they were spotted. Fred pushed Reka behind him and backed away from the hounds. Their cover was blown, but Fred surmised that was the point of the dogs.

He took a second to look at Minerva to see if she had noticed their new situation, and one of the dogs sprang at him and clamped its teeth into the muscles of his forearm. He stifled a yell and smacked the dog hard in the face with his free hand. It reacted by clamping down harder, and he could no longer suppress his scream. He was sure the teeth had gone to the bone, and blood began to drip from the wound onto the asphalt.

Reka stepped from behind him and clocked the dog hard on the side of the head. The animal let go in surprise, and Fred pulled his arm out of its maw and up close to his body, soaking his shirt in blood and dog saliva. The hound regained its composure and resumed its aggressive stance and growling, joined again by its companion. Fred and Reka stood in their own heightened stance. Fred's fight or flight mode was fully engaged, and Reka had a handful of his coat sleeve ready to drag him away at the dogs' first movement.

"Call off the dogs, Diana." Minerva's commanding voice reverberated off the outbuilding and even the few winter-bare trees surrounding the carpark. The other goddess, Diana it would seem, whistled, and the two snarling monsters ran to her, tails wagging like well-fed puppies. Fred and Reka kept their distance, each looking about for additional hidden members of the Huntress's pack, but Minnie beckoned them with a hand gesture.

As the two of them warily approached the goddesses, Fred flinched at the palpable crackle in the air. These women, these deities, were definitely not friends. The second goddess glared at him and Reka.

Minerva pulled Fred closer to get a better look at his arm. His breathing was shallow, and as Minerva painfully prodded the tatters of his coat before returning her attention to Diana, it occurred to him that he might be going into shock. Reka hadn't left his side but had given up her handful of sleeve to wrap her arm around his waist protectively.

"These are the best minions you could find?" Diana's eyes flashed with golden flecks even in the pallid November sun.

"They are not minions. They are friends, met through Črnobog." Minerva's voice took on a honeyed, bass note in her god form. It was a brief distraction from the pain in his arm.

Diana didn't flinch at Črnobog's name, but mention of him hardened her expression.

"You were a fool to allow yourself to owe him." Diana practically spat the words out at Minnie.

"My people suffered less. That was my only concern at the time."

Diana laughed, but nothing about it indicated mirth. "Your people. They only maintain your shrines to pocket the coins of travelers."

"And yours? A few bowls of porridge left in the forest are enough to sustain you and your pack?" Minerva was clearly not having the insult.

Diana shrugged.

"Fred, Reka, this is Dianae Abnobae, the goddess of

the Black Forest and to some extent the Vosges." Minerva pronounced the goddess's name with a smooth transition into perfectly accented French and, he assumed, Latin.

Neither he nor Reka did more than nod to acknowledge the introduction. Fred had already met her dogs, and that was acquaintance enough.

Diana did little more than nod herself and returned her attention quickly to Minerva. "You can't seriously be acting on Črnobog's behalf? His plan, such as it is, will only bring chaos."

"A favor is a favor. His success in reassembling the sword of Charlemagne does not mean he will succeed in the entirety of his endeavor." Minerva cocked her head as if she were thinking about it for the first time. Fred doubted that were the case.

"Goddess of Wisdom, my ass." Diana looked as if she would indeed spit.

"Maybe you should give me a little more credit."

"I won't stop you, but I also won't assist you or Črnobog when this spirals beyond his control. And it will. Surely you see that?" Diana petted one of the dogs as it nuzzled her hand, its muzzle still reddened with Fred's blood.

"Maybe things won't get to that point, but if they do, you may find you have no choice but to act." Minerva smiled, but it didn't go all the way to her eyes.

Diana snorted at her and turned to go.

She'd only gotten a few paces away when Minerva called to her. "Aren't you going to apologize to Fred for your dog mauling his arm?"

The goddess Dianae Abnobae lifted her free hand in a rude gesture and kept walking.

With a blink Minerva was Minnie again and deftly performing first aid on Fred's arm. Once his ripped shirt was off and Minnie had washed away some of the blood, he was relieved to see there was more pain than damage. He was thankful the dog had not thrashed and shredded his arm. There were sizable punctures, and it would take some scrubbing to prevent an infection.

Minnie wrapped her hands around his forearm, and he yelped again. Reka scrunched up her face and looked away as an orange-red glow suffused Minnie's hands and his arm. Slowly he felt the pressure of her grasp more than the nauseating pain that had radiated up to his shoulder. After a few moments, she dropped her hands and surveyed her work.

His arm was mostly healed, the puncture wounds were covered with bright red scar tissue.

"It will continue healing. The scars will fade, eventually." She poured a little more water over his arm to remove the last traces of blood. "Reka, would you get a clean shirt for him from his bag?"

Reka disappeared into the boot to retrieve a shirt, and he sat crosswise on the passenger seat with the door open. She handed him a button-down shirt, and with help from both women he was soon redressed. There was nothing to be done about the blood on his torn coat sleeve. Though his arm no longer hurt, it did feel mostly useless, and he was far too addled to finish the drive.

"We should find a place to stay." He looked from Reka to

Minnie.

"Oh, I'll drive." Minnie fished the keys from his pocket.

"I don't mean to question a goddess, but I had assumed you asked me to drive because you don't?" Fred had no desire to anger her; a woman who could heal could kill.

"I do know how, it's just been a while—at least since the last time I played field nurse—and I don't exactly have a license." She smiled as she motioned the two of them into the car as if they were unruly children who didn't want to go home after an afternoon in the park.

Reka, again less concerned with Minnie's wrath and more concerned about the incident with the dog, asked, "How long is 'a while'?"

"The war, I think."

Fred and Reka looked at each other. Fred couldn't read Reka's thoughts and he wasn't about to say his out loud, but he was guessing "the war" was World War II. He also had to wonder if that's when Minerva Britanna had requested a favor from Črnobog.

CHAPTER 13

Ivanka Novak walked into the courtyard of the building that housed Renegade Tea, Dušan Črnigad's photography gallery, an antiques store that was a cover for a practicing witch, a papered-over empty retail space, and the flat she would now share with Faron. Her sisters had been returned to the care of her Aunt Olga, who had finally copped to having her own supernatural powers. They were subtle but useful, as Olga had some kind of money magic that made her an excellent business manager. After the deaths of her sister and brother-in-law, Olga had inherited Ivanka's parents' business holdings and had joined forces with Gregor Bregant, the increasingly less-silent silent partner in Renegade Tea and by default, Ivanka's new landlord.

Veronika and Ana had had no desire to be separated from Ivanka and Faron, but their aunt's new honesty about her abilities had made staying with her more appealing. Faron had instructed the girls to heavily ward the house with Olga's assistance and to call him when they had finished.

Ivanka was curious as to why Faron, a god or demi-god or whatever the hell he was now, hadn't offered to ward it himself. She figured it was to further unite her sisters with their aunt after the separation and the revelations, but understanding anything Faron did was getting harder. Having waved goodbye to her sisters, she was tentative about returning to the teahouse. They had all come home, but everything was changed, and if her ability to foresee the future meant anything at all, the current situation wasn't stable either.

Fred opened the door of the teahouse while she and Faron still stood in the middle of the courtyard, their next move uncertain.

"Hello, travelers. There's tea made and some soup, too, if you'd like."

Ivanka had missed Fred. No matter how busy the teahouse got or how inexplicable the world had become, Fred was a still point that she could focus her tilting vision on. She hadn't realized how much she had depended on him in the months after her parents' deaths and through all the changes with Faron and her sisters. She ran to him and threw her arms around his shoulders.

"I missed you so much." His clothes smelled of curry spices and baking. Her whole body relaxed in the knowledge that she was truly home.

"I missed you too." Fred turned his head up and said to Faron still standing a distance behind her. "And you."

Ivanka looked into the teahouse. It hadn't changed at all. Dušan sat at a table near the pastry case with a woman with angular features and shining dark hair.

Fred let go first. "I should introduce you."

Reka came out of the kitchen drying her hands on her apron. "It's good to see more familiar faces." Ivanka hugged her then stood back to look at her. The two had become friendly before the events that had driven them all from the city on Dušan's orders, but Reka felt more like family now, having gone through exile as well. Maybe she wouldn't disappear like every other dishwasher they'd ever had at the teahouse.

The woman stood up and offered a hand to Ivanka first. "You must be Ivanka. Dušan has told me much about you. I'm Minnie."

Ivanka shook her hand and heard the snick-snick of arrows escaping a bow, the clank of steel on steel, and felt the hot breath of horses followed by the whirring and grinding of war machines and heavy artillery. Before she came back to herself, she saw the woman embracing Fred and kissing him the way people do before they shred each others' clothes off for the first time. Ivanka opened her eyes and blinked at Minnie. She was a goddess in disguise, no doubt about it.

A knowing half smile turned up the corner of Minnie's mouth. "Dušan said he thought the powers of your sight had grown. I see he was not mistaken." The goddess introduced herself to Faron—whom she addressed as Faron Belinus—as Minerva Britanna. Did deities always introduce themselves with double-barreled names, or was that a British deity thing?

Fred motioned for the new arrivals to have a seat, and Ivanka noticed angry, red scars on his forearm.

"What happened?" Ivanka peered more closely at the marks. They looked to be old scars, but he'd acquired them since she'd last seen him.

"Dog bite." Fred shrugged. There was more story there, but she'd have to dig it out later. It had to be bad seer protocol to slap her hand on his arm and get all the information she needed.

After a round of Fred's incredibly strong tea and fiery curried lentil soup, Dušan offered to walk them up to their new flat. When Faron had mentioned they would be moving into the Renegade Tea building, Ivanka had assumed it would be into Gustaf Lichtenberg's old apartment, but that was not the case. Reka had taken that one, and Fred had picked the small flat next to Goran's on the second floor above Vesna and Jo's apartments. She followed Dušan up the first flight of stairs with Faron behind her. Dušan handed her a key and pointed her to a door across the opening of the courtyard. She led them around the balustrade and slid the key into the lock. The door opened to reveal to a shallow entryway no bigger than a closet and beyond that an open-plan flat with two doors off the main room that served as a living space, dining area and kitchen. It wasn't an exact mirror of Jo's apartment, but close. All of their things were there with new furniture, or at least new-to-them furniture. Much of it looked like it might have been sourced from Goran's downstairs, but she liked the mix of antique and modern.

She didn't want to gush over anything associated with Dušan, but she did thank him. He nodded and suggested she check out the rest of the flat.

The first door was a decently sized bathroom, and the second was to a room she had dreamed of creating for herself in the tiny second bedroom of the flat they had lived in in Šiška before Dušan had sent them to Greece. An altar made from a huge section of tree trunk took up the center of the room. A tall apothecary cabinet—clearly something from Goran's shop—held all of her supplies and some she didn't recognize. A white ring had been painted onto the floor around the stump.

She would truly be an ass not to gush.

"It's perfect. Thank you." She wasn't going to hug him though. There was still a line, and she still didn't trust him as far as she could kick him.

"No need to thank me. Goran set all this up. Matjaž asked him to deal with his mother's things after her death, and Goran had no use for them." He ran his hand over the smooth edge of the wooden altar.

Faron spoke for the first time since they entered the apartment. "Is having Avgusta's things in here a good idea?" Despite being a god now, he bristled when he said the name of the woman who had tried to burn his mother at the stake.

"Goran cleansed everything and destroyed the items that it was best not to let fall into the wrong hands, or any hands for that matter. I assure you all is well."

Ivanka looked at the stump and then at the door. "How exactly did he get this in here?" There was no way to turn that piece of wood to get up around the bend in the stairs leading up to this floor or through the front door, let alone this one.

Dušan shrugged. "I assume the same way he got that monstrosity of a couch into Vesna's flat." He patted his pockets and looked at them. "I'll leave you to get settled in.

Fred has offered to make everyone dinner. Vesna and Igor should have arrived by then, and Goran and Gregor will be joining us."

"Thank you for this." Ivanka meant it, but it didn't erase everything else Dušan was responsible for.

"I'm glad you're pleased." He gave them a small nod and left.

"He's not evil." Faron looked at her, unblinking. When they'd changed trains in Zagreb, she'd noticed he had managed to conceal some of his more obvious god-like qualities. He couldn't do away with those silvered flecks in his eyes though. Dušan's eyes glittered like that, too, but it took longer to notice.

"I don't think he's evil. I think he's an asshole, and I think he has a plan he hasn't shared that is going to endanger us all." She walked back into the living room and realized there wasn't a bed anywhere. "Where are we supposed to sleep?"

Faron walked to the dining table and pulled it away from the wall. She realized then there was a raised area framed with molding painted to match. Faron pushed against it and it popped out. He reached up and pulled down a wall bed made up with some luxury linens that definitely hadn't come from their flat.

"Still an asshole." Ivanka patted her coat pockets for the key and handed it to Faron. "I'm going to go see if Fred and Reka need some help with dinner."

———

Vesna, pounded on Dušan's door. It was almost midnight, and she was long past the point of exhaustion. She had knocked on Jo's door before she'd even gone to her own apartment, but there was no answer. Ivanka had peeked out of her flat and padded over to fill Vesna in on where things stood at *Zajčeva ulica 2*. Everyone had returned except Jo, and though Dušan refused to say where Jo was, Ivanka had shared that her contact in Greece had said Jo was in the Nav.

All Vesna knew of the Nav was what Jo had told her. It was a place of unending gray where the lost dead went to stew. Vesna had imagined it to be like the Catholic vision of Purgatory or an unending wait at a doctor's office. She balked at the thought of Jo having spent months there, and that thought had directed her up a flight of stairs to beat on Dušan's door until he came out to explain why he had imprisoned her friend.

Ivanka had gone back to her flat, and Igor had tentatively followed Vesna up the stairs but stood back while she attempted several styles of knocking, each progressively louder. She heard the deadbolt turn, and the door moved open underneath her last knock.

Dušan was still fully dressed—black pants, black jacket, white shirt pressed to a knife's edge—because of course he was. He nodded at her and opened the door enough to let her in.

"Are you joining us, or would Vesna prefer to berate me alone?" Dušan looked at Igor, who still stood in the gloom outside the puddle of light from Dušan's door.

Igor followed her in without answering Dušan's question.

"Why isn't Jo here? How long do you plan on keeping her in your underworld prison?" Vesna wheeled on Dušan before he'd even had time to close the door behind Igor.

"The Nav is hardly a prison, and I think you would appreciate the changes Mor- ... Jo has made there." Dušan clicked the door closed, and the three of them stood facing each other in the small front room of his apartment.

Vesna noticed the triptych of photographs of Jo was gone and that where there had been two richly appointed chairs there was now a low divan long enough for the three of them to sit comfortably.

Dušan brushed past her toward the flat's kitchenette. "Can I offer either of you some wine? A cup of tea? You have been traveling for some time."

Igor sat on the end of the divan closest to the door. He started to say something that sounded like he was going to accept Dušan's offer but stopped when he looked up at Vesna giving him daggers.

Dušan took his time pouring himself a glass of wine. "Are you sure I can't offer you anything?"

It was his turn to get the brunt of her pointed stare.

He rejoined them and sat on the other end of the divan, leaving her the middle, if she wanted to sit. She was not going to sit on his conjured out of nothing furniture.

"When will Jo be here?" Vesna stood over him, but there was nothing she could do or say to ruffle Dušan.

"When this is over—"

"When what is over? You haven't even told us what you're planning. And seeing how well things went the last time, you'll probably get us all killed." Her voice was going up as her anger crested, and as much as she hated to sound shrill— after years of her mother saying she was exactly that anytime she was upset—she didn't hold back. Dušan's last plan had left more than one person dead, including her mother.

Dušan still wasn't taking her bait.

"We can discuss this later. It's late, and you've been traveling for hours."

"Days. We've been traveling for days." She wanted to shake him, but it wouldn't get anything more out of him.

Igor stood. "Let's get some rest."

"Rest? Don't take his side." Vesna glared at Igor. She could see that he was exhausted, and she knew how much he had given up to be with her the last few months. But her anger spilled over onto him anyway.

Dušan stood then and looked her in the eye. "Jo has been through enough. When this is settled, when things are back to the way they should be, she can come home."

Vesna registered what he said but knew that the words "should be" and "home" didn't mean the same things to Dušan as they did to her. "Where do you get off trying to protect her after all that you've done to her?"

"We can discuss this over breakfast. I had hoped you would join us for dinner, and we could all discuss it then."

"All?" How many other people did he intend to involve in his scheming?

"I'll explain in the morning."

Dušan had finally persuaded her to leave, and she and Igor had gone back downstairs to their flat. The closed door to Jo's apartment felt like a reproach. Vesna paused for a moment thinking the best course of action would be to go back upstairs and berate Dušan until he relented. There was no way to know how long that would take or if it was even possible to persuade a god to do something he didn't want to, but she couldn't help but feel she was failing her friend.

Unlike Dušan, Igor couldn't read her mind. She was grateful neither of them possessed that ability, but he could read her face.

"Let's sleep. You can take things up with Dušan in the morning, well rested." He ran his hand up her bicep and over her shoulder to cup the side of her neck. The motion felt protective but respectful and calmed her, briefly.

She would probably stare at the ceiling for most of the night, but Igor was right about how far she would get with Dušan tonight. She opened the door they'd left unlocked when they'd dropped off their bags and released the cats from their carriers. Antony and Cleopatra greeted them at the door, mewing loudly and happily that they had returned.

CHAPTER 14

Jo and Rok landed hard on their backs in the center of Tromostovje. Jo recognized Plečnik's handiwork in the balustrade of the Triple Bridge immediately. If that hadn't been a giveaway, the electric light comet appearing to race over their heads would have immediately placed her in Ljubljana's city center. It had to be December.

They still held hands and Jo made no move to get up, instead assessing for a moment the feeling of having dropped out of time and space into a quiet but brightly lit city, grateful she hadn't plonked them into the river—which would have been more typical, given her luck.

"I think you need to work on your landings." Rok laughed but there was a bit of breathlessness in it. She'd had the air knocked out of her too.

Jo reached over and tapped him on the shoulder with the knuckles of her free hand. "It's my first solo trip. I'm just happy we are in the right place and not on top of Mount Triglav or something."

"Technically it's your second solo trip." He pushed himself up to stand, offering her a hand when he was upright. "And, to be fair, the landing was a bit softer than last time."

She took it and pulled herself up with his assistance. Her stomach lurched a little as she stood, but it was a marked improvement over any of her previous trips from the Nav. Apparently she didn't get as inter-dimensional travel sick if she was driving. That was something.

She was surprised he was willing to even mention their landing into the Nav. That trip, predicated by him sending her into unchecked rage in her flat, could have ended worse for both of them. Things were still a little iffy between them on her end.

Rok brushed some road dust off her shoulder. "Where to now?"

"My place. I don't have my key, but I'm hoping this Morana magic can at least let me pop a lock." She looked around at the sleeping old city. There was nothing to indicate what day it was, except what she'd gleaned from her earlier observation that the lights were up for the New Year and it was cold. But it was probably one or two in the morning on a weeknight given the dearth of people about. "Do you think anyone else is here?"

"I'm know Dušan came back, but I don't know why anyone else would. The Board can't be any happier now than they were in the spring."

Jo pulled the heavy velvet cloak around her, gathering as much of it in her hand as she could so she could walk without tripping over the puddled hem. It was bit unfair that Rok had popped back into the Now in the clothes he'd been wearing when they fell through the hole in her apartment floor. Given that hers had rotted into the bog, she was glad for the velvet and the thin shift she been given. Shoes would have been nice, but at least she wasn't completely naked. The two of them made their way through the quiet but festively decorated neighborhood along the river toward Zajčeva ulica. Her street was dimly lit, and the solid doors that sealed off the courtyard to their building after dark were closed.

She had assumed Rok would stay with her, if just for the first night. Faron and Ivanka had moved into his old apartment the previous autumn, and all of his things were packed away in storage. She still had reason to be angry at Rok for hiding who and what he was to her all those years and for assisting Dušan in spying on her, but it was hard to stay mad when Dušan had played him too. And if she was being really honest with herself—because she had to be at this point, because no one else seemed to be—she did love Rok. As a friend. With benefits. And he and Gregor and Vesna were the closest thing she had to family other than her son.

"I'm guessing you don't have a key for this door either?" Rok laid his hand on it and gave it a push, to see if it would open.

The tumbler in the lock turned and the door stuttered open over the cobblestones in the inner courtyard. The scent of freshly mown hay and sun-warmed linen drifted over her.

Jo squinted at him. "Did you mean to do that?"

Rok shook his head. "I guess there are a few benefits to taking a trip into the realm of the gods."

"That's a positive take." She pushed the door open wide enough for them to walk through.

"It will probably come in handy." He followed her inside and closed the heavy door behind them, locking it again with his new skills.

The darkness of the courtyard was punctuated with the smells of cold stone, a little bit of damp from the river, and Rok's lingering magic signature. She hadn't expected a welcoming party. Despite Rok's assumption that everyone but Dušan would still be away, she had hoped someone would be there to greet them.

A yawn surprised her and after she'd infected Rok with it, she headed for the stairs. The stairwell light was out again as it didn't switch on with her step up onto the second stair where the motion sensor usually caught her. They climbed to the first floor as quietly as possible in the dark. If Dušan was there, she didn't want to talk to him tonight. She was as certain that he hadn't believed her capable of getting herself out of the Nav as she was that he would be pissed about her doing exactly that.

Rok started to put his hand on her door above the deadbolt but Jo stopped him.

"My turn."

She laid her palm on the door, but nothing happened. "How did you do it?"

"I didn't do anything. I just kind of assumed the door was open." Rok shrugged and offered by gesture to do his trick again.

"Let me try one more time." She thought about pushing the door open and put her hand above the deadbolt again.

The wood around the lock exploded inward, propelling the

deadbolt against the inner door before it fell to the floor with a solid thud.

"That's one way to do it." He was probably smiling as he said it, but it didn't amuse her. She had god magic all right but it was turning out to be rather unpredictable. At least her miraculous healing powers meant she didn't have a bruised ass and a concussion from smacking down on the bridge earlier.

Behind her, several lights cut through the dark courtyard as doors clicked open. By the time she turned around, multiple familiar faces were either peering out from those cracked doors or down at her from the railings of the floors above.

Vesna, in pajamas and slippers, rushed out from next door and flung her arms around Jo's head. "You're home."

Her words were immediately echoed by a fully dressed and very unhappily surprised Dušan. "And how exactly did you manage that?" The look he gave Rok would have melted iron into slag.

"I clicked my heels together three times and said 'there's nothing like pissing off Dušan,' and here we are." Jo leveled her own metal-melting gaze at her ex.

Vesna stepped back and shook her head before turning on Dušan. "What did you do to her?"

A breeze wended its way around the first floor balustrade, and Jo watched as it picked up wispy locks of Vesna's dark hair. That was not good.

"Vesna, it's—" Before Jo could get the rest of her protest out of her mouth the breeze gusted enough to slam the open doors shut and a bolt of lightning crashed its way to the ground, dead center in the courtyard, exploding a few cobblestones where it contacted the earth.

The divine, or even partially so, stood staring at Vesna, unaffected by the sudden electrical charge in the air. Those who were mortal covered their ears and crouched down waiting for the building to fall in on them.

"What the f—" Rok shook his head as if shaking water out of his ears and gave Jo a dirty look, quickly followed by one of surprise and concern.

"I wasn't me. It was her." Jo pointed at Vesna.

Vesna stood stock still. Her hair fluttered back to her shoulders from the dark nimbus it had created around her head. "I didn't mean to … do that."

"Impressive." Dušan gave Vesna a condescending soft clap with his false praise.

"God, you're an asshole." Jo marveled again that she had hooked her wagon to that particular star in this life and apparently in a past existence as well. Clearly, not shacking up with self-absorbed, snarky deities was a lesson she still needed to learn.

Vesna walked toward Jo and took her hand to pull her toward Vesna and Igor's flat. "I think you need to see this to understand."

"See what?" Why was everyone staring at her?

"Your face."

Jo tapped tentatively at her cheek with the fingertips of her free hand. "What about my face?"

Vesna didn't reply but gently pulled her into the bathroom

in her flat and pushed her in front of the mirror. "That."

Jo recoiled from her own image before peering in more closely to inspect the changes. Almost everything was the same except her eyes were a shiny black, including the sclera. Spidery black veins radiated from her sockets onto her cheeks and temples. Jo gently prodded the lines branching under the soft skin of her eyebrow. "So that's what it looks like."

"What did he do to you?"

"It wasn't Dušan, but it's a long story. Can we talk about that pyrotechnic display out there first?" Jo blinked a few times and sensed that her face had changed again. Vesna visibly relaxed, and a quick side peek at the mirror confirmed that she was back to her new, old self. Still Jo, but a little less gray and a little more dewy-skinned.

It was Jo's turn to pull her friend through the apartment, and they rejoined everyone on the flagstone landing outside. Everyone now included everyone in the building at that point. Anyone who hadn't been awakened by Jo magically kicking her door in had been shaken from sleep by Vesna's bolt from the blue.

Goran, in a comically fluffy bathrobe, surveyed the assembled crowd. "Dušan, I don't know what you've got planned for this army you've assembled, but I seriously hope you know what you're doing."

Dušan might have had a plan, but it was clear to Jo her arrival hadn't been part of it.

CHAPTER 15

Bettine sat up straighter at her desk. The person on the other end of the call couldn't see through the speaker phone, but Bettine knew attitude could be projected and a straight back was more authoritative than a desk chair slouch.

"When you've contacted all the Observers, I'd like you to reach out to the Witchfinders as well." She resisted the urge to fiddle with the pens on her desk. This part was boring grunt work but necessary, and she didn't trust Otto to do it. Not because he couldn't follow orders, but because this wasn't his crusade and the Observers would sense his hesitation.

Alessandro, the Observer in Venice, had been the first she'd appointed to her new Board. He was smart enough to get things done and malleable enough to not ask too many questions. There were benefits to the Board having kept their inner workings secretive, one of them being that Alessandro had never had any interactions with any of the others. He didn't ask her why a vacancy was open.

His voice was distorted by static on the connection. "This will be a bloody business, if what you say is true."

"I am, of course, hoping it won't come to that, but you

know what demons are capable of." Bettine smiled at her own lie. The Observers had all been taught to fear a demon like no other thing behind the Veil. Fear made people easier to manipulate. And besides, they should be afraid. Črnobog might not be an actual demon, but he had ignored every treaty and protocol set by the Board. It was time to put him down.

"The few Witchfinders who remain don't have much use for the Board." Alessandro wasn't telling her anything she didn't already know.

"True. But they do have a certain thirst for dispatching anything supernatural that threatens their imagined authority." Maybe that was too far. She didn't have any use for any religion. Magical thinking was magical thinking in her book, no matter the dogma that came with it, but Alessandro had Catholic leanings.

There was a long pause on the line. "I'll do what you ask, what is expected of me as an Observer."

He wasn't offering a ringing endorsement of her plans, but she would take it. She believed they could get rid of most of the things Črnobog might convince to join him. The scattering of Witchfinders who remained would probably react in their usual way once things got started anyway. More than a few of them would be happy to clang into their righteous armor for a little bloodshed.

"Thank you, Alessandro. Please alert me when you've completed these tasks." She started to hang up, but he asked a last question.

"When will this begin?"

"I don't know, but soon I think."

She ended the call and looked out her window across the dark rooftops of Paris to where the sparkling lights of the Eiffel Tower stood above the city. With all of the new security measures enacted after the terrorist attacks, the tower had taken on a greater aloofness in her imagination. It had become less the heart of the city she had made her home in and more of a lightning rod.

Her own lightning rod was on his way to Ljubljana. Otto had been sent on reconnaissance. Word had trickled in through her network that Dušan Črnigad had invited a few of his friends back to the city. She expected that small band to start showing their true colors soon. In her experience, two witches couldn't be in close proximity and not make themselves obvious.

Otto would be there to report, and Alessandro's network of Observers in the surrounding districts could be summoned to sweep in and put down the rebellion. That would give the new Board the excuse to clamp down everywhere else in Europe and convince their counterparts on other continents to do the same. It might take a few human lifetimes to rid the world of the supernatural completely, but the work would have begun in earnest. When it was complete, if she survived to the end, she could figure out a way to finally get Death's attention.

———

Jo woke up to the sound of Rok snoring lightly. It was still fully dark outside. She turned over to press her back into the spoon of his body and watched the light summer curtain she hadn't been there to change out flutter in the thermals from the radiator. Her body was tired, but her mind wasn't. She thought being home would have put her at ease, instead it had done anything but. Vesna was vastly changed. Dušan was angry. She'd expected that. She hadn't expected the look he'd given her before returning to his apartment.

His expressions had progressed through a quick series, and though she hadn't been able to name them all, she caught disappointment and worry. Faron's reluctance to meet her gaze or speak to her were equally disorienting. The thought that he had shifted his allegiance to Dušan came with a dull pain in her chest.

Before she set off on an hours-long rumination on what Dušan had taken from her—and what he had given to her—Jo closed her eyes tightly and took a few deep breaths. She turned her senses to the weight of Rok's arm over her waist and the warmth of his body pressed against hers. She matched his breathing and drifted back into sleep.

She was lying in the tall grass of the Ljubljanica barje. The river was swollen with autumn rains, and the first frost was burning off the changing leaves. There was an old-fashioned basket piled with apples on the edge of a dark cloak laid out to create a bower among the reeds. When she reached out to take one of the fruits, it was her hand she saw. The amethyst ring that had been a gift from Faron and Rok glinted at her in the bright moonlight. She had expected her other hand, the pale one she could trace the veins in like the multi-hued rivers of Slovenia.

Another's hand took the apple from her, and she watched as Dušan brought it to his lips to snap into it. Juice ran down the corner of his mouth, and before he could wipe it away with the back of his hand, she was on him. Her lips brushed over his, tasting all the summer sun and the nectar of the flowers that had become the fruit. She could taste his longing, and she could taste his fear. She pushed him down onto the cloak, her cloak with the tiny sparkling jewels creating a galaxy of stars underneath to reflect the constellations in Dušan's eyes as he looked up at her, hungry and surprised.

There was no tenderness in her in seduction. They crashed against each other, skin to skin, muscle against muscle and bone to bone. She willed him inside her, to be subsumed by her as Deity Vesna had been on the banks of that other, deeper river. But he didn't give. He was still separate, still his own being. Until she opened her eyes again and looked down into his face, into those fathomless eyes, and lost herself instead. She tumbled through his memories, watching her leave him in his studio that last time, watching her run through the orchard the night they had conceived Faron. He had watched her burn, watched her break under the strain of centuries of fear and neglect. He had watched her scream in betrayal when Dažbog had first sent her to the Nav, feeling guilty for his part in the sun god's scheme.

He had planned this all. Planned it for her, with her. He'd come to her in the cell the night before she had burned. She was delirious with hunger and the disease the Portal she had possessed had acquired in her imprisonment. She had thought him a hallucination until he had kissed her, held her filthy body against his to soothe her fever with his cool flesh. He hadn't offered to save her, but she didn't want saving. He had promised her vengeance. He had promised her a future where they would be loved again. He had told her of the sisters who would come.

Jo woke again and slid out from under the protective weight of Rok's arm and out of her bed, out of her apartment, up the stairs to stand in front of Dušan's door. It opened before she could knock and centuries of longing propelled her through the threshold into Dušan's, into Črnobog's, cold embrace, half of her thoughts still screaming for her to run away from him, from this place, from what she was about to do.

"I knew you would come."

CHAPTER 16

Dušan welcomed Jo into his flat, into his arms. He found her mouth with his. He tasted the same longing that he had in that connection at the gallery months ago, but there was an urgency now. She was his Morana again, but wrapped in Jo's flesh. His goddess had returned, but she was human now, too, and as much as he wanted to believe that didn't matter—it only mattered that she had returned to him—he knew better. He'd spent too much time as a human to not understand how that experience changed a person, even a divine one.

Jo kicked the door closed behind her with her bare foot. She had come to him from sleep, dressed too skimpily for the cold night air, her shoeless feet carrying her up the stairs and over the stone landing to his door. None of that seemed to matter to her as she kissed him more deeply, running her hands into the thickness of his hair at the nape of his neck. He wanted to savor this moment.

He wanted all of Jo, all of Morana. He changed into his god form under the light pressure of her palms, hoping she would join him. She looked up at him, the dark tendriled lines feathering out from her eyes over flesh gone the color of sun-baked marble. She didn't change fully and maybe that was this place or her hesitancy. Once the Veil was opened, she would have no difficulty.

He cupped her face in his hands, midnight against winter frost, and drank her in. His own thoughts spiraled away from him to the many times he had loved her, to the thousands of embraces they had shared, and before falling fully into the trance of her being, he encapsulated them in a warded bubble—their own miniature universe, out of time—lest they bring down the building on the heads of their mortal, and much less so, friends.

It didn't matter that there could be an infinite number of moments like this if his plan worked. He had waited for this reunion, planned for it. The strong scent of vanilla wafted over him, coming off Jo in waves as Morana's magic and memory flooded her. That she smelled of the fruit of an orchid from another continent was a product of her human rebirth, but if he cast his memory as far back as possible, he could no longer recall a different scent on her skin.

Dušan stopped her as she started to work open the front of his robes. She jerked back into the moment from wherever her thoughts, or lack of them had been, and stared at him with Morana's limitless black eyes. He wanted her, both in his weaker human form and in his stronger true one. But they had work to do. Once that was done, there would be nothing to prevent them from being together forever.

"We have to go to the church first."

Jo laughed, her usual lilting scale counterbalanced with the deep-throated peals of Morana's amusement. "I hardly think we need to proclaim ourselves before the Christian God."

Dušan slipped out of her embrace, piercing the enchantment he'd enveloped them in, and walked to the other room in the flat to pop open the plain wooden trunk at the foot of his bed. Inside, the sword of Charlemagne, reconstituted from the parts he had collected over the previous months and finished with the grip and pommel Minerva had acquired for him, lay on a bed of black silk velvet crackling to contain the magic of the sword. It was no gilded coronation sword. It was a weapon forged in fire and hardened with the blood of Charlemagne's enemies both mundane and magical. Dušan carried it back to the main room and laid it at Jo's feet.

Her eyes widened as she squatted down to pick up the sword, holding it as if she had held it often in battle and knew exactly how deadly it could be. He looked into the fathomless black pools that had replaced her stormy blue-gray human eyes, and she nodded at him. Words weren't necessary.

She dropped the sword to her side and turned to go out into the night.

Morana's spirit may have flowed through her, but she still didn't seem to have full rein of her abilities or didn't think to use them. Črnobog called Morana's cloak and some shoes to her to keep Jo's human body warm, and the two of them walked toward the barje, toward Plečnik's Church of St. Michael in the Marshes.

The center of the city was still asleep under the bright holiday lights, though the first movements of early morning had begun as vendors made their way to the market to fill their stalls and cooks made their way to the restaurants along the river that served breakfast for tourists. No one disturbed them as they walked in their own bubble, invisible to the denizens up before daybreak.

Jo walked ahead of him, the sword on one side, her other hand filled with the extra fabric of Morana's cloak. She didn't look back but kept on as the sky changed from the low black ceiling of a clouded night to the first hint of royal blue.

When they arrived at the church, the caretaker was just stirring. The smell of coffee made in the Turkish manner drifted on the morning air from the priest's quarters on the ground floor. Jo hesitated for a moment at the foot of the strangely humped-looking staircase that led up to the entrance of the church with the cutwork belfry towering above. The doorways in the stone glowed faintly as the first hints of rose gold entered the sky. It was a simple building for a church, a double-stacked box with the organic curves of the long stairs leading to the first-floor entryway. The belfry, modeled on the churches of the karst, was a narrow façade, pierced with arched windows or doorways capped within a platform for the church's bell under a square section of roof and a stylized double cross pinnacled at the very top. Simple but surreal, as if dropped from an Escher print into the flat landscape of the marshland.

Jo practically glided up the steps until she stood at the base of the tower.

"You have to go to that door." He pointed to the smaller window on the right side where a narrow set of steps ran diagonally from one lower window to a window halfway up the tower.

She nodded at him but looked up at the base of the smaller staircase. It didn't connect to the first-floor level outside the tower.

Dušan raised his hand and Jo lifted into the air, the cloak billowing out around her feet before she touched down on the small landing. She took the stairs slowly as though the weight of what she was about to do pressed down on her. It was an undertaking, and one he had decided she must do.

When she reached the second small landing, she faced the arched doorway and held the sword aloft. As the first golden rays of the morning sun shot through the sky, Jo brought Charlemagne's sword down through the thickened air inside the opening. Dušan heard the sword tip clank on the stone before a percussive wave burst out from the rip Jo had made in the Veil.

The pressure had knocked her off the steps, and she fell backwards, nearly striking the edge of the landing below where she would have broken her back on the staircase. Dušan's magic caught her and held her long enough for him to take her hand and pull her standing next to him, the sword still clutched in her other hand.

The caretaker threw open the sanctuary doors behind them and stared open-mouthed at the two figures standing at the top of the stairs. Črnobog, now swathed in the black robes of his true god form, held the hand of Morana, Queen of the Witches, draped in darkness glinting with tiny jewels scattered like dew at the hem.

"St. Michael the Archangel, defend us in battle, be our protection against the wickedness and snares of the devil. May God rebuke him we humbly pray; and do thou, O Prince of the Heavenly host, by the power of God, cast into hell Satan and all the evil spirits who prowl about the world seeking the ruin of souls. Amen." The man crossed himself and stood firm in the doorway as if Črnobog and Morana were set to storm the sanctuary.

"We are no devils." Črnobog waved to the man as he descended the staircase with Morana at his side. As far as the dark god was concerned, all deities were welcome in the Now. The world was theirs again.

———

Morana held Črnobog's hand in hers as they walked deeper into the marsh. Frost sparkled on the browned grass and the carpet of fallen leaves under their feet. Jo was there, but she was no longer in control. Morana's will was steering the good ship Jolene Wiley. Jo had been there when she'd split the Veil. It didn't feel like an out of body experience, because she was definitely still in her body. It was more like one mind having a conversation with itself, but the other voice wouldn't answer Jo's questions about what the hell was going on.

Morana was pleased though. Jo had gotten that message loud and clear. The Queen of the Witches was basking in the glory of the world returned to her. Morana wondered if Jože Plečnik had known that was the spot where the Veil had been thinnest. He must have and had set a church to the glory of the Christian God's warrior archangel on the spot to protect it. Morana was rifling through Jo's thoughts and memories, pulling up bits to look at like sorting someone else's laundry. The woman whose body she had taken hadn't grown up Catholic. Aside from her grandmother occasionally dragging her to Sunday school, she hadn't grown up much of anything, but having lived more than half her life in Ljubljana and earning a degree in art history had educated her a bit on the lore. Morana was surprised the woman hadn't put things together more quickly, but a god's vision was sharper.

The St. Michael of art carried scales as well as a sword, in order to weigh the souls of the dead on Judgement Day. The idea irked Morana a bit, considering the time she had spent away from the Nav while all those departed humans had languished, failing to accept their deeds and misdeeds in order to transition into the Next. Where was Michael then? Why didn't he offer to help her? It didn't matter now. The gates were opened, and the dead could move more easily to the Nav or the Next depending on the state of their souls.

Surely Jo would be pleased with that, though Morana saw Jo's thoughts were more concerned with how what they had done might affect the living people in Ljubljana—who were just now waking to a changed world.

Morana pushed Jo's thoughts to the side with a hard mental shove. It was impossible to contain her joy. The world was glistening around them even as it began its long winter slumber. The two gods made their way deep into the marsh, to the source of the Ljubljanica. Now in the quiet season, the river gently bubbled up from its underground course. Morana knelt at the edge of the pool and cupped her hands in the water for a drink.

———

Vesna woke early, trying not to disturb Igor's sleeping form as she extricated herself from under the duvet and circled bodies of two sleepy cats at the foot of the bed. Fred had planned a market run for the teahouse for a grand reopening and had invited her to join him before they'd all shuffled back to bed the night before.

The night before. There was a lot to process there. They had all come back from their exile changed; she'd sensed it and had seen it in the auras of her friends. Jo was most changed, but perhaps that wasn't surprising given she'd spent the last several months in the underworld. Like Persephone. No, like Morana, Queen of the Witches. That is the story Fand had told her as they had pored over her grandfather's book with its marginalia scribbled in his looping hand. He'd written long poems to the lost queen, invoking her to return to sustain the witches.

Vesna took a second to rail again against her mother's lifetime spent hiding what she was, denying Vesna the knowledge of her magical ancestors. It didn't do to dwell on that too long. Her mother had gone to her rest in the Next, if Jo's telling were to be believed. And there was no reason to believe her mother hadn't earned it. She had sacrificed herself for them all. And she had told her that her job as the new Witchfinder wasn't to persecute the witches as her father and all the Witchfinders before him had done. She was to take her Uncle Leo's work to its logical conclusion and protect the witches. But how?

Vesna dressed quickly and warmly in the dark, listening to rhythm of Igor's deep breaths and the sleep murmurs of one of the cats. She hoped Igor's and Cleopatra's dreams were kinder than hers had been.

Coffee would've been welcome, but she didn't want to make that much noise in the kitchen. She pushed her arms into her coat and walked out of her apartment into the first light of the morning.

The hairs on the back of her neck stood up immediately.

The morning air felt different, like it had thickened, or curdled, and she could almost see the currents that swirled in the space at the center of the building. Every sense was on high alert, yelling "Something is very wrong!" She stepped out tentatively to the railing to look down into the courtyard.

Fred stood with his back to the door of Renegade Tea, keys in hand, watching two spectral dancers in 18th-century clothing glide around each other in time to music only they could hear. A pale blue light infused their forms but didn't cast onto the cobblestones that still lay in morning shadow. Fred could see the ghostly revelers. She could see the ghostly revelers, in detail, right down to the flutter of ribbons on the woman's ornate gown. Had her bolt from the blue disturbed some haunting presence? They must be relatively benign, or surely the wards Goran and Jo had set wouldn't have allowed them to manifest.

Unless the wards had faded in the months they'd been away.

But even if the wards had evaporated, she'd never been able to see a ghost or a shade, even with Jo in the room talking to one. And as far as she knew, Fred didn't have that ability either.

Vesna went back and closed the apartment door without locking it and made her way down to the ground floor. The dancers were slightly more gossamer when she was looking at them from the bottom of the staircase. She could see Fred clearly through their twirling forms. Unwilling to walk through their new ghost neighbors, she made her way to Fred along the edge of the courtyard.

"Maybe it is a bad idea to have so many gods and witches

in one place. The ghosts must be drawn here." Fred looked at her like she could confirm his deduction.

"Your guess is as good as mine. I thought it might have been my accidental weather magic."

Fred shrugged. "Should we still go to the market?"

"I honestly don't know what else to do. They're just dancing. I don't think they're going to hurt anything."

Fred opened the door to the teahouse to retrieve the rolling market bag and closed it again, locking it.

The two of them made their way through the open courtyard doors— Vesna assumed Fred had already flung them wide when he'd come downstairs—and out into the watery light of the Old City.

It wasn't only their courtyard that had been visited with the weird. The cobblestones crackled with magic in a way they had only ever done when she'd been very drunk or very newly in love, and a thick mist rose from the now-pale-green, glowing river in fantastical columns like the turrets of Bavarian castles.

Fred glanced at her, that questioning look plastered on his face again, before turning back to the river as a Roman barge floated by, its crew yelling in what she thought might be Latin and scurrying about the deck. A wave of nausea overcame her as a faintly glowing hand burst from her chest, swiftly followed by the body it was attached to. A priest dressed in robes of the medieval church walked through her, gesticulating to his companion who was nodding along as they continued down the embankment.

Her impulse not to walk through the courtyard specters

was spot on. She could taste the priest's last, very fish meal in her mouth, flopping her stomach over again. It would probably be smarter to go back to bed, hoping she would wake up again into a less interesting day, but she took Fred's arm and they pressed on toward Prešeren Square.

Prešeren's cast bronze muse who usually sat at his patinaed shoulder, her breasts exposed, had abandoned him, leaving his statue standing alone, looking bereft on his platform. A quick glance up revealed that Julija, long the object of his unrequited desire, had left the darkened picture frame of her window on the building opposite. Despite the story of star-crossed lovers, she had not closed the gap between them after all these years of longing glances. Vesna couldn't blame her; she wouldn't have enjoyed being stared at forever either.

It hadn't taken Vesna long to normalize what was going on around them. Apparently things weren't going as smoothly for others. There were no other people on the streets, no other living ones at least. Ghosts bustled about, and she and the hairs standing at attention on the back of her neck got a sense there were darker things hiding in the shadows. Police sirens wailed in the distance, and more than a few shopkeepers were plastered to the front windows of their businesses looking out in wonder and horror at the bizarre sights that had greeted them on their way to work.

A scream pierced Vesna's wonderment and forced her and Fred's gaze to the sky where a verdigris dragon, another statue come to life, held what looked to be a meat vendor from the market in its talons as it made a swooping circle over the river before it landed on the walls of the castle on the hill above the old city. It nestled between two other dragons in a line on the parapet like pigeons on a wire. They were the dragons from Zmajski most, the Dragon Bridge, come to life and apparently terrorizing the market. One of the four was missing, which probably meant it was out looking for breakfast. The dragon on the right of the one who was now greedily devouring the poor vendor was preening its scales and licking between its toes like a cat. Vesna guessed that monster had already eaten.

It was definitely time to turn back. She pulled her mobile phone out of her pocket and tried to call Igor. No luck. A canned voice let her know that the system was overloaded with an unusually high volume of calls. No surprise there.

Vesna and Fred made their way back, slowly, toward *Zajčeva ulica* and the teahouse. She finally took a full breath when they reached the doors leading into the courtyard of their building. When she glanced back up to the castle as the fourth dragon took its place on the parapets, she knew the dancing ghosts twirling inside were going to be the least of their worries.

CHAPTER 17

Bettine attempted to calm Otto. It wasn't as if he hadn't seen stranger things in his long life. He shouldn't be afraid; he should be angry, furious even, that Dušan Črnigad had managed to put his plan in motion so swiftly and now they were going to have to deal with the fallout before they'd had time to put all their own plans into motion.

Otto described a city in panic as bronze statues came to life with the magic and adoration they had absorbed over the years and the dead roamed the streets. Hopefully dragons were the worst they had to deal with. If she was being honest with herself, if no one else, she wasn't overly fond of demons and had little desire to have to confront one that she didn't already have under her control. And Ljubljana held demons. Of that she was certain.

There was no way to know when exactly the Veil had torn, or more likely been ripped wide, but Otto estimated early morning. He had gone to bed after his travels, and the city had only been infused with the mundane magic of the holiday markets and light displays. She instructed him to try to make contact with Alessandro in Venice to see if the ripple had already spread. It would give her an idea of how fast things would go.

Alessandro had sent out a message to the list of European Witchfinders one of the former Board members had compiled, and he had copied Bettine. A few had returned terse messages that amounted to thinly veneered "fuck yous," some even including a blessing in Latin to the same effect. She guessed they would be more willing to assist when one of their own dragon statues rode into the sky with a tourist in its maw.

She had no idea how quickly the Veil would disintegrate now that it had been opened. To be fair, she had thought Dušan would just show up in the city center of Ljubljana as Črnobog and unleash the myriad demons he'd absorbed into that cloak of his. Ripping open the Veil was a bold move.

———

Ivanka made another pot of tea as more sleepy faces made their way into the shop. Igor had pounded on their door and filled them in on what was going on. He'd woken with a sense of dread after Vesna left and found Veronika of Desenica sitting at the foot his bed looking none the worse for having been burned as a witch.

After his long dead ancestor had coaxed Vesna's terrified cats out of hiding and had them purring in her lap, she'd given Igor a warning about his love being in danger and disappeared into the ethers leaving the cats mewling for their new friend. He'd gotten up with the intent of finding Vesna in the market and seen the ghostly dancers in the courtyard. After that he'd started waking everyone, telling them to meet in the teahouse. He was going to go find Fred and Vesna.

It hadn't taken anyone long to realize Fred and Vesna weren't the only ones missing. Dušan's door had been wide open, and Rok had rushed into the teahouse looking for Jo. Rok, disheveled with his eyes blazing, had been disconcerting. And he wasn't the only one. In addition to Faron no longer being able to cover his own dazzling eyes at all, Minnie had emerged into the courtyard in full Roman regalia, pike in hand.

Ivanka had met a goddess in Greece and knew Dušan skulked around in human form, but standing in the presence of Minerva left her awestruck. No wonder Fred had fallen so hard. Minnie—could she still call her Minnie?—joined their group after dismissing the ghostly dancers through an ornate door that appeared on the cobbles and disappeared as the trailing hem of the woman's voluminous gown crossed its threshold. The Roman goddess immediately went to Rok to calm him, calling him something like Hors Dažbog in that funny way she had of referring to the other gods present with double-barrel names like they were landed English gentry out of a movie. Rok, as far as she had known, was not a god. But he had gone to the Nav with Jo. Ivanka really wished she'd had more instruction in European mythology. It definitely would have been more useful to her now than calculus.

Faron in his god form, or what passed as such as he seemed to be perpetually in between being fully human or fully divine, sat at the table closest to the bakery case and tea station, not hovering over her so much as being watchful. That glimmer in his eyes was fully on display and had a flinty edge to it that made her a little nervous. It was like he was spring-loaded for battle, and she had to wonder what he had seen coming or what Dušan had shared with him when he had disappeared all those times.

By the time Igor returned with Vesna and Fred in tow, everyone in the teahouse was on edge despite, or maybe because of, the amount of tea they'd blown through. Ivanka and Reka had started to throw some breakfast together out of what they had left in the kitchen.

Vesna's face was pale but set as she scanned the assembled crowd, which now included everyone who'd slept in the building the night before except Jo and Dušan. Vesna marched straight to the table where Faron sat. He'd been avoiding looking at her and staring into the depths of his tea like it was a scrying bowl.

"Where are they?" Vesna sat down in the chair opposite. Her tone, though angry, held a note of sympathy.

Faron looked up at her, and Ivanka caught the almost imperceptible recoil when Vesna saw his eyes. Ivanka understood why he'd been so absorbed by the tea, or had pretended to be. His eyes had gone from flinty sparkly to full on glowing with a silvery white light.

"She wasn't supposed to come back." He looked at Rok and Minnie sitting together at another table as incongruous as an ancient scruffy bearded man and a Roman goddess could be, snuggled up drinking tea out of mismatched china in a punk-rock teahouse in the middle of Old Town Ljubljana. If the situation hadn't felt so dire, Ivanka would have laughed.

"Dušan said we could open the veil without her and that once things had settled, he would go and get her. He said mundanes wouldn't want the 'weird' back in the world, but they would get used to it and it would make it easier for people like us, like Mom." Faron narrowed his eyes, concentrating the glow to slits. "He lied to me."

Minnie floated across the room, her brilliant toga billowing slightly as she walked, if one could say a goddess of such stature could do something as mundane as "walk." She took the third chair at the table and laid her hand over Faron's. "It is Črnobog's way, to be the trickster."

She turned to face the others in the room. Ivanka moved to stand next to Igor where he had sat at a table with Goran, who'd been one of the first to wander in.

"Črnobog has taken his Queen to open the Veil." No one reacted. "That is why you see Faron Belinus, Hors Dažbog, and myself as we are. In the realm of the gods we can only be our true selves. That means this now is the realm of the gods. And spirits …" Her voice trailed off.

And very quietly Vesna whispered, "Among other things."

Minnie nodded. "Yes. Worse things."

———

Morana had drunk her fill at the pool and turned to Črnobog with a different thirst in her dark eyes. He knew the city would be in chaos and that the chaos would slowly spread over the next few hours and days to every coastline of the continent before seeping into the oceans and spreading to the rest of the world. There was plenty of time to revel in the destruction of the secrecy the Board and the Witchfinders drew their powers from. What was time to him now? It was nothing, as it should have always been, as it was before materialism outstripped magic.

He cupped Morana's white face in his hands and kissed her deeply. His senses filled with her presence. The scent of vanilla on her skin and the taste of the sacred river on her tongue. Her thousand names echoed in his thoughts. She pressed against him, her nakedness revealed as quickly as she thought it into being and he luxuriated in the chill of her skin against his own. As she pushed him down onto the frost-covered ground he continued to reach for her, pulling her to him from his dreams over the intervening centuries from her last death. He blinked against the dappled winter light that played through the last few dead leaves clinging to the branches above them, and for an instant, in his mind, it was Jo astride him, her dark blonde hair flowing out like it had against the orchard floor.

———

Morana had missed the feel of him. Missed his skin that could bring a shiver or warmth depending on his disposition. She had missed the world and the stark beauty of the dying season. Inside her now she held that darker magic close to the brightness the spring goddess had given back to her. She also felt Jo's roots in her veins as they sought to find purchase in the earth again. Images of Dušan as the man he had pretended to be for so long played through Jo's thoughts as if Morana were turning the pages of a photo album. Jo had loved him, almost idolized him, and he had abandoned her. Hurt her like no one else had. But even that wasn't true, there were other wounds, older ones that had made his blow so much less of a surprise.

Jo, like Morana, had drawn herself in two. Walling off that part that had been soft enough to be hurt. But it had seeped out. It had found others like Rok, who was now made semi-divine. There was also a tall priest with a lion's name, a dark-eyed woman, and a man named Milo. All dead now. There was so much guilt there. And a ghost, Henry. That was not really his name, but it was the name Jo carried and burnished in her mind. And still there was Dušan, the father of her child, their child. That light had burned at the center of that walled garden in her heart.

Maybe it would have been easier for Jo if she had known Morana was there all along, walking the boundaries of that garden, waiting for the walls to finally crumble. Morana felt a flash of Jo's presence. She wasn't going to subside as easily as Morana had imagined. Never mind, perhaps it would be convenient to have a human face if she ever needed one again.

———

Was this what it meant to be a Portal? Jo had only vaguely understood what it meant to be a threshold that could be crossed only once. But Morana hadn't crossed a threshold. According to Dušan and Deity Vesna, and Morana herself, the Witch Queen of the Universe had been there all along. Jo tried to push her senses out to the edge of her body. It was still hers after all, whatever Morana or the dark lord thought. That body that had been solely hers to control was now, under Morana's management, fully engaged in fucking Črnobog's brains—or whatever gods had between their ears—out. There had been a time when Jo might have enjoyed reconnecting with that lost love, but not now. And she didn't feel connected to anything, not even enough to care about what she guessed was some hot god on god action.

Morana's will had put her in a neat little box for the time being then turned on some virtual reality porn. Jo could push against the sides, and they gave a bit, but she couldn't get out.

Deity Vesna may have returned what had been taken from Morana, but what had been taken from her, Jo, in that process? She hadn't asked for this. Hadn't asked to fall in love with Dušan. Had that been Morana's doing way back when? Jo didn't want to believe that. However painful his abandonment at the end had been, she had enjoyed her time with him. She punched the thought that it hadn't been her choice and her experience down into her own memory box to protect the past from being tarnished by the present. And because it hurt to remember. If it still hurt to remember, those feelings had to belong to her, didn't they?

It hadn't just been that day in the orchard that was magical, or the time in his studio spent honing her craft behind the lens, talking about light and framing. They had talked about everything, even to the point of heated debates on what, at the time, had seemed desperately important to her—like what was the purpose of art and how responsible were artists for the images and ideas they put out into world. He had listened to her, and he'd been a god with all the answers all along. Gods did have all the answers, didn't they? Somehow that made the memory even more bittersweet, an ancient god nodding at her explanations and laughing at her jokes.

Whether or not gods had all the answers, they weren't perfect. And maybe that was the whole point. Dušan had come to her as a man, imperfect and cocky as hell, but in that bad boy, alluring way of his. She had built the fairytale around them, imagined a life where they made art and fixed the world's problems lying in bed together in the afterglow. She'd peed on a plastic stick in Vesna's bathroom and watched a blue line emerge, still thinking there was some kind of future where there was a "them."

Jo had never imagined it would look like this, the ultimate third wheel experience.

Morana rolled them off Črnobog and lay next to him on the ground staring into the naked canopy above them and the low, clouded sky beyond. The occasional electric blue streak erupted as a cloud billowed out from its compatriots, reminding Jo of Southern heat lightning. But those flashes were never blue.

The window and the sword.

Dušan had given her a sword. She'd cut open the sky with it.

No. She'd cut open the Veil.

She'd cut open the Veil that Charlemagne's magicians had drawn over the world before he'd slaughtered them with that same sword. She'd unleashed the In-between on the Now. On the city and everyone in it, including everyone at the teahouse, everyone she loved.

Demons.

She'd unleashed demons so Dušan could get his rocks off with Morana in the woods.

God fucking dammit.

CHAPTER 18

Vesna looked from Faron to Minerva and around the room at the anxious and confused faces. The very real thought that they were at war, and that her dearest friend might be fighting for the enemy, settled itself in Vesna's mind. Fand had warned her that what was to come wouldn't be easy, and that she would be called upon to lead. She had no interest in being a general. Not in Črnobog's army, as Goran had suggested the night before, or in the forces against him. But she also wasn't down for letting innocent civilians get eaten by dragon statues come to life or letting the people she cared about die at the hands of whatever else lay out there waiting.

Her gaze rested on Minerva again. She was a warrior and a god. Surely having her with them at the teahouse meant she was ostensibly on their side. "What do we do now?"

Minerva leaned back in the chair and looked around the room at all the faces now intent on hers. "You can hole up here until the worst is over, or you can stand against Črnobog and try to close the Veil again."

"Is that even possible?" Ivanka stepped closer to the table, still holding a teapot in her hand like it was any other day and she was going to offer Vesna, Faron, and Minerva a top-up on their Darjeeling. The tiny normal things made the bizarre world they'd tumbled into harder to bear.

"Almost anything is possible." Minerva smiled ruefully.

"Possible means we try." Igor spoke for the first time since Faron had told them what he knew of Črnobog's plan.

Several heads nodded in agreement.

Minerva sat back up and folded her forearms on the table in front of her. "Rok and Faron and I can go deal with the dragons and whatever else might be out there wreaking the worst of the havoc. Vesna, you should contact the other Witchfinders if you can and warn them. And you should get in touch with the nearest Observer to let them know what's going on."

Vesna balked at involving the Board, or even any of the other Witchfinders. The last group were at least as likely to murder her or Ivanka just for being witches as they were to send out demonhunters to help them.

Vesna felt the goddess's mind reach into hers like little icy tendrils creeping along her scalp and into her ears. "We can sort out allegiances later. They can prepare for whatever is coming where they are. Now that the Veil has opened here, it will begin to disintegrate elsewhere. Though things may be bad in Ljubljana, there are places where the Veil has been keeping much worse things at bay." Minerva's eyes flashed even brighter for the briefest moment, and a wave of fear washed over Vesna with images of war and destruction.

They couldn't let it get to that.

Vesna stood up without addressing anyone present

any further and shut herself up in her office. The mobile phone system was still trashed. Either the line stayed dead after dialing, or a bland, robotic-sounding woman's voice explained that they were receiving an unusually high volume of calls and to try your call later.

She might not have a later to call.

The computer booted up without too much struggle, and she began typing under the assumption that email messages would go through. The first was to the Witchfinder in Vienna. She had met him once, at her father's funeral. He was barely older than she and seemed far too fragile and sickly to push a demon back into a jar, but he was a Witchfinder she knew how to get in touch with. There were very few of them left, and they generally kept to themselves.

She sent another email to Alessandro—the Observer who had contacted her in the time between Gustaf's and her mother's deaths and she and all of her friends had disappeared to the corners of Europe at Dušan's whim. He seemed nice enough, for an Observer, but he was still an agent of the Board. After Bettine's treachery earlier in the year, Vesna had even fewer reasons to trust anyone involved with their evil empire. Still, Minerva had suggested it, and Vesna had to trust a goddess of war knew what the hell she was doing.

It seemed like seconds after her mail program made the whooshing sound of her words being transported away into the ether, that it chimed with an incoming message. Alessandro must have been sitting on top of his computer, or the mobile signals in Venice weren't yet bothered by what was happening in Ljubljana.

He breezily, or as breezily as one could in reply to an email explaining that bronze dragons had come to life and were eating the villagers, relayed that a member of the Board, a man named Otto, was either in Ljubljana or on his way and he would give him her contact information and location to find his way to them.

Vesna replied as quickly for him to just put her in contact with Otto. There was no need to brave the streets. She left out the part about not wanting anyone from the Board anywhere near the teahouse or her friends. After hitting send, she closed the laptop again and stood, tucking the machine under her arm, and rejoined everyone gathered around the table where Minerva—it was impossible now to think of her as Minnie—was still sitting explaining to a group of demi-gods, witches, and teahouse staff how they could close the Veil.

Vesna sat the laptop down on the next table. No one had noticed she was standing there as they were held rapt by Minerva's words and those flashing god eyes.

"We need to find Jo first." Vesna spoke quietly, or thought she had, but almost every head turned to face her despite the glittering eye thing the goddess had going on.

Minerva spoke first. "We can do that, but I think it's clear she's with Črnobog. If she is, then she is responsible for what's going on outside."

"I don't care. Jo would never do this. She's fought against a demon. She's been possessed by Achelous. She knows what a revenant is capable of. She would never set those creatures on mundanes in general, let alone us." The image of Jo curled around Leo's corpse on the forest floor flooded Vesna's thoughts, and she couldn't imagine for a moment that Jo would unleash anything from the In-between on the world on purpose.

The goddess smiled ruefully. "Do you really believe that? Jo is a god now, like Faron or Rok." Vesna noticed Minerva didn't include herself in that list. "She could no more be under Črnobog's sway than I am."

"You brought him what he asked for." Fred spoke up across the table. Vesna could see that it pained him to correct Minerva. He was in awe of her, and if his aura was anything to go by, in love with her as well.

"That was different." Minerva adjusted herself in her seat like a bird settling its ruffled feathers. "I owed him the favor."

"For what?" Vesna stepped closer and looked down into the face of the still-seated Minerva. "What could he have done for you that you would risk being party to that?" Vesna pointed to the front door of the shop to indicate everything that was going outside their building.

Minerva got very quiet. "He and a circle of British witches helped me stave off the Germans. London didn't fall."

"I guess that's a pretty big favor." Reka took a sip of her tea and looked at them all. "So how do we even find Jo?"

Vesna looked between the three gods, or demi-gods— if that's what Rok and Faron were—hoping one of them would fess up to what they were eventually so she could arrange her mental family tree accordingly. Rok looked back at her, his face openly confused by all that had taken place. No help there. Faron looked guilt stricken. Minerva it was. Vesna leveled her gaze at the goddess. Of the three currently present and accounted for deities she was definitely the most intimidating. Maybe that was the difference between a god and a demi-god.

"She's with Črnobog. But she isn't your Jo. She is Morana, the goddess of life and death, who has had her full powers returned to her." Minerva emphasized the last bit about having her full powers returned. Vesna didn't know exactly what that meant, but given that she herself had managed to call down a bolt of lightning by accident, Morana at full power was probably terrifying. But Jo had to still be in there somewhere.

———

Jo pushed against the mental box Morana had tucked her into without making any progress in regaining control of the situation. Črnobog walked beside Morana, but it was clear that Morana was leading them back into the city. She had said something to Dušan about wanting to return to the place of her execution and watch whatever was there now crumble into the river.

Where was the goddess of spring and all that vague sense of goodness? Had Morana always been so dark? That didn't line up with what little information Deity Vesna had shared with her, or what she'd been able to glean from this mind meld business. She was in no way equipped to deal with wrestling a goddess for control of her own body. How had she regained control after Achelous left? Oh, right, he'd burst out of her, leaving a saucer-sized burn in the middle of her chest that she'd covered with a giant tattoo of an eclipse. Did Morana's form still bear her tattoos? All those marks would look garish against that paper-white skin. She tried to look at her forearm to see if she could see the sparrow on her wrist, but there was no response in the limb.

Morana and Črnobog were making brisk time, as if the gods could cross the distance more quickly. In the outer neighborhoods, the streets were weirdly empty with random cars stopped in the middle of the road, one door open as if the driver had fled without looking back. The air crackled with what Jo now knew was magic. She hoped that the weirdness of the weather and the sense of dire impossibilities had kept most people inside. But people were people, and surely there would be a few who had to investigate, like those who ventured into blizzards and floods, determined to witness the destruction.

The smell of rotting cabbage hit her and Morana's nose, she guessed, like a garbage-splattered alley wall. Demon magic. Jo would never forget that smell. It had drifted over Zelena Jama the night Tomaž, Ivanka and her sisters' father, had been exploded all over their pristine IKEA catalog kitchen. It had followed her down the street to the shop where she and Maja's ghost had hid in the disgusting bathroom waiting on Leo to collect her. Leo. Even the thought of his name hollowed out her chest, or Morana's chest, or whoever the fuck's chest it was now.

Morana stopped her long strides, Črnobog having stopped a step behind her.

"It will only take a moment to take care of these." Črnobog stepped away toward where the scent seemed to emanate from.

"Why bother?" Morana's voice rang in Jo's thoughts like being on the inside of bell when someone pulled the rope.

"It's better to dispatch with them now. I would prefer the city not be in total ruins." Črnobog had barely turned to address her question.

"Is it better to be feared or loved?"

He did turn then. "I've been feared long enough." Without waiting for a retort, he walked toward two inky black clouds of wingbeats and eyes drifting in the shadow of an apartment block. They rushed out of the shade to greet him, like dogs do when their owner returns after being away at work all day. He raised his palms to them, and they disappeared in the folds of his robes. Maybe that's why everything about him was blackened. He absorbed all those demons and the void that seemed to exist at the center of them where your eyes could never focus—like those pictures Fred had shown her of objects coated in Vanta black. He had joked that they should have some teacups made with it in keeping with the theme of the teahouse. It probably wasn't food safe though.

Why did her mind keep drifting away from her? It was like it didn't have an edge, despite the box she'd imagined, and if she wasn't careful to rein it back in, it would dissipate into wisps, taking her will with it. Morana and Črnobog would be pleased, she guessed, if they didn't have to deal with her again.

Črnobog returned to Morana's side, and they continued their journey into the city center, to the Old Town.

"I would like to meet your son." If Jo's mind didn't drift off into the ethers, it was going to be pulverized into dust by Morana's voice clanging around in her head.

Črnobog froze.

Jo watched him react through what little space she could see; it was a little bit like watching through two eye holes cut into a Halloween sheet. His face didn't change, but his presence shifted.

He continued to hesitate before he finally answered with a flippant, "That can be arranged."

Was he worried about Morana meeting Faron, or was he worried about how Faron would react to Morana being in charge of the body more recently animated by his mother? Jo would be more likely to bet on the second, but the possibility that Črnobog gave an actual shit about either option surprised her. Maybe there was some hope there.

Or maybe he was worried about how she would react to Faron transformed fully into his god form, like Črnobog and Morana. That was, indeed, another thing for her to worry over, but there was precious little she could do about it. Morana had her locked down hard enough that she couldn't even use her own mouth to speak, let alone scream.

———

Ivanka stood in the courtyard looking up at the square of sky framed by terra cotta roof tiles. The cloud ceiling was unusually low, but not like a recently lifted fog—more like an actual ceiling that couldn't be pierced. Branching veins of blue light zagged between the clouds often enough that the crackle had become background noise.

A loud thud landed against the wooden doors to the courtyard. They had been closed behind Fred and Vesna when they'd returned, and the seldom used, old-fashioned beam had been lowered into place in addition to the more modern lock. Knocking followed a moment after the thuds. Insistent knocking.

She moved toward the door and got close enough to hear two people speaking softly but fervently at each other on the other side.

"Who's there?"

"Thank god. Who's that?" It was a man's voice, but three inches of wood and who knows how many layers of paint muffled it too much to know if it was familiar.

"I asked you first." The city was overrun with ghosts and ghouls. She had no idea who or what might be trying to get an invitation through all the warding they had done. She looked up again as a bronze dragon looped over their courtyard before flying away. She didn't fancy opening the door and accidentally letting in something worse.

"Gregor and Janez."

Ivanka started to lift the beam but stopped and shouted through the door. "Prove it."

"Maybe you need to tell me who you are first." The door didn't hide the irritation.

"Faron's girlfriend."

"Ivanka, can you please let us in?" The other voice said something, but she couldn't make any of it out.

"Prove you're Gregor."

Two driving licenses slid through the slim gap in the doors and fell to the cobblestones at her feet. A very good photo of Janez and a truly awful one of Gregor graced the two pieces of laminated plastic.

She raised the beam up and turned the lock. Gregor pushed the door open just enough for the two men to slip in and quickly shoved the door closed again and turned the key in the lock. Ivanka moved the beam back into place and looked the two men over.

"How did you get here?" Gregor lived in a village on the outskirts of town. He and Janez could have walked there, but it would've taken them some time.

"We drove as far as we could and then stashed the car near Tivoli. We walked the rest of the way." Both men looked fashionably disheveled, but not as terrified as the people Vesna had described hiding in the shops watching the sky.

"Do you have a death wish?"

Gregor answered with a quick no and Janez shook his head. "We just thought there might be safety in numbers, and we couldn't get anyone on the phone to tell them we were coming, or to find out if you all were still alive."

It was Ivanka's turn to nod in understanding. "I'm sure Vesna will be glad to know you're okay. There's some tea made and some leftovers from breakfast in the kitchen."

Gregor indicated Janez should go inside, and he lingered in the courtyard with Ivanka.

"Any word from Jo?"

Her face must have given her thoughts away as he looked immediately stricken.

"Is she dead?" Ivanka watched the color drain from his face.

"No. Or I don't think so." Ivanka really had no interest in

being the bearer of bad news. She'd much prefer Vesna or Faron handle this one. "Why don't you come inside, and Vesna can explain what we know."

Gregor held the door to the teahouse for her, and they found Janez already seated at a table with Goran and Fred. Reka was walking toward them with a fresh cup and a pot of tea.

"Who else is here?" Gregor looked around at the empty tables.

"In the teahouse? Just us right now. In the building, Vesna and Igor. Faron, Rok, Minerva—"

Gregor stopped her. "Who's Minerva?"

"A friend of Fred's he brought back from London." Ivanka's thoughts slid back to that image she'd had upon meeting Minnie, Minerva's human disguise, in the teashop when they'd arrived. Fred definitely wanted to be more than friends with Minerva. "The three of them are out trying to do what they can to keep people from getting killed. Have some tea, and I'll go get Vesna to fill you in."

The bells clanged as the door opened again.

"Fill him in on which part?" Vesna stood behind them dressed like she was going skiing with a bunch of goths.

"On Jo." Gregor's color still hadn't quite returned, and Ivanka could easily imagine how Gregor must feel. He was practically a brother to Jo, and she knew exactly how it felt to have your sister go missing when there were more things in the world than you had dreamed possible.

"You better sit down first."

Gregor did as he was told, and Reka brought another cup to set on the table in front of him and fill with tea. Darjeeling by the scent of it.

Vesna filled him in on what they believed had happened and where they thought Jo was or at least who she was with.

Gregor stared in disbelief. Janez put his hand on Gregor's thigh to comfort him but it didn't lessen the pained look on his face. Goran and Fred just listened. They had heard this already.

"Jo would never do that." He had repeated the same phrase throughout Vesna's retelling.

Vesna leaned back in her chair and studied her folded hands in her lap before looking back up into Gregor's face.

"I'm not sure if Jo even still exists."

All of Gregor's disbelief and sadness recoiled and struck back out at Vesna as anger. "How can you even suggest that?"

"Morana is a powerful goddess. More powerful than Črnobog. She's been worshipped for longer than memory or records in multiple forms across the continent and possibly into the East. Goran thinks that she is the daughter of Hecate or maybe even Hecate herself transformed by the beliefs of the early people who lived here. Can Jo survive being possessed by that? Portals weren't meant to survive if the gods overtook them."

"But Jo is different, because of Faron."

"She was different. She—"

"Don't say 'was.' Don't act like you're certain she's gone." Gregor said it in anger, but there was resignation mixed in with the resolution.

The bells on the door rang again and Minerva returned to the teahouse. She had gone to do what she could to protect the mundanes from the immediate dangers, like hungry dragon statues.

"Jo isn't gone." Minerva strode to the table, doing that goddess walk thing that made it impossible to look away from her.

"How can you know that?" Fred seemed to be the only one of them willing to question Minerva now.

She smiled at Fred, almost wistfully. "Morana did not possess Jo as a god would possess a Portal. To do so would make Morana mortal, again. There was always something of Morana in Jo, waiting to come to life, to return. I don't know what triggered it. As much as you'd like to think I know everything, I am not omniscient."

"If Jo is still in there, can't she take control?" Gregor looked hopeful for the first time since he'd sat at the table.

"That depends on how strong Jo's will is. Even then, I'm not sure she can do it while the Veil is open. It's not something I've ever needed to consider." Minerva sat down and looked up at Reka, who had been standing still holding a pot of tea and listening through the whole exchange. "Could I have a cup of that?"

———

Bettine angrily tapped the top of her computer shut. Otto had emailed to tell her the phone lines were completely jammed. Alessandro had also messaged to tell her that the tear in the Veil had not yet reached Venice but that the streets were filled with people gawking at the storm clouds gathering beyond the lagoon and at the strange blue cloud-to-cloud lightning ricocheting inside the thunderhead.

It was spreading more slowly than she had anticipated, but it was spreading. The next nearest Observer and one of the remaining Witchfinders were in Vienna, and neither had replied to Alessandro's messages. Alessandro had apparently received a message from Vesna Kos letting him know about the situation in Ljubljana and asking what assistance he could offer.

Otto refused to leave his hotel room to see if all of Črnobog's minions had returned to his little enclave around the teahouse. She had no intention of going to Ljubljana, but if Otto believed death was waiting for him outside the confines of his lodging, there was little else she could threaten him with. Night would fall soon, and there might be as much to frighten him inside as there was outside. She would be curious to see who or what survived the first night.

She opened her laptop again and fired off a message to Alessandro to string Vesna along until they could gather enough Observers and Witchfinders together to enter the city and take back whatever Dušan had used to open the Veil. She had to hope it was still there and that no mundane military decided to level the place thinking that would stop it. The only thing leveling the city would do now is destroy the one thing they might be able to close it with.

—

Morana had halted their journey to the city center again to marvel at the changes in the world since she'd last walked in it. There were things she was unsurprised by like the shining glass façades of buildings, and then there were relatively pedestrian things like discarded product wrappers and the occasional plastic cap that held her enraptured. Ljubljana was relatively litter-free considering how messy humans were, but Morana had been fascinated with the few brightly colored bits of flotsam on the roadside.

"Why would they make things out of a substance that will outlast their family lines to just throw it in the gutter?" She was crinkling a candy wrapper in her hands, repeatedly folding it over and watching it snap back into place.

It was amusing to watch. And he was glad for any delay in getting to the teahouse, whatever the cause of it was. In all his conversations with Faron, his son had never asked what would become of Jo when she returned from the Nav. Faron had known that his resurrection of her on her birthday after she'd been killed by Veronika's dilettante revenge magic had made her immortal. Črnobog had neglected to tell Faron that his mother had always been something like a Long-Lived, and that she would change further.

He hadn't been prepared for his own feelings about a forever-changed Jo. Morana was still angry and out for vengeance, and he did believe she should have that revenge, but his disappointment in losing Jo for Morana to fully reappear had surprised him. As he watched the goddess bending down into the storm drain to let the last of the dead leaves fall between her fingers to strain out a cigarette butt and smell it before making a face in disgust, he had to wonder if his Jo was still in there.

His Jo. He had always thought of her that way, but she wasn't really his. Not after he had let her walk out of his studio that night. Even when she had come to him still half dreaming last night, she hadn't been his. It had been Morana's longing that had carried her to him. If she did regain any ability to communicate through or around Morana's presence, she would not have kind words for him. It probably didn't matter. With the Veil open, it was impossible for Jo to reemerge. Almost.

He shook his head to clear it, as if doing so would work, and took Morana's hand as she offered it to him after standing and shaking the debris from her fingers.

"Shall we?"

Shall we walk into the city center to the business Jo had built with her friends to support herself and Faron, and tell them that Jo was no more? Vesna and the others would fall on him like a swarm of wasps, not caring what might happen to them. Minerva would most likely be there, and unlike Rok and Faron, she was not a demi-god. He could not best her, even at the height of his powers. Morana might stand a better chance though.

They continued on along the river into Trnovo, where Morana stopped again at the bridge to watch the ghost barges of ancient Roman Emona float by, guided by men with long steering poles shouting across the piles of amphora and other goods in a language he hadn't heard spoken so freely and casually in over a millennium. He let her watch and bask in the glory of their work, like a child at a fair, as the sun sank closer to the horizon.

CHAPTER 19

The courtyard had gone fully dark and, despite the wards, Vesna had made everyone promise not to turn on any of the courtyard or stairwell lights. As far as she was concerned, it was much better if no one thought they were home. She stood at the railing on the walkway outside her apartment and looked down into the darkened courtyard. A rectangular puddle of light leaked out of the shop front windows onto the cobblestones. Everyone had regrouped at the teahouse; it had come to feel like a safe haven since they had all returned. Truth be told, it had always been her safe haven, but now that concept took on a more life or death reality.

There was still no sign of Jo or Dušan, or whoever they really were now. Vesna hadn't decided if that was a good thing or a bad thing. She should go join the others in the shop. Ivanka and Reka had made an effort to put together something for dinner, a soup of some sort. They would need more supplies soon. Between what little dry goods everyone had in their flats and the stores at the teahouse, they probably only had a couple of days of soups and bread left.

"I want to tell you everything will be okay, but there's more than one ending to this story." Rebecca Wiley, Jo's American Civil War-era great, great, whatever grandmother and the current embodiment of Death, stood next to her and put both hands on the railing, following Vesna's gaze into the courtyard below.

As they watched, a well, like those that must have at one time been in the center of almost all the courtyards of the city, rematerialized as a large granite ring with the rigging for a bucket over the side.

"I can tell you to expect more of that. The past overlapping with the present. The ghosts coming out. Not just of people, but of this place."

Vesna turned to look at Rebecca. She looked like a ghost herself in the gloom of the balcony. There was no moon to offer additional light, only the weak glow from the teahouse below. "I had guessed that darkness would make a few things that had been unwilling to come out in the daylight braver."

Rebecca nodded. "I'm glad you are all together. You might want to keep it that way tonight."

"Will you stay with us?"

"I would like to, but I expect to be busy." There was no humor or concern in her voice, it was just stated as fact. Death had a job to do. "She's still in there, don't let Morana forget that."

Rebecca disappeared as silently as she had come, and Vesna began to pick her way slowly down the dark stairwell to the teahouse, though she didn't feel much like food or company. Another figure was waiting for her at the bottom of the stairs.

"Jesus, you scared the crap out of me."

"I didn't mean to." The voice was a deep basso, like a cello string vibrating as the bow was drawn across.

"It is Milo, isn't it?" Vesna peered into the gloom. She could just make out facial features and the shape of a tall man.

He stepped back and into the teahouse light. He looked well for a shade. Jo had described him as haggard and still bearing the bruises of his death, but he looked as good as he had in life.

Milo must have noticed her staring at his neck. "I've cleaned up a bit."

She nodded and invited him to join her in the teahouse. He wasn't another mouth to feed, but he was another ally in whatever the night held. Most of the people seated at the tables had met Milo when he was alive, and there were audible gasps as he came in. Vesna wondered if this is how it had felt for Jo over these last long months.

Milo, unfazed, gave a small wave and pulled up a chair next to the goddess Minerva like it was any other evening.

———

Morana stood with Črnobog's hand clutched in hers in front of the wooden door that lead into the courtyard of Zajčeva ulica 2. The building had been heavily warded. She could see the magic like pale lines of blue script swathing the doors and licking out onto the stones of the archway. Human magic she could have dispatched as easily as brushing it aside, but this wasn't the simple conjuring of a witch.

"Didn't Minerva bring you the hilt of Joyeuse? Why would

she work with the witches to keep you out?" Črnobog's dark visage was hard to read, but he seemed somewhat relieved that they couldn't enter.

"She brought it to repay a debt owed." He was matter of fact. "Let's enjoy the city. We can make an attempt tomorrow."

"I'll be curious to see if their wards are as good as they seem to believe." Jo's thoughts, a bubble of concern, intruded briefly, but Morana pushed them back down.

She adjusted Charlemagne's sword in the scabbard she had fashioned to carry it and followed Črnobog into the darkened Old Town streets. The holiday decorations stuttered on, but most of the buildings remained unilluminated as the shadows came to life.

———

Ivanka nodded along to '90s riot girl punk and stacked the last of the bowls on the rack to dry. Goran polished the flatware and stood it in the baskets behind the service area. He and Igor had insisted on helping to clean up after dinner, reminding Ivanka that they weren't customers. She was happy for the company, and she didn't have too much time to let her thoughts wander out to investigate all the terrible things her imagination could conjure up.

Over dinner, the crew that had gathered at the teahouse had agreed on a watch schedule. Vesna had shared Rebecca's warning with them, and they expected problems overnight. There were wards in place for malevolent people and spirits, and Minerva had added to their strength. Ivanka's blood ran cold at the thought of other things that might be able to skirt or break those wards. Could they stand up against Črnobog and whatever Jo had become?

Dishes done and kitchen cleaned, she and her helpers rejoined the others in the seating area of the teahouse. Ivanka had to wonder if they would ever reopen. It was a funny thought given she had doubts that they would all survive the night, let alone the plans that were formulating if they made it to daybreak.

Goran left first, with Gregor and Janez in tow. The couple would sleep on his futon, and he would take the second watch with Rok. Ivanka and Faron had agreed to take the first couple of hours. As everyone else left and headed to their flats, if not their beds, Ivanka thought of her sisters and aunt. It was better that they were together and probably better that they weren't there at the teahouse. Her aunt's house was off in a suburban neighborhood, where she hoped there were fewer awful things in the history of the pavement and parks than the center of the city must hold. Ivanka had been able to get an email message to them and received a quick reply before the internet service crapped out. She was surprised they still had electricity at the teahouse but didn't expect it to last. When the power went out, it would get very dark and very cold. While they still had it, she made a pot of tea and decanted it into one of the insulated press pots they sometimes used for catering. It might not be enough to get all of the watchers through the night, but it might help the humans stay awake.

She and Faron unstacked one of the outdoor cafe tables and a couple chairs and parked them in front of the shop window. They had a clear view of the courtyard doors, or as clear a view as one could have with only the dim light from inside the teahouse. Her eyes were still adjusting, but Faron assured her he could see fine. She'd bundled up, but her legs were already cold. She guessed that by the end of their two-hour watch, every other part of her would be too.

It was the first time she and Faron had been alone since the morning and the revelation that his parents had potentially released hell on earth. Could she bring that up in casual conversation? Did she need to be casual about the fact that he had known part of Dušan's plan all along?

"Where did Dušan take you all those times the two of you disappeared?" He had refused to tell her when they were all floating together on that island in Greece, but she was determined to get it out of him now.

"Mostly back here. We went to Vienna once to look for the sword blade."

"And what did you think the two of you were doing?" Ivanka tried to make her question sound neutral, she wasn't sure she succeeded.

"Bonding maybe?" He helped himself to a sip of her tea and set the cup back on the table in front of her. "And I thought he would take me to Mom or tell me where she was."

"Did he?"

"He told me eventually."

"And you were okay with the fact that he'd dropped her into the underworld?"

"He said he was protecting her from what was coming."

Ivanka stared at him in the darkness. Demi-god or no, Faron was still human, still the little boy who hadn't known his father and wanted to protect his mother from further harm.

"What about protecting the rest of us from what was coming?"

"I didn't realize what was coming was him. I—"

"Shh." Ivanka peered into the darkness at the center of the courtyard.

"What?" Faron leaned in and whispered it closer to her face.

"Can't you hear that?" Ivanka strained to hear the sound again, a faint scratching or scurrying.

Faron nodded that he heard it too. Something, or several somethings, were climbing up from the bottom of the ghost well.

———

Vesna heard the first crash just as she was dozing off curled into the corner of her overstuffed couch. She and Igor were both to the door in the next heartbeat and heading down the steps into the courtyard.

Faron was tangled in a fight with a shadow that looked like a giant rat. It was hard to tell in the dark if it was corporal or a shade of a thing. Ivanka was trying to ward the well, but another dark shape had attached itself to her leg and was attempting to pull her over the edge into the darkness.

Igor threw himself into the fray with Faron. Vesna had to hope for the best there and went to Ivanka.

"Finish the ward with you or get this thing off your leg?" Vesna wedged her body between Ivanka and the well, facing the opening.

Through gritted teeth, Ivanka voted, "Ward. There are more coming."

Vesna raised her hands and began reciting the words Goran and Minerva had taught them as they re-warded everything that morning. Vesna kicked herself for not realizing the well was a new opening into the building when it had appeared earlier.

As she finished the first part of the charm, another creature emerged from the well. The smell of rotted cabbage and sickly sweet flowers, lilacs, gagged her.

She didn't know what the things were that had come out first, but that smelled like demon.

A breeze collected around her, and as she started the second part of the ward, it whipped itself into a swirling wind. Faron called out to the others in the building, and Vesna heard footsteps on the walkways and stairs before the others emerged into the courtyard. The courtyard funneled sound. There was no way anyone was still asleep.

Vesna shouted at Faron. "Can't you do something?" She had watched Dušan as Črnobog dispatch two demons into his cloak in Bettine's hotel room when Bettine had held her hostage to get at Jo.

"I can't control them. Not like him."

Vesna assumed by "him," Faron meant his father. Faron could read her thoughts. Noted.

Minerva appeared, giving off a faint glow in the darkened courtyard. She took a few seconds to assess the situation and first drove her pike through the shape that had been trying to drag Ivanka back into the well. Whatever it was yelped as

Minerva picked it up like skewered cheese on a cocktail stick and shucked it off her pike over the opening.

It landed with a soft thud that seemed to momentarily distract the demon oozing over the side of the granite enclosure.

Minerva turned her attention to the demon and began shouting at it in what sounded like Latin to Vesna. It stilled but didn't retreat. Without further warning she thrust her pike into it.

A horrific roar erupted from it and reverberated off the stone walls of the courtyard. They didn't have a demon jar to secure it, and Vesna, deafened, had no idea what to do next.

Minerva shook it off her pike again into the depths and shouted over the opening, creating a lid on the well like a sheet of faintly glowing cling film. Faron had finally gotten a purchase on the creature he was struggling with and flung it onto the lid. It fell through, and the membrane resealed itself with a disgusting slurp.

Vesna took a deep breath in the silence, but it came ragged as her heart was still racing with her fight or flight instinct still fully engaged.

"I don't think that's the only thing we'll see tonight. Gather everyone together in the teahouse. We'll be better off to stay together." Minerva waved her hand over the demon gore on her pike. It glistened in the low light before being absorbed into the metal.

As Vesna watched the last few drops of blood disappear, an open-throated yell filled the courtyard. A door banged against a wall above them, and Goran's body fell from the banister and landed next to the well with another black, shapeless mass on his chest pressing Goran's dead weight into the cobblestones. Minerva and Vesna ran to him, the goddess kicking the demon off with lightning speed. Vesna knelt to tend to Goran while Minerva piked the creature and tossed it down the well to join the others.

Vesna couldn't find a pulse on Goran's wrist or neck, and his eyes were wide and staring up into the dark square of night sky. Faron joined her and knelt next to the body. He reached out to lay his hands on Goran's chest, but Vesna stopped him.

"He wouldn't want you to bring him back. The cost is too high." Goran's shade rose from his body as she finished her sentence.

He looked down at his corpse in surprise, then around at all of them. His shade was faint, still almost translucent compared with Milo's very solid presence at the bottom of the stairwell. Vesna watched as his door, one almost identical to the door of the antiques shop, except faintly glowing, appeared in the courtyard. Before he reached it, a woman with long white hair materialized near it, her shade as strong and solid as Milo's. She smiled a sad smile that showed large, white even teeth, and she held her hand out for Goran.

Vesna heard Goran whisper "Mother" before the door opened wide, and the two of them disappeared together into the Next.

Vesna looked up at the walkway where Goran had gone over the railing. Two figures were peering over the banister, but Vesna couldn't make out faces in the darkness.

"It came out of the wall." Gregor spoke, and his words sank

heavy in the air down to them.

"Everyone needs to get in the teahouse. Now." Vesna stood and began herding those around her through the doorway.

"What about Goran's body?" Igor stopped and stood at the dead man's feet.

Vesna looked from Igor to Minerva as if the goddess should field that question. Vesna's heart was tight in her chest, and every synapse pulsed with the instinct to protect the others, to get them away from the well and to safety or at least to where she could see them all.

"Go. Have Faron and Rok begin warding every inch of floor and wall and ceiling. I'll take care of him. His body should be safe in his own warded circle." Vesna watched as Minerva lifted Goran's limp body into her arms like he was a child and disappeared into his shop across from the teahouse. She'd been in Goran's ritual working space one time when she'd slipped behind the heavy velvet drapes to help him raise power for the ward that now hung over the door of the courtyard. That was before she knew she was the daughter of a witch as well as a Witchfinder. He'd trusted her, knowing what her father's family had done, how many witches they'd tortured and murdered. She stood looking at the well, the reality of Goran's death heavy in her chest. Why hadn't she seen what would happen? What good was the burden of sight if she couldn't know this would happen and try to stop it?

Vesna finally followed Gregor and Janez into the teahouse and closed the door behind her, the bells jangling on the wood. The sound startled her as if she hadn't heard them a thousand times, and she started to unloop the braided cord from the door handle. Minerva opened the door and stopped her.

"Leave them. They are a powerful talisman." Minerva closed the door again and began weaving her words into the fabric of the wood and glass. The wards glowed in the darkness as they radiated out from the bells that had announced every customer coming in for tea for more than a decade.

When Vesna turned, she watched Faron's and Rok's magic spread out from where they stood twisting into each other's words when they met to form a skin or a bubble around them. The scent of god magic—burnt sugar, freshly mown hay, and lavender—made her lightheaded. She wobbled before sitting heavily on the nearest chair. Large, warm hands caught her before she hit the ground, and everything went dark.

CHAPTER 20

Alessandro watched as the thunderhead roiled toward the entrance into the lagoon from the house that Venetian Observers had lived in since the 13th century. The citizens and tourists went about their business, but he noticed the people traversing the acqua alta in their high gum boots were moving a little more briskly than even the temperamental floodwaters of Venice called for. He knew what the clouds heralded, and nothing good would come of them arriving at nightfall. Even the mundanes must feel that something was wrong.

Lightning flashes, blue against the darkening gray of dusk, illuminated the water as the turmoil leading the storm rolled slowly over the Lido and engulfed the few vaporetti still out on the water as they taxied people back from the other islands. Venice was a city of secrets despite the Disney-fied veneer it had taken on in the past twenty years or so—twenty euro just to sit at a cafe in San Marco before you even order a coffee!—and all those monsters were about to be laid bare as the Veil subsided.

What did gouging the tourists matter now? That storm

could swallow the city whole that very night, and he would have front row seats to watch it happen. His computer screen still held Vesna Kos's message when he turned back to his desk. Bettine had asked him to enlist the Witchfinders and other Observers to put down Črnobog's rebellion. As Alessandro saw it, the world was already going to hell in a handbasket. A supernatural shitstorm laid over the top of the chaos humans had already unleashed seemed almost fitting to him. Set a ghoul on every fascist and be done with it.

Still, there were those he cared for, and despite his cynicism he wasn't ready for Venice to sink into the sea just yet. He dashed off a message to Vesna, closed his computer, and filled his pockets with a few things from the desk's top drawer before heading off to meet the Witchfinder of Venice at his home near the Peggy Guggenheim museum at the mouth of the Canal Grande. It was as good a place as any to watch the end of the world.

———

Vesna felt the earth quiver under her feet, and she braced herself against the stones of the arched doorway that led into the courtyard of the building in which she lived and worked. The motion felt like standing on a duvet as it was being shaken out across a bed. Earthquake? Blast? She didn't know, but she could hear distant screams and the unmistakable sounds of glass shattering—on the scale of windows, not wineglasses.

There was no one else left in the courtyard. Everyone who had come to shelter in their enclosed corner of the city was gone, and she didn't know if she was the lone survivor or the person who had volunteered to stay. She stumbled down the cobblestone street to where it met the river embankment and marveled that there were still a few street lamps glowing to illuminate the tendrils of fog wending their way up over the balustrade like the tentacles of a Lovecraftian nightmare. She stuck close to the buildings and slid along storefronts and restaurant windows, watching as the fog's appendages sought out anyone or anything to curl around and drag down into the river.

Where was Jo's river god when she needed him? And why did she need him? Why was she even out there?

Jo. She was looking for Jo. No one had believed her that her dearest friend had not been subsumed by some dark goddess with her asshole ex-boyfriend sidekick hell bent for leather to unleash their goth version of paradise on the world. Maybe that was why she had found herself alone. She was the only one willing to risk her own life to save Jo's. But that didn't sound right either. Any number of them would have done the same.

There was a gap in the buildings at *Novi trg*, the New Square, and she was going to have to make a run for it if she didn't want to be out in the open for river Krakens or bronze dragons to summarily end her. She didn't know where Jo was, but her instinct told her to keep heading toward the Triple Bridge where she could cross to *Mestni trg*, the heart of the city.

She took a deep breath and ran flat out from the cover of the sports bar on the corner of the square. As she made it to the other corner, her heart firmly lodged in her throat, a hand covered her mouth and a well-muscled arm pulled her into the doorway of the restaurant she had momentarily been panting against.

"Furrrck." She tried to bite the hand over her mouth, but it was quickly pulled away by its owner.

"Manners, woman." A very large man towered over her in the doorway, his skin glowing a coppery green from within.

"Achelous?" Apparently thinking the name of a god in this magical weather was enough to summon him.

"I would say 'at your service,' but I am here on my own mission." He made a half-assed attempt at a bow.

"I don't need much from you. I just need to know where Jo is." She didn't want to get chatty, but she wasn't going to pass up any assistance he might offer.

Achelous laughed, the sound coming from deep in his chest then bubbling up like the source of the river itself. "Vesna, dear woman, you know exactly where she is."

"I have an idea of where I think Jo is, mentally, spiritually, but I need you to tell me where she is physically." Irritation was swiftly overcoming the adrenaline shakes she had from being assaulted by him.

"You know you're dreaming, or visioning, or whatever it is you mortal seers do, don't you?" Achelous absentmindedly pushed a strand of hair off her face and tucked it behind her ear.

The doorway and the open square spun around her, tilting in the prehensile fog, and she was standing back in front of the teahouse again with Achelous. He was looking much more human, dressed in dark jeans and the coziest looking oatmeal-colored half-zip sweater. Her head was spinning with the scenery.

"That fog would have had you swimming down in my world if you had left the confines of your warded little bunker for real." He directed her to one of the outdoor cafe tables that had been set up. "And I think you'd be freezing, dressed like that."

She looked down and found that she was wearing the flannel pajamas Jo had brought her back as a gift from the States. Orange and black cats tumbled over each other on a field of blue sky with fluffy white clouds.

"What is going on?" She crossed her arms and tucked her hands into her armpits, suddenly very aware of the cold.

"I suspect that's what you came to find out." He looked around. "Now that the In-between has fully bled into the Now, you just conked yourself out to figure out what to do next." He picked up a teacup out of nowhere and took a sip; steam escaped the upturned rim in the shape of little fish swimming in a school.

"So what did I 'conk' myself out to learn?"

"Conk is a word, isn't it?" He tilted his head and cocked his eyebrow, a disconcertingly human expression on his still uncanny features.

"Who cares? Where's Jo?"

"I didn't come to tell you that. I did come to tell you that you need to take Ivanka when you go looking for her." He reached across the table and cupped the side of her face with his hand. It was surprisingly warm given he was part fish. "It's very important that you and Ivanka go to Morana together."

She hit the floor with a thud and opened her eyes to a roomful of people, letting that word "people" cover numerous kinds of beings, standing over her looking very worried.

——

The city was deserted except for the figures of shades and other things that went bump in the night lurking in the many shadows cast by the few holiday lights that flickered on as night fell. Jo was surprised any of the city still had power. Maybe magic was keeping the racing comets and twinkling stars illuminated against the low ceiling of leaden clouds.

Morana was leading Črnobog to *Mestni trg* in front of the town hall. Jo was party to the goddess's thoughts, but it was like being lost in her own dreams: she knew it wasn't real, but she couldn't wake herself up either. Centuries ago the square had been the place of Morana's execution as a witch. Those who had burned with her had feared the Christian god and just been too old or too poor or too knowledgable with the local herbs to escape the overzealous Witchfinders. Morana had made a bargain with a Portal who had managed to get caught up in the witch craze despite knowing better.

Jo couldn't sort out if Morana's anger was directed more at those who had died around her screaming to a god who wouldn't save them or the men who had lit the pyres. Either way, a lit torch appeared in Morana's pale hand before the goddess hurled it up toward the window on the first floor of City Hall.

Through her limited perspective, Jo watched the torch make a graceful arc over the balcony railing then bounce back onto the cobbles as sparks shot out from the impact. Morana turned her face up to where a goddess stood swathed in a dazzlingly white toga and crowned with a seriously badass looking helmet. Her eyes flashed with golden god light.

"Not tonight, Morana."

Jo expected some wordy diatribe from the Queen of the Witches, but instead there was a very clear, "Who the fuck are you?" Maybe Jo was having an effect on Morana after all.

"Does it matter?" Rok joined the woman at her left elbow.

Jo guessed that really she should think of that person by some other name, but to her Rok didn't really have any other names, whatever he pretended. Dušan on the other hand? She was happy to refer to him as the Dark Lord as sarcastically as possible.

"Friend of yours?" Morana cocked her head at said dark lord. Jo had rubbed off on her.

"Where's Jo?" Rok still sounded like Rok, despite having acquired the sparkly god eye thing. Thank all the gods, the last thing she needed was another voice sounding in her mind like someone ringing the Liberty Bell while she was standing in it.

Morana didn't answer.

Dušan didn't answer.

"I'm in here. Somewhere." Jo said it as loudly as possible, but it didn't ring in the mental construction she thought of as her head, so she had to assume no one heard her, except maybe Morana.

"My Jo, hold on." It was Rok's voice, but his lips hadn't moved. Jo was certain she had heard him and was too distracted with trying to figure out how that worked and if Morana had heard it as well. She didn't have time to get pissy about that fact that she wasn't his Jo, had never been his Jo, and would never be his Jo—even if he seemed to be on the side of the angels now.

"I don't need a torch to burn the place down. It just seemed fitting." Morana threw her arms wide, palms facing the City Hall, and released an arc of individual little fires, like a perfect line of flaming tennis balls, flung toward the front entrance of the building.

Achelous joined the pair of gods on the balcony and unleashed a waterfall over the railing, snuffing Morana's magical Molotov cocktails before they had much of a chance to ignite the few flammable items in the portico on the ground floor.

"Why is this building so important to you?" Morana screamed in what seemed like an undignified fashion for a goddess. "Just let me fucking burn it."

Jo wished she had imaginary cotton to jam into the imaginary ears of her imaginary head. Why the hell did Morana need to scream?

"Why is it so important to you that you need to risk burning all of Staro Mesto to the ground?" Achelous cocked his head at her. "That seems rather petty for the so-called Queen of the Witches."

If Achelous's words were meant to shame her, they had done anything but. Jo could sense the goddess's anger grow, her memories replaying the lighting of the pyres and the screams of the women around her as they cried out for deliverance from the flames. The anger flooded out any other thought the goddess or Jo could have, and Jo felt herself slipping into the raging river of Morana's vengeance. She had her own reasons to be angry. She had been so wronged, by Dušan, by Rok, by her mother. Lied to by so many. Had so much taken from her. She'd even had her own time at the stake and knew what it felt like to have fire licking up her flesh.

Rage filled her thoughts, along with two words, spoken first in Rok's voice, then Achelous's. *Hold on.*

———

Ivanka handed Vesna a cup of tea and watched in case her boss started to list to the side again. Minerva had left, dragging Rok with her, and calling behind again to ward every inch of the place as they disappeared before even opening the door.

It had only been half an hour or so ago, but it felt like Minerva had been gone longer. Faron had stayed, and he and Ivanka and Igor had woven wards into every inch of wall and floor and ceiling and window. Igor had even gone back into the kitchen and downstairs into the bathroom to ward the taps and drains and the toilet, just in case. Good idea, given the demon porthole the ghost well had turned out to be.

Vesna had finally come around, though she hadn't made much sense when she started talking. None of them had seen Achelous, but Vesna had insisted he had been there outside at the table.

After a few sips of tea and deep breaths, Vesna made a little more sense. She explained her vision, or what she could remember of it. It all seemed consistent with what was happening, except the part where Ivanka was supposed to go with her looking for Jo.

Faron had gotten very quiet while Vesna spun out her dream.

"If anyone is going to go looking for my mother, it should be me." He said it very quietly, but there was no mistaking the finality behind the words, in his mind at least.

CHAPTER 21

Otto shifted the curtain aside and looked down into what he could see of the narrow square in front of the hotel. Part of the pink Franciscan church was glowing faintly in the light the holiday decorations cast onto the Baroque façade. The electricity had been off inside the hotel for some time, but the swags of municipal lighting burned on. Housekeeping had come around almost immediately with flashlights and lanterns for the guests. He had to admire the Hotel Lisica staff's commitment to customer service when ghosts were drifting up and down the halls and the main entryway had turned into a dripping cascade of blood over the worn marble steps and out onto Miklošičeva Street.

He had nothing to ward his suite with, and the occasional specter drifted through the room without making too much of a fuss. He wasn't worried about the shades of the dead. He had spent his life dealing with terrified mundanes being visited by their long-departed aunties. He was more worried about the creatures no living mundane had seen without dying of fright. There were much worse things that prowled the night than restless ancestors.

He closed the curtain and paced the floor. No electricity had meant no further emails from Bettine, and the phone lines—cellular and wired—were hopelessly overloaded. The last message he had received had been from Alessandro, the Venetian Observer Bettine had elevated to her new Board. Vesna Kos, the local Witchfinder in Ljubljana, had contacted him asking for help. Otto didn't have much help to give either of them. He had no special skills or powers other than those granted by his position on the Board and the psychoscopy he'd acquired, as many of his kind did over their long lives.

He had no intention of leaving this room now that things had gone awry much sooner than Bettine had expected. He had hoped to connect with some superstitious member of the local clergy to collect something to protect himself with when he had arrived, but the situation had changed too rapidly. Now he had only his wits and his wakefulness to get him through the night. He wasn't sure what his personal demons looked like, but he knew they would come. It wasn't that he wasn't ready to finally go, but he would have preferred his life not end with being ripped apart.

———

Morana was tired of being thwarted. First by that upstart of a misplaced Roman god and now by some watery asshole. What did these immortal beings care for the trappings of humans?

You cared once.

No. That voice no longer existed. That part of her had been returned and had no right to speak up for anything. Vesna, the Goddess of Spring and Hope and rainbows and fluffy bunnies had been loved and revered even to the point of her followers carrying an effigy of her, Morana, Goddess of Winter and Death, to the river to drown it. All while Morana and those few who still believed in her and still followed the old ways had suffered. Her lighter half was not allowed to plead for these murderers.

That's all these humans were to her now. They raped and murdered each other, poisoned the earth and water and every living thing that depended upon them. They even fouled the air. They had cut down the old gods with the sickles of their new faith, mostly abandoned their brave new god, and then had become death themselves.

A cascade of images flooded her mind. Witches alone in their rooms, in clearings in the forest, on beaches, and even gathered with others like them, lighting candles to her and singing for her return. They had kept her thousand names on their tongues even when she had been too weak, too broken to continue.

Did Goddess Fluffy Bunny wish their lives spared because they'd said a few words in her honor before brewing up their love potions or while fucking in the grain fields?

There are others. They have always been here.

Morana screamed with the same piercing rage that had dried up the Nav after she had been cast there by Črnobog and Dažbog a millennium ago. Fuck them all. They could all burn and sort themselves out in the Nav.

Every window in *Mestni trg* shattered, sending the oldest handblown panes and sheets of storefront plate raining onto the cobblestone streets. She would not have her revenge taken from her as well. Not even to spare those very few who still believed in her.

The other gods present had cowered with their hands over their ears, as if that would help. She left them and wended her way through the gently curving streets and back across the river toward Črnobog's nest of accomplices. If she wiped that little den of vipers out, Črnobog would have no one to continue his human charade with, and she could go about her business untroubled by his indecisiveness. He had her now. His precious human pet was gone, or at least pushed as far down into the recesses of her thoughts as possible.

—

Otto startled awake. He had drifted off too many times sitting down, but he was tired of pacing a track in the floor. He stood up again and ran in place for a moment to get the blood flowing and sat back down with his back to the window. He didn't expect his demons to come through the door or from the outside. They had always taunted him from under his bed, and he suspected that's where they would emerge now that the way from their realm to his was standing wide open.

His phone chimed with an incoming message. He picked it up and looked at its bright face, almost blinding after the dim light of the lantern. How could Bettine possibly have gotten through? She had spent her long years forcing the most powerful witches she could find, and confine, to teach her their ways, but surely even the most powerful human magic user couldn't manipulate satellites.

The speech bubble his phone displayed messages in read: "Go. Now. Find Dušan Črnigad. Only your death is waiting for you in that room." He clicked the button on the side to darken the screen again and swore in at least three languages before quickly asking God for forgiveness.

Perhaps she was right. It would be better to face his death as a man out on the street rather than cower in his room waiting for a demon to drag him by the ankles into hell. He found his shoes under the edge of the bed and put them on before sliding his arms into his coat sleeves. He picked up the flashlight on the nightstand and slid it into the pocket of his coat, took the lantern, and headed out into the hallways of the hotel, hoping he could find his way to the side street entrance in the darkness without a staff person trying to stop him. It would only take a word to convince him not to embark on this foolishness, even though he knew there was no going back now.

As he made his way down the interior stairs to the ground floor, he kept looking up into the shadows above him, certain someone or something was following him.

———

Bettine watched the France 24 newsreader describe the freak weather that was spreading from central Slovenia into the neighboring countries. A reporter with a sleek blonde ponytail and the latest season's coat stood in a flooded San Marco Square looking chic in her expensive knee-high rain boots as she described the tourists running back to their hotels as the unusual electrical storm approached. "*Je n'ai jamais vu cela,*" was repeated multiple times into the camera. A flash of blue lightning struck the bell tower behind her, and her feed went dead.

The newsreader calmly commented they had lost Marie and went on to another feed in Vienna, where the locals were still watching the storm in the distance. There was no mention of ghosts roaming about or statues coming to life.

She suspected no news director was ready to run with that over live television just yet. Humans, mortal ones especially, were very good at pretending anything they couldn't explain didn't exist. Even with a witness.

She clicked the television off and sat in the immediate silence. She had forgotten how much of her own energy was sucked into a communication spell. Breda and the other witches she had learned from drew on the energy of the gods they believed in, but Bettine wasn't about to reach out to a withering deity for assistance. Her will was enough. Otto would get the message, even if the phone on his battery had died. She was drained, and though her bed looked very inviting, she felt the need to keep on top of things. If Otto and Alessandro couldn't enlist the help of the Witchfinders and Observers to close the Veil again soon, she would have to go to Ljubljana herself.

The thought had occurred earlier to her to go to Venice and watch more closely from there. Now it would be difficult to travel, and the longer she waited the harder it would be to get there. Communications were only the first thing that had been disrupted. Flights were cancelled into and even over the area, and soon no driver could be found in all of Paris who would be willing to take her into the edge of that storm—no matter what she promised them as payment.

It was truly a shame her fetch had been destroyed and, along with it, the last vial of her summoning elixir. That would have been the easiest way to transport herself to Ljubljana. Ironic that it had been Breda, a witch of Ljubljana herself, who had finally gotten that spell in Charlemagne's illicit collection of grimoires to work. No other witch had been able to transport so much as a leaf. She missed that old woman, if for no other reason than she was certain there had been more to learn from her before she died. It was a shame her son Goran didn't seem to be as talented. No matter. He probably wouldn't last the night.

———

Črnobog stood again after Morana had left the square. He suspected she was heading for the teahouse and his gallery, but it wouldn't be any easier for her to get past the wards this time. He looked up at the City Hall balcony to find Minerva, Achelous, and Rok all glaring down at him.

"You are even more pathetic than I remembered." Minerva insulted him in the most dignified way possible. If they hadn't shared a common language, he would have guessed by her tone that she was praising him. She drifted down to join him in the cobblestone square, followed by Achelous. Rok watched them with a dubious expression on his face and disappeared back into the building before appearing again at the doors on the ground floor.

"What are you going to do about this monster you created?" Achelous turned his attention back to Črnobog after tsking at Rok for his unwillingness, or inability, to use his full powers.

Črnobog had no answer for him. He had not created Morana. He had simply summoned her from within Jo. And Vesna, the deity of spring, had sacrificed her stolen life to return the dark goddess to her full power. That had been a surprise. He had hoped to keep Jo in the Nav until the worst of the transition was over and humanity had a moment to adjust to a reenchanted world. He had admittedly not expected her to be so willingly swayed by the spring goddess and quite so driven to avenge herself. A small oversight on his part.

Minerva couldn't hear or see his thoughts, but she could apparently read his expression. She laughed. "You hadn't planned for this either. You truly are an idiot." She pivoted on her sandaled foot to follow Morana.

A pyre of logs and brush and broken furniture with three stakes standing like sentinels appeared in front of Minerva. They were clear as day, even in the darkness—clear enough that Črnobog could see the small platforms nailed into the tree trunks where a heretic's feet would rest above the pyramid of fuel. With the appearance of the pyre, the square changed around them. The advertisements for the funicular up to the castle and the modern storefronts had been replaced as the buildings reverted to their older forms, the Baroque overtaken by the early modern. They were now in Ljubljana, Laibach, before the earthquake, before the Enlightenment. The smell of horses and their excrement, and probably that of humans as well, filled the air.

Night had truly fallen, and the city had sunk into its own shadow.

—

Ivanka didn't think it was possible, but the gloom in the courtyard had gotten darker. Vesna had insisted on hoarding their candles and batteries, and only the dimmest light was allowed in the kitchen and her office, as far away from the shop windows as possible. None of them wanted to draw any attention to themselves. They hoped the wards on the courtyard doors and the well outside held, but Goran's death had proven there were gaps and that big plate glass window that had seemed to disappear with the absence of the any light to allow for reflections hadn't put Ivanka at ease.

She stood as close to the window as she could without touching it, as if she could deduce what was going on in the city from the air that found its way in around the gaps in the door. Her sisters and her aunt were out there. Her friends whom she hadn't seen in months. Regular customers. Her grandparents, even if they had disowned her and her sisters after their parents had been killed. So many people had been caught up in this pissing match between a bunch of old gods who couldn't accept that the world had moved on—and was even now moving on from the new gods.

A bubble of anger rose in her throat. Minerva and Rok, or whoever he was now, were out there. Minerva had not taken Faron. He hadn't completely transformed like the goddess had when the Veil had been split. Was that because, like Rok, he was still mostly human?

But was he? His mother was out there with Črnobog. Minerva had called her Morana, Queen of the Witches. How human had she ever really been?

Hushed voices chattered behind her. Maybe they were making plans, maybe they were asking for more tea. She didn't care. Part of her was petrified by what could be out on the streets she couldn't see, and part of her wanted to scream at everyone there for holing up and having a tea party while people died. As if they could stop it. Goran was gone. A chill ran from the top of her head down the small of her back, and she flinched. There would be others to bury before this was over.

She turned from the window to look for Vesna in the

darkness. Maybe she had seen more, or seen more clearly. A pounding knock sounded in the courtyard. The chattering voices stopped, and she felt every eye in the teahouse on her as she slowly turned back around to the courtyard.

The knocking came again, heavy, almost desperate against the thick wooden doors she and Fred had repainted in the spring before they all left. Faron appeared at her elbow.

"I'll go see who it is." He pulled a coat from the row of pegs on the wall that just happened to be his and opened the shop door, slipping out before anyone thought to stop him. Even her. It did briefly cross her mind that it was such a human thing, to reach for his coat before stepping into the cold.

She pressed her face to the glass and tried to focus on the doors. A small light glowed level with the doorknobs as the two black slabs parted. Three shapes slipped in, and the door closed again. The light blinked out, and the doorknob on the shop door turned.

Faron opened the door again, and Ivanka let her senses snake out as far from her as she could, like Clotilda had tried to teach her. Nothing seemed out of place or wrong. Instead she felt relief.

"It's your sisters and Olga." Faron's words cut through the silence, and Ivanka let out a breath she didn't realize she'd been holding.

Good thing or Veronika and Ana would have knocked it out of her with their tackling hugs.

Ana let go first. "Breda left. She said she had to go to take Goran away. But before she left, she said we should come here. That we'd be safer all together. She said it was time for the witches to come together. Goran's dead, isn't he? He and Breda went into the Next, didn't they? She doesn't come when I sing 'Blackbird.' Olga and Veronika saw her before she left. They saw Breda. She looked so beautiful, Ivanka. I'm sorry you didn't get to meet her. Why are Faron's eyes sparkly?" Ana took a deep breath, and Ivanka tried to get a word in before Ana had a chance to launch back in.

"Yes. Goran is dead, and I did see Breda. She came for him, and they crossed into the Next together." Ivanka thought it would have been hard to say, hard to say out loud again that her teacher was dead, but she was numb.

"What happened?" Veronika had let go of her during Ana's monologue and stood shoulder to shoulder with Olga, as tall as her aunt now. Ivanka hadn't realized her sister was still growing.

Ivanka hesitated. Ana had to be terrified already. She didn't want to make it worse. Though to be fair to her baby sister, she was holding up pretty well.

"He was trying to fight off a demon that had come into the apartment. He was protecting Gregor and Janez, who don't have any magic to fight back with, and he fell from the walkway." Faron said it as gently as possible and gave Goran's death the dignity in the telling that it deserved.

"Couldn't you bring him back, like you did Ms. Jo?" Ana, always direct.

"I could have, yes, but that was not what Goran wanted." Faron squatted down as he spoke so Ana didn't have to look up at him. She was still so small for her age.

Ana nodded hard and wiped the back of her hand over

her eyes. The gesture stabbed at Ivanka's numbness, but she wouldn't break. There was too much to come.

"You didn't answer my other question." Ana's voice didn't crack, but it had that edge it got when her sister was trying to sound grown up or braver than she felt.

Faron laughed softly. "About my eyes? No, I didn't."

"Why are they like that?" Veronika was less sentimental but much higher strung than either Ana or Ivanka. Her sister tried to cover the tightness in her own voice with snarkiness.

"The Veil is open, and gods can't hide." He stood up and shrugged, which Ivanka felt more than saw.

Olga, who had been quiet during this whole exchange, finally spoke. "That's what Breda said when she appeared. How long is this going to last?"

Olga had the least amount of experience with the reality Ivanka had been introduced to the night her mother, possessed by a demon, had burst into Faron's flat and thrown her against the wall before disappearing into the night with her boyfriend. Things had only gotten stranger from there. Olga hadn't wanted to believe at first. She'd spent a night in Dr. Struna's Hospital for the Weird, as Ivanka had come to think of the doctor's clinic, crying her eyes out after they had rescued Ana from a revenant. Yeah. Things had changed.

Vesna had joined their little conclave by the door. "Why don't you all sit down? I can get you some tea and a sandwich."

The butane burners they had for catering gigs had come in very handy once the power had flickered out for good. Hot tea on demand. One of Fred's soups on standby and all the tea sandwiches they could make until the frozen bread ran out.

"Tea would be nice." Olga quickly deduced there wasn't an answer to her question about the duration.

Vesna whispered Ivanka's name and motioned for her to wait while Faron ushered the newcomers to a table in the back of the shop.

"What have you seen?" Vesna spoke so close to her ear, Ivanka could feel her lips move.

"I was going to ask you the same question. Did you tell us everything about your little vision quest?" Ivanka didn't mean to be derisive, but she was agitated and suspected they were all holding back so as not to induce panic in the ranks.

"I did. Now it's like looking at a blank wall. I can't see anything of our futures."

"I didn't see anything, but I have that feeling. Like when you know something you really wish you didn't." Like when she'd seen Vesna's Uncle Leo die in a vision.

Vesna nodded and took her hand. "What do you know?"

Ivanka's stomach sank to the floor when Vesna touched her. "I felt… We won't all survive." You and I. We aren't going to make it.

CHAPTER 22

Otto slid into the alcove of a bar entranceway on the riverbank. He looked over his shoulder into the darkness behind the glass front and saw two faces illuminated in a match flame. Both sets of eyes were wide with surprise. They attempted to wave him in. He guessed they thought they were safer inside than he was on the street, but he knew better.

The layer of mist over the river was rising and thickening as it slid over Jože Plečnik's embankment, built to tame the water and contain the seasonal floods. No amount of marble was going to keep that river at bay tonight. Tendrils of fog worked their way across the cobblestones to snare a café table or abandoned bicycle and drag it back into the water where it made the smallest of splashes.

He gave the two people holed up in the bar a dismissive wave and made his way onward. He said a tiny prayer for them that sunrise would come before the mist made its way under the door.

Moving doorway to doorway and running flat out across the open areas where streets or squares met the embankment got him to *Zajčeva ulica*. Or at least he thought that's where he was. The city had begun to change around him in the dark, and when he'd stepped back from the wall to shine the hotel flashlight against the corner of the building where the street sign should be, there was nothing. The river on his right had also changed. The holiday lights still hung in the air between buildings and burned brightly with the modern glow of LEDs, but the embankment had subsided. All of Plečnik's work to tame it and separate the watercourse from the city had disappeared, and Otto found himself looking down a gently sloping bank right into the roiling mist. The tentacles that had been creeping out and following him as he made his way down Breg were flailing up at the decorations, temporarily ignoring his progress.

He took the opportunity to dash up the street and look for the courtyard door marked with a number 2. The rectangular green signs marking the addresses were also gone, but he managed to count his way to what he hoped was the right door.

It was locked, which he had expected. He knocked, tentatively at first, unsure of what he might be summoning from inside, or outside.

No response. The only sounds he could hear were his breath coming fast and the blood pulsing in his ears. He knocked again. They were smart not to come to the door, but he hoped someone inside had enough compassion to invite in a lost traveler, especially on a night as strange as this.

He was beginning to wonder about what he would do next if no one answered when a voice on the other side asked who he was.

How did he respond to that? He could lie and claim to be a tourist caught out. Better to start with the truth; it would leave him more room to lie later if he needed to.

"I'm with the Board."

Silence. Then a second voice swearing. He thought he heard a snippet of his name before the sound of a beam being lifted and the lock turning.

The door on the right side opened, creating a crack between the two ancient looking slabs of arched wood. The air rushing out from the courtyard smelled different that the air in the street, and he realized that the smell that had crept up to him wasn't just the river but included the scent of horses and the filth they left in their wake.

"Are you Otto? Did Alessandro send you?" It was a woman's voice, wary and angry.

"Yes, I'm Otto. Alessandro asked me to look in on you." That wasn't a lie either. He doubted this woman knew that Bettine was still alive. Given who Bettine was, he didn't want to take the chance of pissing her off before she opened the door all the way.

More hissing whispers punctuated with, "We can't just leave him out there."

The door opened enough for him to enter and was quickly closed behind him and barred and bolted before there were any words of welcome spoken. He heard something scurry across the cobblestones at his feet and assumed the rats of Ljubljana must be enjoying the darkness.

The woman introduced herself as Vesna; the man with her was Faron, whom he knew to be Jolene Wiley and Dušan

Črnigad's son. The man wouldn't look at him directly, which made him suspicious. The other man who joined them and was quickly herding them toward a storefront just inside the courtyard was introduced as Igor, Vesna's partner. She had hesitated before using the word partner, so he assumed there was some ambiguity there.

The door to the teahouse opened and just as quickly closed behind them. He thought he heard the rat again but decided his brain was playing tricks on him. It was easy to imagine things when you couldn't see clearly, and there were more immediate concerns than a few city rodents enjoying what must be a rat Carnivale to them.

More introductions were made, and it became clear that this was a tightly knit community made up of people who had lived in the shadows of the Veil and those who had existed happily without any knowledge of its existence. One of the people he was introduced to was unmistakably a corporeal shade. His handshake had been ice cold as the man gave his name as Milo.

Vesna parked Otto at a table away from the others and began her interrogation.

———

Črnobog trailed Minerva with Achelous and Rok bringing up the rear. They wouldn't beat Morana to the teahouse and the others, but they would arrive not long after. As they walked through the streets, they encountered ghosts of the long dead, a few ghouls slinking in the shadows, and many horses left to their own devices as the denizens of the modern city were not out. Even if they had been, few of them would have known what to do with a cart horse.

It didn't take long to get from *Mestni trg* to *Zajčeva ulica*, a street named for a rabbit or a poet. He found it poetic now that Jo's friends and family had holed up on Rabbit Street. Though it was usually a quick walk, time was moving differently as layers of Ljubljana's past bubbled up through the pavements. The air moved thickly around them, and he had to wonder if a god could get caught in one of those currents, looping for hours looking at a single window or a stone on the road.

Though he didn't much care to take responsibility for things he believed were out of his control—he wasn't omnipotent, after all—he did have a twinge of something that might be guilt when his thoughts turned to what could happen to Jo's friends if Morana did manage to get through those doors. The goddess had every right to be angry, every right to seek revenge, though those most deserving of her wrath were mouldering in their graves or sitting in the groves she had restored in the greened Nav. These mortals were hardly blameless, but they also hadn't set fire to any witches lately. There were definitely places where that still happened, and those who practiced the old ways were often looked at as eccentrics at best and supping with the Christian Satan at worst.

A tiny part of him wanted to let her burn it all to the ground. But that hadn't been his plan—their plan. He'd spent enough time ruling over the desolate underworld in Morana's absence. Now that the goddess had returned, he found he did miss Jo. Parts of her, her vocabulary at least, were seeping into Morana's personality. He appreciated that Jo had grown steel in her spine over the years. The new, improved version of her that had met him on the landing after accidentally blowing up her apartment door the previous night would not have gotten entangled with the man he pretended to be. He didn't linger too long on that thought, as it didn't sit well with his own sense of who he was—as a man or a god.

The quartet of deities made it to the mouth of Jo's street, but there was no sign of Morana. He wasn't sure if that was good or bad. It did mean she could be anywhere in the city or returned to the Nav or who knows where. The hole in the Veil would have expanded beyond the borders of the country by now. In the hillsides and mountains to the west, the memories of war would be waking up. Jo might have spent her time sending lost soldiers into the Next, but no Voice was capable of exorcising the things their spilled blood had leached into the soil. Every atrocity left a mark in the In-between, a demon or a ghoul born of hatred and torture and pain.

Minerva shouted at him, her voice reverberating off the stone buildings. "I said, where would she go?"

"I have no idea."

Achelous shook his head. "You unleashed her on the world, and you don't know what she's up to?"

"I hadn't planned for her to come back until the worst was over."

It was Rok's turn to chastise him. "Did you really think Jo was going to stay in the Nav? Even before she was Morana, she wasn't going to do anything she thought you wanted her to do."

Rok might think he had known her better, but Črnobog guessed he was just as familiar with her obstinance. What he hadn't counted on was the spring goddess playing into Morana's hand so perfectly.

"There are many places she might go." Črnobog shrugged.

Minerva rolled her eyes at him. Perhaps she had been spending too much time as a human, as well, given her petty reaction to him. Jo would have been proud.

Would have been. Was that what he wanted, what he had intended in all this? It had been his plan, but he hadn't thought he would lose Jo completely.

"Rok and Achelous, you should stay here and protect the others. Črnobog and I will find Morana." Minerva turned to go immediately, shooing Črnobog ahead of her as if he were a child.

"You trust him? If you find her the two of them might gang up on you." Rok said what Achelous was thinking, given his nod in agreement.

"I don't trust him for a second, so I'm not taking him inside that building either." She made the same dismissive hand motion at them, and the river god and the demi-god disappeared through the bolted doors into the courtyard beyond.

———

Morana had found herself walking in large circles around the center of the city. Now she was standing in front of a communist-era block of flats in Šiška after wandering through Tivoli Park as it shifted through the many decades of its existence. The apartment building was nondescript, and she had only the slightest glimpse at a memory of why she would be there.

A horse pulled a driverless cart through the parking lot behind her. She turned to watch it try to make its way out onto Vodnikova cesta, banging into cars as it went, setting off alarms with screeching sounds and flashing lights before bouncing over the curb into the street. This was ridiculous; she had work to do.

Jo was exhausted. Pushing her will against Morana's took every bit of reserve she could muster. She tried to think of meaningful places away from the teahouse. Jo wasn't willing to take any chances that whatever wards were there would hold against a goddess as pissed off as her current roommate. Morana would turn toward the river, and Jo would imagine the strongest memory she had tied to a place in the opposite direction.

Thinking of pouncing on Rok in the week after Helena had been killed when she didn't yet understand what she was, had gotten them to the parking lot in front of his building. She wasn't even sure she knew what she was now. He had left the next day, disappeared into the wind. It was a strong memory but not necessarily a good one. She'd scratched him to the point of drawing blood while they were having sex. The image of the two of them sitting on the edge of his tub while she dabbed his back with vodka would've made her cringe if she still had control of her own fucking face. She had lost control of herself then, too, in a different way and thrown her body against his to get out of it, out of her head. She'd used him. But she'd copped to it.

Soon after that she had been fighting for her life, and Faron's, in the bottom of the City Museum. That was the first time a god had taken over her body. Achelous had poured himself into her and used her to put the demon back into its vessel before blasting out of her and leaving her to nearly drown in the flooded basement. And for what? He could have just appeared and yelled at the thing, surely. Instead, she and Faron had almost drowned, and she'd—

No. No. No!

Morana was walking again, headed back to the city center. The City Museum wasn't even a two-minute walk from the teahouse. Damn. That was not the plan. But Jo was tired, and all she could think about was the choice Achelous had offered her as she'd been on the edge of giving in to the water trying to keep Faron's dead weight afloat. Achelous had offered to take her. She could have gone to live with him in his watery bower in the river. Under the river? Maybe she should have said yes. Then none of the rest of this would have happened. And Faron would be dead. She hadn't fought the weight of her waterlogged clothes and screaming muscles to save herself.

Her thoughts flipped back a number of years to a different river to the day her father had drowned and Achelous—she knew it was him now—had whispered in her ear, "Don't let them in." His advice didn't help much now that the call was coming from inside the house and she couldn't get out. Maybe Achelous should have just taken her into the Tennessee that day, and she would never have met Dušan. Faron would have never been in danger. He would never have been. She was so tired.

———

Ivanka startled as Rok and what had to be another deity appeared in the teahouse. Gods who weren't specifically warded out could just pop through the barrier they had erected. Good to know. Also, not good. Who else was roaming around out there? How many old gods were left? Were Jesus and Mary going to show up on the teahouse doorstep asking for a cup of Assam?

Otto, the newest addition to their ragtag collection, stood up, knocking his chair over and making a racket as it banged onto the floor.

"Achelous." Vesna sounded surprised, but also like she hadn't been certain Achelous was real.

Ivanka had assumed he was as real as Faron's father being the dark god of Slavic myth, or at least Slavic myth as related by Christian monks trying to put the "uncivilized" locals to shame. Those lessons with Clotilda had been incredibly useful. Achelous's blessing of the River Ljubljanica had saved Ana when she'd gotten caught in the crossfire of Veronika's revenge magic against Jo. Ivanka still wasn't down with the idea of worshipping a deity. She had her own ideas about what deities were, and as of yet none of them had proven to her that they were any better than humans. More powerful, yes, there was no denying that. But better? Črnobog, for one, was a first-class asshole. Despite her misgivings about Črnobog, she had a soft spot for Achelous on Ana's account. She wasn't ready to sink to her knees in his presence though.

Achelous's verdigris skin glowed softly in the teahouse like the sun reflecting on the surface of the glacial rivers running through the mountains. Rok had his own glow, but it mostly came from his eyes, like Faron's.

Faron appeared at her elbow. The others who had gathered in the teahouse, Gregor and Janez, her sisters and their Aunt Olga, Fred, Reka, Milo, and Igor all sat in silence. Ivanka couldn't make out their eyes to see where they were looking, but their faces all seemed intent on this new deity among them.

It was hard not to stare. She had accustomed herself to Faron's strangeness, and that had made it easier to accept Minerva and Rok. Achelous had an otherworldliness that made the deities she had previously encountered seem almost ordinary.

A smile broke across Achelous's face. It was beautiful and terrible, and she had to remember that there were words now used for mundane things that had once been reserved for the gods and she finally got it.

Achelous's smile broadened into a laugh. "Very old gods carry their own strangeness."

Ivanka wasn't sure if she imagined it or if Achelous had set the image there, but she saw him as a one-horned bull raging against a champion and as a merman swimming in the depths surrounded by his siren daughters. As uncanny as his presence was, he could be stranger still. And he could just be a person like Dušan when he wasn't Črnobog, though in her imagining he preferred jeans over Dušan's black suits.

Achelous finally seemed to notice Otto—the only one who had stood when he and Rok had appeared. He tilted his head in an almost birdlike way and asked Vesna, "Can I ask why you let a traitor in?"

Otto made a sound somewhere between a gasp and a hard swallow and went to sit down again, forgetting his chair had turned over. He sat hard on the side of a leg, startled, then scrambled to right the chair and sit properly. He didn't speak or make another sound, though he looked desperately like he wanted to explain himself.

"He's from the Board." Achelous casually pulled out a chair and sat down, sprawled out like a sullen teenager on a bus seat.

"We know. He told us." Vesna had regained her cool and took the lead again.

"I think there's more he needs to tell you." Achelous rolled his hand in the air in Otto's direction. "Out with it. You don't have the luxury of secrets at this point."

Otto opened his mouth and closed it again a few times like a fish gawping at the walls of an aquarium. When he finally collected himself enough to make words come out, he was met with dead silence.

"Bettine is gathering support to come and fight Dušan Črnigad and close the Veil."

"Bettine is dead." Vesna said it as if she were simply correcting a misstatement by Otto, but Ivanka could see her anger like a cloud of crimson dust rising up around her.

As Ivanka realized it was Vesna's aura that she could see, a dark cloud formed over Otto's head crackling with electricity. The man moved to the side to avoid the downpour the cloud brought with it, but he couldn't dodge the bolt of staticky lightning that shot out and zapped him. He glared at the cloud and rubbed his shoulder.

"Be glad she's restraining herself, or you'd be dead." An amused expression flickered across Achelous's features.

"How is Bettine alive? I watched her self-immolate in front of the Hotel Lisica." Vesna was looking straight ahead. Otto probably would have burst into flames himself if Vesna had looked directly at him.

Otto took a deep breath. "That was her fetch, a projection—"

"I know what a fetch is." Vesna was breathing in and out at a controlled pace, but another bolt from the miniature thunderhead licked out and struck Otto in the ear. She hadn't known anything about fetches until Fand had told her what the magic she'd pilfered from Bettine's room was for.

"Of course." He now rubbed his ear with the hand that had been massaging his shoulder. "She intends ..." No one interrupted him this time, but he didn't continue. Ivanka guessed they'd gotten to the part where he couldn't say any more without getting in trouble with his boss.

Vesna stood up and walked to where she'd hung her coat on a peg by the door. Otto's cloud disappeared while she rummaged in her pockets.

When she returned, she held up the stoppered glass vial containing a shimmering red-gold liquid that glowed with the blue light of magic when she tilted it at eye level.

"Fand said this might come in handy."

Vesna smashed the glass on the wooden floor and ground it to bits with the ball of her booted foot.

Otto stepped back and looked at her in horror. "What have you done?"

———

Morana walked back down *Vodnikova cesta* toward the shortcut to the city center through Tivoli park. The trees were bare now this far into December, but there were still drifts of leaves in the gutters and in the overgrown areas. The smell of vegetal rot hung like a curtain where the road gave way to the path into the park, and Jo thought of Helena's brother Matjaž walking her to Rok's that night she'd pounced on him. Her attraction to Matjaž and her inability to shake it, along with all the weird shit that had happened since Helena's murder, had been the trigger for her breakdown when she'd gotten to Rok's door.

Matjaž, in his own grief, had kissed her. She had not wanted to involve him in her weirdness, but he was already up to his eyeballs in his family's weirdness without any help from her. He and Helena and their mother—witches, the lot of them. Only Matjaž was left. And if Dušan had sent Matjaž away like he had everyone else in the spring, she hoped he was still safe out there somewhere in the world. She hoped he was living his best life up to his knees in mud trying to save a crumbling building from time and water. If she disappeared into nothingness so Morana could fuck up whoever she wanted to fuck up, Jo would dissipate into the ethers with that small regret piled onto the others. She would have enjoyed whatever would have existed between her and Matjaž had they met at a different time, a different place. A completely different life.

One of those other regrets would be not having been able to thank Helena. She'd been a bit of a pain as a spirit guide, but she'd also done her best to look out for Jo. And she'd taken the risk of tackling a revenant and plunging through someone else's door into the Next in an effort to save Leo. Her sacrifice hadn't worked, but Helena had tried. She, probably more than anyone else, had understood how difficult it had been for Jo to admit to herself that she had fallen in love with Leo.

Morana stood silently in the bower of naked branches as if she were listening. Jo had to believe Morana knew what she was thinking. No matter how many entities were in this body, there was only one brain up there, and they all had to be sharing it. Morana stepped into the park, crossed the open expanse where there should have been sports buildings, and found a seat in a well-tended rose garden overrun with glowing shades and smaller dark things hiding in the shadows.

She untied the sword from her waist and placed it under the bench before laying down. Her eyes closed, leaving Jo without the windows she'd had on her surroundings. Had Jo managed to exhaust a goddess trotting her back and forth on the edges of the city? Or had her disordered thoughts about all the people she'd damaged been too much even for the Queen of the Witches?

"I think she's just tired from trying to keep you at bay." It was the voice of the spring goddess who had stepped into Jo's body like Alice through the Looking Glass in the Nav.

"Can she hear us while she's sleeping?" Whatever part of the mind or brain Jo had control of was at its breaking point, trying to understand what the hell was going on.

"No. But she won't need to rest long." The voice seemed to be in her head and coming from outside in full Dolby surround sound. "You need to keep trying to take control. This isn't who she wants to be."

"How can you possibly know that? She seems pretty bent on making someone pay." Truth was Jo didn't know how much longer until she was the one giving in and passing out for good.

"Because I'm as much a part of her as you are."

"Did you forget the part where you two hijacked my body and—"

"No. Morana was always you. She came back into this world with your first breath. I just returned her full divinity, her full powers, to her."

Jo started to rail some more about not choosing this bullshit, but she heard footsteps on the gravel path into the rose garden.

"She almost looks peaceful." A woman's deep honeyed voice came from above as if she were looking down on the sleeping form on the bench. It was the goddess from the City Square who had rained on Morana's pyromaniacal parade. Despite the goddess's late-night radio voice, her words reverberated in Jo's thoughts with all the clang of standing inside a church bell as the hour struck.

"Hmm. I wouldn't bet on it. Not until she's had her revenge." Dušan. She'd recognize that voice anywhere, but why weren't his words banging around in her head like a herd of alpine dairy cows?

"I'll leave you here to talk some sense into her." The goddess again. Then footsteps receding on the path.

Dušan sat on the bench and stroked Morana's temple, her temple. Jo had to keep reminding herself that Morana was not the real boss of this body.

"You need to stay alert. She isn't going to give up easily." The spring goddess again. Jo imagined her words as butterflies flitting through her thoughts. Word forms and wings. She could sleep, just for a few minutes.

"No!" It was a chorus of voices now. Demanding she be awake. If she'd had control of her body she would have bolted upright, as guiltily as if she'd fallen asleep at her desk in school. She must be hallucinating now, the chorus of voices chimed again, "Just stay awake."

Morana woke, and Dušan took her hand. "I think it's time you met the others."

———

Fred watched a blue mist rise from the remains of the vial on the teahouse floorboards. The others stood and backed away to the edges of the room. Otto seemed especially frightened, which Fred took as him knowing exactly what was coming.

The smoke curled and spun in on itself, thickening and pulsing until it was too dense to see through any longer and had begun to take on a human form.

"What did you do?" Igor was the only one who stepped closer to Vesna when she hadn't moved away from the mist.

"If Fand was correct in her assessment, I just summoned the fetch's witch." Vesna toed a bit of broken glass and waited. Fred expected her to tap her foot in impatience. "Fand thought Bettine had the vial with her to summon a fetch, but the magic works both ways."

The form fully coalesced, and a face emerged from the general area of the head. Fred recognized it as Bettine, the woman who had come to meet with Vesna and Gustaf in the spring. As she became more flesh than mist, Bettine's expressions ranged between murderous rage and shock.

"How did you do that?" Bettine spit the words out at the

closest person, Vesna.

Igor didn't step between them, but he stepped shoulder to shoulder with Vesna. Fred appreciated a man who understood his partner did not need protection but support.

"I broke the vial I took from your servo." Vesna shrugged. "And now that you're here you can tell us how to close the Veil."

———

Alessandro made it to the Witchfinder's lodgings through the dwindling crowds of tourists as night fell. The staff at the Peggy Guggenheim were evicting the few stragglers so they could close the gates. The *Dorsoduro sestieri* stood highest above sea level in the city and was generally spared the worst of the destruction wrought by the *acqua alta*. He was unsure if that bit of geographical luck would spare the museum and the district from the storm roiling on the edge of the lagoon, but he could think of no other place to wait.

Paolo greeted him at the front door in a coat with a leather satchel in his hand. "We're leaving."

"So I gathered," he gestured at the bag, "but where do you intend to go, and how do you imagine getting out of the lagoon?" Alessandro patted down the pockets of his coat. He was prepared to leave if necessary, but that hadn't been his plan.

"The last email I got was from Christoph, my compatriot in Vienna. The new Witchfinder in Ljubljana contacted him. The storm began there." He closed the door behind him and locked up with his back to Alessandro.

How much should he tell him? What loyalty did he owe

Bettine? Whatever she said, he knew she had somehow been responsible for the deaths of the previous Board members. Paolo was a good man, and his allegiance to the Church—unlike those zealots like the Kos family in Slovenia—had not made him ruthless. He harbored no bloodlust for the unfortunates who lived beyond the Veil.

"I know." He paused.

"I believe you know more, friend. But we should discuss these matters on the boat. Captain will take us to Koper, and we will have to find our way to Ljubljana from there." Paolo's expression was one of determination, but Alessandro recognized the fear as well.

Alessandro looked at the leading edge of the storm itself, which had breached the Lido and entered the lagoon. Getting past that into the Adriatic would be a dangerous crossing. He wasn't ready to think about what creatures from the deep the storm would have summoned to the surface.

Paolo led him to a side entrance of the Guggenheim Museum grounds. Paolo pushed the talk button on a keypad hidden behind a planter spilling over with greenery. A scratchy electronic voice responded with what sounded like a question about the weather on Wednesday, and Paolo said, "*Neve*," close to the speaker.

The gate buzzed, allowing them to enter the grounds, and the human owner of the voice they had heard escorted them to the private pier where a sturdy boat and a sturdier looking woman waited for them. Her face was deeply tanned, but she still seemed young to him despite the sun damage.

She hailed them in badly accented Italian. An American.

"Captain will get us there, friend. Don't worry." Paolo seemed to believe absolutely in this woman's ability, and Alessandro put his life in her hands.

Alessandro stuck his hand out in greeting and introduced himself.

"Just call me Captain, everyone else does." She turned her attention back to the small stack of what looked like supplies.

Once the cases were loaded, the trio boarded the boat, which seemed more suited to ferry wealthy tourists back and forth to the mainland than weather a storm at sea. Captain unmoored and steered the boat back out toward the lagoon, minding the speed limit for boats. Alessandro had to ask himself if that mattered now. But of course it did. Paolo wouldn't be taking this risk if Venice no longer mattered to him. But much more than Venice was at risk.

Captain turned the boat south, away from the general entrance of the lagoon.

"I'm going to try to get us out of here between Lido and Santa Maria del Mare."

Her accent was truly atrocious, like something out of a bad film.

"We can speak English if you prefer." Alessandro hoped she took it as a friendly invitation instead of criticism.

"I knew Paolo spoke English, but I wasn't sure about you and I always hate to ask." Her eyes never left the water. "Hate to be *that* kind of American."

Alessandro smiled and nodded, relieved that her voice was much more pleasant when speaking in her native tongue.

"It's admirable of you to learn the local language." Or to at least try.

She nodded and guided the boat between the two islands. They were still headed straight into the storm but seemed to be flanking the worst of it.

Alessandro got the distinct impression that the storm had its own plans, and those didn't involve the barrier islands.

CHAPTER 23

Bettine looked around at the many faces turned toward her. She couldn't tell if they were more surprised to see her than she was to find herself there. She would have preferred to arrive on her terms and without most of the people in this room knowing she had, but this did solve the problem of how she was going to get there.

"Why do you think you can stop it?" Answering questions with questions wouldn't give her the upper hand for long, but it might give her a better idea about what exactly was going on.

"I don't think I can. I think *we* can." Vesna turned as she said it and was met with several nods.

"You may not operate like your father, but you may be as foolhardy." Bettine pulled out a chair from the nearest table and sat down. "Is it possible to get tea in this teahouse?"

Vesna was unmoved by her request. A young woman stood up in the shadows toward the back of the shop and said she could bring something.

"No, Reka. I'll get it for her." Vesna turned and disappeared behind the counter display.

"Otto, I assume you have been introduced. Would you care to do the honors?" Even in the darkened dining room, his face was unmistakably pale.

"I just arrived myself and …"

"Never mind then. What fancy dress party are the two of you headed to?" The inclusion of gods in this menagerie surprised her. It could make things more difficult. It didn't, however, make her any less likely to be antagonistic toward them.

The green one, seated at the next table answered her. "Achelous." He paused briefly. She had expected him to give the full descriptive "god of all waters and blah blah" as deities, especially old defunct ones, needed to do to make sure their full glories were understood. He instead continued the introductions around the room, reserving descriptives for the humans present.

Bettine caught herself raising an eyebrow a few times at "Ivanka, seer of the Three Sisters and consort to the resurrected Belinus" and "Milo, shade of some renown." This Achelous was entertaining, if nothing else.

"And you Bettine? Who are you?" He tilted his green face at her, and she saw a stomach-churning flash of his many other faces.

"I don't trade in honorifics—"

"Then perhaps I should introduce you." He made a sweep of his arm to indicate his audience. "Assembled friends, this is Bettine, Governor of the Board of Observers, originally appointed by Charlemagne himself at the Council of

Frankfort in the Christian year of 794, secret adept witch, and murderess." He looked straight at her with his last words.

"I could have told you the last." Vesna returned with a cup of tea in a mismatched cup and saucer and set it on the table in front of Bettine. She pulled out a chair and joined her. "I am a little surprised by the rest."

"I almost forgot. Bettine, murderess, this is Vesna, Witchfinder of the Duchy of Carniola officially, but these days we just use Slovenia. But you knew that part. She is also the Measurer of the Three sisters."

Vesna seemed surprised by the last but hid it quickly.

Achelous turned his glowing green gaze on Bettine again. "Would you like to explain to them how the Veil can be closed again?"

She hadn't come prepared to be interrogated by a god. Let alone one that still seemed to wield power. She knew Achelous as a faded river spirit embodied in the Water Man of Prešeren's poetry, decidedly not a deity with worshippers. Or at least not enough worshippers to matter.

"Where is Jolene Wiley?" Bettine didn't bother to look around the room. She hadn't been included in Achelous's introductions.

No one spoke.

She waited a few beats before answering her own question. "She's with Dušan Črnigad, isn't she?"

CHAPTER 24

Črnobog led Morana through the park toward the entrance where the museum of modern art should be. The museum was currently missing, having been replaced with a horse paddock and a small outbuilding. Ljubljana was still shifting through its many centuries, though it was harder to notice in the darkness. The holiday lights still blazed on, almost in mockery of the havoc the night creatures wreaked on anyone fool enough to wander out into the night. There were those who were smart enough to hide but had been left out in the open when the building they were cowering in disappeared as that area reverted to an open lot undeveloped during the time of Emona or the middle ages. The city would sort itself by daybreak, but that was probably little comfort to those being rent to pieces by ghouls. He did try to save the few they encountered, but Morana marched single-mindedly back to the teahouse, leaving him little time to play at rescuer.

The two gods walked along the river where the embankments flickered between the early-modern sloping banks and the concrete abatement of Plečnik's architecture. Taverns and restaurants appeared then faded again as peddlers' wagons replaced them. The ghosts around them conversed in Latin, German, a smattering of Italian, many versions of Slovenian, and Old Slavonic. Morana stopped at the entrance to *Zajčeva ulica,* and Črnobog was again reminded of the image of Jo's friends and family, including his son, hunkered down in a warren on Rabbit Street waiting in the dark for sunrise and the promise of some kind of safety. But the all-clear wasn't coming. The goddess of life and death was waiting outside their doors.

Morana walked the few paces to *Številka 2* and hesitated again. Was she reconsidering her actions? Or was something—someone—interfering? He wanted to believe Jo was still part of Morana, but he had seen the determination in the goddess's dark eyes and there was no compassion there. Not for those she sought out. Not for Jo. Not yet.

Morana laid her hand on the latch to the arched wooden doors, and a faint blue glow radiated out to form tendrils that vined themselves around the wards still visible in the In-between. The protections that had been laid previously to keep him and Morana out allowed what was left of Jo to enter. The goddess had figured out that her friends wouldn't ward Jo out of her own home, even if it was Morana who arrived.

———

There was no stopping Morana now. Jo thought of every place she'd ever been in the city far away from the center. She thought of a play she had seen years ago at an experimental theater that had popped up in the train yards where she'd first met Nico—before he'd opened the bar in Metelkova—and nights spent trawling that same bar for someone to keep her bed warm. She thought of the day she had met Leo in the cathedral and had walked with him through the rain to the rectory where he'd made her Turkish coffee and listened when she had expected him to douse her with holy water or call the attendants at Polje. She thought of the catering event where she'd first encountered Helena and mornings when she'd bundled Faron up and they'd gone to the bus station to escape the city for the day, choosing a route at random. None of it was enough to turn Morana away from the teahouse. The goddess hesitated, even stopped at the entrance, but Jo had failed.

Jo felt the reverberation in her body, in the body she was sharing with Morana, as the wards opened on the doors leading into the courtyard. She imagined the latch shattering and bits of metal and wood falling to the street at their feet, but aside from that first jolt, the door had given no other resistance. Only the wards had fallen at her, at Morana's touch, and now anything and everything could find its way into her sanctuary. Jo sensed Dušan—Črnobog—there in the darkness behind them. She hadn't seen his human face since the Veil had been opened. No, since she'd opened the Veil. She couldn't think of him that way anymore, couldn't think of him as human. He wasn't. He was the dark lord of Slavic myth, the trickster, and she had fallen for his lies. She'd fallen for him, and that was why they were standing here, her body hijacked and breaking into her own house, her thoughts disjointed and spinning out away from her as she tried to focus.

That's new.

There was a well in the courtyard with a glowing membrane capping it. Was that to keep things out or in?

Morana walked to the teahouse door. There wasn't much light but enough that Jo could see their reflection in the glass. Two towering figures in black. One as dark as the robe he wore and the other an unearthly pale with eyes like holes burned into a sheet. Inside the teahouse was only darkness, but the wards showed on the large plate window and the door, glowing as they had on the outside of the building. She guessed Morana would pop her way through these as well. And then what?

And then all hell would break loose apparently.

Morana swiped her hand over the knob and walked inside, banging the door against the wall and chiming the heavy bells Jo had tied on the day they had opened so they could hear customers if they were in the back cooking or making tea.

The goddess from the square followed them into the teahouse. Minerva. Morana knew her name, though Jo hadn't. Minerva walked through the gathered crowd in the center of the teahouse and stood in front of Morana, eye to eye. Her toga gave off its own faint glow, and her movements left the slightest sense of tracers, like a sparkler.

"These people are under my protection." Minerva's voice rang inside Jo's head. God, she hated that.

"You and what army?" If it was possible, Morana's voice sounded even louder. "You have no hold here."

Minerva laughed, and the deep peals pushed through Jo's mind like concussive waves. "They believe. That is all that is necessary." The goddess swept her arm out like she was revealing the prize behind the curtain. The prize was her friends.

Morana moved to walk past the goddess, but Minerva turned and grabbed her arm. Morana threw her off easily and knocked the goddess to the floor. "You will find that your small band of believers is not enough when you are on land consecrated to me before you even existed."

Črnobog put his hand on their shoulder to stop her, but Morana shrugged him off. Morana's eyes didn't need to adjust to the darkness, so Jo's view was clear inside the teahouse. Achelous in his green merman form stood shoulder to shoulder with Rok and Faron. Vesna and Ivanka lingered behind them with Bettine. Bettine? What the fuck was she doing here? Had all the upheaval roused her ghost?

"And you must be Faron." Morana moved so she was in front of him, looking down and definitely in his personal space.

"And you must be Morana. Are you enjoying your walkabout before my mother returns?"

Jo expected Morana to throw her head back and laugh maniacally like a cartoon supervillain, but she just cocked her head and looked past him to Vesna and Ivanka. The two women where putting on brave faces, but Jo knew they were doing exactly that. Morana pushed past Faron to stand in front of Vesna.

"And you are Jo's friend. Her confidant. A weather witch and a Witchfinder's daughter by the smell of you." Jo could feel Morana's anger rising again, and she tried to think of puppies and rainbows or rotting leaves and snowfall, whatever would be Morana's happy place.

"I am the daughter of Witchfinders and a witch." Vesna's voice was steady but Jo could hear the fear there too.

"Not enough of a witch to make up for the blood on your family's hands."

Before Vesna could respond, Morana pushed her hand out hitting Vesna square in the chest with her palm. The light went out in Vesna's eyes before her body crumpled to the floor. Ivanka rushed toward Morana, the others too stunned by what had just happened to stop her, and put herself between Vesna's body and Morana.

Jo was screaming, but she didn't have a mouth of her own or any control over what was happening. *Stop it. Stop it. Stop it,* ran through her thoughts until the words lost meaning, but the goddess didn't stop. She struck down Ivanka with the same gesture before the others could react.

Morana turned toward Faron and beckoned him to come to her. Faron's eyes were blazing with god light and anger. Jo could see both the man he was and the little boy he had been. He didn't respond to Morana but went to Vesna and Ivanka, kneeling between their bodies and placing a hand on each woman's chest.

Morana didn't give him time to revive them but grabbed him by the shoulder and pulled him to her. "They don't need your comfort or your death magic."

Jo stopped keening and looked through Morana's eyes at her son. *This is not happening.* She was not going to let this fucking interloper take him.

The other voice she'd been hearing spoke up, quietly. The spring goddess reminded her that she shared Morana's power just as Morana shared her body. *Take it.*

How the fuck am I supposed to do that?

With her own anger surging past Morana's, Jo pushed her senses out as far as they would go and imagined her fingers sliding into her own hands like gloves. Stepping into her body like a coat, she let out the most bloodcurdling scream she could imagine. The sound ripped through her like Morana's scream had done in Town Square when Minerva and Achelous had stopped her setting the buildings on fire.

Everyone around her covered their ears and tried to move away, cowering under tables and trying to protect each other. She felt two hands solidly on her shoulders and turned around, still screaming at the top of her voice, and had to look up to see Črnobog's face.

She looked into his star-strewn eyes and stopped. The hollow in the immediate absence of the sound was almost as deafening. She shrugged out of Črnobog's grasp and knelt between Vesna and Ivanka. They were both dead. There was no light in either set of staring eyes, and she wanted to scream again. What had Morana done?

What have I done?

The voice spoke up again. *You have her power. And mine.*

The Goddess of Life. Jo mimicked Faron's actions and laid her palms flat on Ivanka and Vesna's chests. She sensed their hearts, sensed them having stopped, and willed them both to beat again.

Nothing.

Beat, *dammit.*

She splayed her fingers out, concentrated on the sound of her own blood coursing in her ears, and willed their bodies to restart. Every death since Helena's played through her thoughts, and her anger and sadness rose up together until she was screaming and crying again. She tried to hold her rage and Morana's as close to the surface as she could before, but it spilled over.

No! *Take me instead.*

She imagined both women gasping and feeling life ebb back into them again before she was pulled off of their still bodies. Golden strands spun out between them, growing taut but not severing, tying her to them as long as she drew breath. She was being carried away through the darkness, stumbling and falling through nothingness before landing curled into a ball like a rabbit, hiding.

CHAPTER 25

"That's the friend you're trying to protect?" Bettine spat out the words at Vesna.

The woman had been dead less than an hour ago, and now she was trying to convince Bettine and the others to go out into the city while it was still dark to find Jolene Wiley.

"She murdered you. And her." Bettine pointed to Ivanka, who was staring at her with an equally determined and stupid face. She threw her hands up in the air. "You're both fools."

"You saw her." Faron had quickly joined the chorus defending his mother. "And it will be light soon."

"She just murdered your girlfriend."

"No. That was Morana." Faron shook his head at her as if he were still trying to convince himself.

"Jolene Wiley is Morana." Bettine said it as clearly as she could, but it was worse than talking with children. And Jo, Morana, or whoever she pretended to be, needed to be put down as surely as Črnobog, or Dušan, or whoever the hell he was.

Vesna's boyfriend joined the idiot chorus. "She wasn't Morana when she left."

"Clearly I can't stop you on your suicide mission." Bettine was resigned to them doing whatever the hell they wanted, but she also knew she couldn't close the Veil by herself. Charlemagne had required 13 magic users to lay the shroud and seal it with their blood. There were enough people there now, but four of them had no abilities whatsoever. It was a shame that Goran had gotten himself killed. He would have been useful, for that at least.

She took a deep breath to keep her voice as even as possible. "It will take all of us, plus more to close the Veil. I would prefer you not get yourselves killed again until we can do that." *It's going to be enough trouble to spill all your blood afterward to keep it closed.*

"You know how to close it?" Ivanka glared at her. The faintest shimmer glowed in the depths of the young woman's eyes. Maybe it was anger, or Bettine's meager aura-reading abilities had been bolstered by the magic infusing everything with the Veil opened.

"Of course she does." Vesna stood, placing her hand flat on the table to steady herself. "It's why I called her here. She was there when they closed the Veil the first time."

There was no way Vesna could have known she was alive, let alone that she had been there when Charlemagne had last wielded Joyeuse to seal the membrane, creating the In-between.

The others were looking at Vesna. Bettine saw skepticism and a little fear in their faces. She knew death could change a person, and Vesna appeared changed.

———

Vesna stood up straighter and let go of the table. Her legs were still a little wobbly, but a core of anger and determination burned at the center of her being. Jo was alive. She had caught a whirling glimpse of her as Črnobog had gathered her into his cloak and disappeared into the darkness with her. Vesna didn't know where he had taken her friend, but now that she was certain Jo was alive, she would find her.

Fand had been right about everything. Vesna knew better than to dismiss the visions of a goddess, but she also knew from Črnobog that the gods could see the many ways a situation could end. Vesna had believed Fand had followed the brightest thread in her predictions but held onto the possibility that another path could be taken.

Vesna looked around the room at the others. The teahouse smelled of fear and like someone had poured a bottle of vanilla extract across the wooden floor. God magic. Jo's magic. Jo had saved her and Ivanka. Saving them meant there had been a sacrifice, or there was still a price to be paid. She wasn't sure which she feared more.

"Two more will join us." Ivanka said it, looking unsure of where the words came from but with full conviction that they were true. "And another is already here."

As soon as the second sentence fell out of her mouth into the room, Rebecca Wiley appeared wrapped in a winter white traveling cloak, her hair gleaming red-gold in the low candlelight.

"We still aren't thirteen." Rebecca's gaze travelled around the room, her head nodding as she counted. "Or at least not thirteen who can do the work."

"The last will arrive at daybreak." Vesna said it flatly, directed at no one and everyone. She had seen Ivanka's vision as if it were her own.

Rebecca nodded and took a seat at the nearest table. "So we wait." She opened the lid on the teapot next to her and looked inside. "So what's the plan then?"

Vesna and Bettine spoke at the same time. Bettine tried to continue to speak over her, but Vesna wasn't having it. "You don't have any authority here."

Bettine looked taken aback but regained her composure quickly. "The Board has authority across—"

Achelous interrupted her. "The Board has no authority over me or Minerva Britanna, and besides, whatever personal power you had to make decisions about anything were forfeit when you and your accomplices murdered the rest of the Board."

Bettine sputtered in protest.

"Sit down and shut up." Minerva continued, "Vesna is the local authority, and Achelous and I support her."

Achelous nodded and smiled at Vesna. His show of subtly pointed teeth was meant to be encouraging.

"We wait for the last two and for daylight." Did she really want to be in charge? Her father had meant the role of Witchfinder to fall to her, and her Uncle Leo had left it vacant. They would both be disappointed if she didn't at least try to do right by the power vested in her. Her mother had charged her with finding the witches—not to persecute them but to protect them, and she had spectacularly failed at that in Goran's case. For him and for her mother, if no one else, she needed to get her shit together. And if two gods thought she was in charge, who was she to say different?

"We have to find the sword." Minerva still stood out in her god form, a faint glow about her, but Vesna no longer found her as otherworldly.

"So you'll have to find Morana next after all." Bettine snorted.

"No, we will have to find Jo." Vesna glared at Bettine. She knew now that it was Bettine's fetch that had watched while her demon-possessed guard broke Gustaf's neck, but Bettine had been in control. Bettine was also responsible for the magic that had killed her mother.

"Suit yourself. Your friend is dead." Bettine was determined to not make any friends in this room. Vesna wondered if the woman thought they would just let her go once they'd resealed the Veil. As Witchfinder, Vesna had the power to detain her.

"My mother is not dead. And you will speak of her with respect." Faron had been sitting quietly next to Ivanka for the last volley of arguments, but he'd clearly had enough of Bettine.

"Or what?" Bettine sneered, but Vesna could see the fear creep into her eyes.

"I don't know what you think we're capable of, but I'm happy to lock you in the office until you're needed." Faron spoke with a level, almost passionless voice, but Vesna knew better and Bettine would be smart to pay attention.

Instead she shrugged and shrank into herself, momentarily chastised. Vesna doubted it would last. They needed Bettine to close the Veil, but she couldn't be trusted beyond that.

"Is there anything else we need to do now?" Igor reached out and squeezed Vesna's hand. She could feel the care and concern in his touch.

"We need to be certain we can protect Fred and Reka and Gregor and Janez. They'll have no one here to defend them when we leave to find Jo." Vesna racked her brain, but she had no idea what would work now that Morana had been able to breach the wards they had set.

"I could arrange for some *vodnici* to watch over them." Achelous smiled his fishy smile again. Vesna would be glad to have him back in his human disguise when the Veil was closed, but perhaps that was an assumption. Would he stay? Would any of them after all that had happened?

CHAPTER 26

Alessandro looked out over the dark water. Under the storm clouds that hung low, glowing with their own internal light, the sea was a sheet of obsidian. The boat's motor roared along, carrying them at top speed across the Adriatic, closer to the port of Koper.

Paolo sat across from him on the low bench that wrapped around the back for passengers or sightseers or fishers—whomever it was that Captain generally ferried about in her luxuriously appointed vessel. He held his rosary in his hand. Alessandro watched the younger man cycle through the beads multiple times. Alessandro had shoved his own rosary into his pocket before leaving his house, but he felt there was more than one god steering their futures that night and he didn't care to pray to any of them at the moment.

Captain cut the engine and lights without warning, then whistled low and told them to get down in a harsh whisper. Alessandro did as he was told. Captain crouched next to the wheel. Alessandro watched over the gunnel as a tall wooden ship drifted by. It was hard to gauge the distance in the glaucous light, but he would've sworn he could smell pitch as strong as freshly poured tarmac. Voices carried over the water from the ship. Italian, but not any dialect he'd ever heard.

He had worried that creatures driven into the depths by the casting of the Veil would find their way to the surface, but it never occurred to him that ghost ships would join them in the crossing.

The boat disappeared into the fog. Captain waited a few beats then turned the key. Before the engine engaged, something bumped against the hull. Alessandro couldn't tell if it was that large or if the hull magnified the sound. He and Paolo looked at each other, still flattened against the bottom of the boat. Paolo's eyes were wide in fear, and Alessandro assumed his face must look the same. Captain opened up the engine and did whatever the maritime equivalent of flooring it was. He pulled himself up onto the bench and maneuvered back into the protective pocket the windshield offered. When he looked to their wake for any signs of the ghost ship having followed them, he saw an enormous tentacle reach up from the water, the tip curled as if it had meant to grasp something that was no longer there.

Alessandro closed his eyes and crossed himself.

CHAPTER 27

Jo woke in total darkness. Disoriented and stiff, she sat up as best she could. Soft earth and maybe straw shifted beneath her. She reached out and touched more dirt, but it was compacted and smooth under her fingertips. She assumed it was dirt as it left a coating on her skin that felt gritty when she rubbed her fingers together. There wasn't any difference between having her eyes open or closed, except when she squeezed her eyes shut, there were at least the colors of her retinas reacting to the pressure.

"Hello?"

Bright light flooded her little cave, and she had to shield her eyes against it.

"You're awake." Dušan. No. Črnobog. *You have to remember who he really is.*

"Yes, Lord Obvious, I'm awake." She braved standing and found the ground was much more solid now. "Care to explain where I am?"

Before Črnobog could answer, the image of Vesna and Ivanka lying on the teahouse floor, their dead eyes staring into the vaulted plaster ceiling, washed over her. She almost collapsed back into a heap on the ground, but an arm caught her around the waist and pulled her close.

"Whoa, there."

She opened her eyes again, a little less light blind. Dušan's face, not Črnobog's, was looking into hers, with something like worry on it.

Jo pushed him away, gently. She didn't want to wind up on her ass because she was being stubborn, but she didn't want him getting handsy with her either. "Where are we? How are you?"

"I'm fine. Considering." He smiled, and it was almost pleasant.

"Stop it. Stop that." Her head was spinning a bit. "I didn't mean 'how are you?' I meant, how are you that." She waved her hand at him indicating human-looking Dušan decked out in his usual black suit and overly starched shirt. "I thought you couldn't be human in the 'realm of the gods' or whatever."

He cocked his head at her. "We aren't in the realm of the gods."

"You closed the Veil?" How long had she been asleep? Could he even do that by himself?

"No. We are in the realm of a god." *Why does he look sheepish?* She didn't like it when he looked sheepish.

"Or something like that." Mary—Jesus's mom, not hers— appeared and smiled a much less disconcerting smile at her. The golden nimbus that usually glowed above her was significantly smaller and contained, like she was wearing a circlet of light on her head. "You're in the cathedral, the one near the market."

Jo looked up at the dense woods around them. Dappled summer sunlight filtered down through the canopy, and she felt the forest floor under her bare feet. This was definitely not the cathedral she walked by to Zsophia's stall on Saturdays. There were no pews where Leo had sat waiting for her. There was no jewel-encrusted, gilded everything everywhere above the definitely not there marble floor.

Mary laughed. "It's your cathedral. The cathedral you would imagine. But it's also St. Peter and Paul in *Staro Mesto*. Let's just say that big-G God has some pull in the In-between, and the small-g gods," she chucked Dušan on the shoulder like they were drinking buddies and continued, "have to mind their manners in His house."

Sure. Why the hell not?

Mary, bless her, offered Jo a Girl Scout canteen. Jo looked at it with a crooked eyebrow before taking it and unscrewing the lid. "Taking this whole hiking through the woods thing a bit far, aren't we?" She took a long drink of the water. It was perfectly chilled without making her teeth hurt with the cold.

"That's on you." Mary took the canteen back and slid it into the little shoulder strap carrying case made out of Girl Scout green fabric and a red tartan. It was just like the one Jo had seen in the box of her mother's things at her aunt's house in Chattanooga.

Jo pulled her mental focus back to the moment. "Is this the part where big-G God sends me to hell for murdering my best friend and my son's girlfriend?" If God wasn't going to punish her himself, she was pretty sure she could whip up an imaginary hair shirt and a cat o' nine tails to get the flaying started, given her ability to perfectly render a sixty-year-old canteen.

"You didn't murder them." Dušan tried to reassure her.

"They are dead, and I did it, so whether or not I 'murdered' them seems like a semantic argument."

"Well, you did kill them, or rather Morana did, but then you brought them back to life." This new, kinder Dušan was making things worse. She didn't believe for a minute that things weren't worse than she knew.

Mary winced at Dušan's explanation. *See, that's not good, but maybe they aren't dead.*

"Okay. So what does that mean?" Between Mary's expression and Jo's own knowledge of the price Death extracted when thwarted, there might still be hell to pay.

"It means Ivanka and Vesna live." Dušan shrugged his shoulders, as if were that simple.

Jo looked down at her hands. Boring, human ones that looked like they'd probably done too many sinks full of dirty restaurant dishes with no gloves on. "And Morana? Where is she?"

Mary made another, harder to parse, face and looked to Dušan. "Are you going to tell her?"

"I think you have a better understanding of what's happened." Dušan Črnigad, class-A asshole and eternal thorn in her side, was not only deferring to someone else, but to a woman. Okay, a demi-god or something, but still. This had to be bad.

"Let's go for a walk." Mary offered Jo her arm.

"How big is this place?" Jo nestled her hand into the crook of Mary's elbow and looked back at Dušan as they walked away.

"How big is your imagination?" Mary laughed, and they followed a deer path deeper into the forest.

———

Alessandro had never thought that images of people kissing the ground after disembarking from some sea- or sky-going vessel were anything more than hyperbole, but he felt the overwhelming urge to do just that when they finally reached the docks in Koper. Captain moored the boat and motioned them off before she clambered up onto the dock herself.

"Are you coming with us?" Alessandro looked from her weathered face to Paolo's more child-like one.

"Nope. But I'm not staying on the boat to wait for you while this shit is brewing." She pulled her slicker up and walked ahead of them down the planking to where a single lantern hung on the piling closest to the shore.

"She has a *friend* here. She'll stay with her." Paolo stage-whispered into Alessandro's ear.

"And did you arrange for us to get to Ljubljana?" Alessandro would have chastised the younger man's scandalized tone had they been in different circumstances. What Captain did with her time ashore couldn't matter less to him, and it shouldn't matter to Paolo. Perhaps Venice's Witchfinder wasn't as progressive as Alessandro had believed, or perhaps it was a blinkered spot.

"Yes. Though I expected to be met at the dock." Paolo looked around in the dimly lit mist.

"I'm here." A man twice the size of either of them stepped into the puddle of light cast by the lantern.

He spoke English with a heavy Slavic accent. Alessandro wasn't particularly good at deciphering one Balkan dialect from another, but he assumed the mountain of a man was Slovenian, given their location.

"This is Uroš."

Alessandro shrugged and offered his hand to Uroš, who didn't take it but gave him instead a silent nod before turning and walking away.

Paolo produced a flashlight, and the three of them followed a path toward a small parking area near one of the many import/export offices in the docks. Captain set off on her own with a wave and left Alessandro and Paolo with Uroš and a decrepit, lime green Polski Fiat from Yugoslavia days.

Uroš climbed behind the wheel and left him and Paolo to sort themselves out. Paolo insisted Alessandro take the passenger seat and wedged himself into the back.

"The roads have been … difficult." Uroš backed the car out of the space and putted out onto the main road headed inland. "But I think we'll be there before morning."

Alessandro guessed it was still before midnight. The ferry crossing from Venice to Koper took no more than three hours in good weather, and Captain had moved across at a steady pace, with only the one pause. He shivered again at the thought of the great tentacle he had seen rise up from the water. The drive from Koper to Ljubljana should take even less time than that, even in the dark. But if such leviathans had been awakened in the deep, what waited for them on land? He nestled into the hard seat and tried to get what sleep he could.

Whatever was out there left them unbothered, and Alessandro awakened in Ljubljana as the Fiat came to a lurching halt in a roundabout.

"Good luck." Uroš got out and came around to open the passenger door; the inside handle had broken off at some point in the car's history.

Paolo tried to give the man a neatly folded stack of euro notes, but he shook his head and closed the passenger door with a tinny thud.

Uroš paused before getting back into the car and grinned at them over the roof. "I assume you will find your own way home."

Alessandro could have sworn the man's eyes twinkled when he said it but chalked it up to grogginess after an uncomfortable nap. He watched the car careen out of the roundabout, narrowly missing a cart horse that had appeared out of nowhere. Modern LED holiday lights strung between gas street lamps cast harsh shadows against the mishmash of buildings lining the street that would carry them further into the central city. He had no clue, really, how the world functioned with the Veil opened, but it seemed as if all the ages of Ljubljana that had existed were slipping past one another jockeying for position.

"Do you know where you are going?" Alessandro had only an address and no familiarity with the city.

Paolo laughed. "No more than I have at any point tonight." He walked away from the roundabout past a hulking ecclesiastic building walled off behind heavy doors and headed toward the scent of the river. Alessandro hurried to follow him. "I've trusted God will take us where we need to be."

Alessandro looked back over his shoulder at the roundabout and wondered if Uroš had been more than he had appeared..

CHAPTER 28

"You aren't going to tell me anything, are you? I mean that's the way it's been from the beginning of this. Bad shit happens. Gods, demi-gods, witches, and humans shake their heads at poor me, so sadly, and leave me with zero information." Jo cringed a little at her own whininess, but she was tired and had been trapped in her own body for the better part of the last 24 hours. It had all started to mash together in her memories like a really bad acid trip from her teenage years.

Mary patted Jo's hand, still tucked into the crook of her arm. "You have every right to be angry."

The validation pissed her off more than it soothed. Of course she had the right to be angry. She was a grown-ass person with agency when it wasn't being usurped by "divine beings" who really ought to know better.

"I just thought you could use a break from Dušan." Mary shrugged and walked on, but Jo stopped and stood staring at the woman's back before she turned around.

"I don't need a break from Dušan. I mean, I do, but what I really need to know is how much damage did I do? How long do I get to be me before Morana comes back? How do

I fix this mess? Have you seen what's going on out there?" Jo flung her hand out to indicate everything beyond the make-believe woods she'd apparently been responsible for conjuring. "I opened the fucking Veil. The Veil I didn't even know about less than two years ago." Less than two years but so much death and destruction.

"Death and destruction are part of the—"

"Don't 'circle of life' me. And don't root around in my thoughts. I don't need a lecture. I've had months and months of object lessons. Would you like me to recite the litany of the dead that plays on constant loop in my head?" It began to snow in her made-up forest, now populated with winter-bare trees and a carpeting of fallen leaves where there had been thick moss.

Mary nodded her head almost imperceptibly, as if responding to a command. "Here's what I can tell you. You need Dušan to close the Veil. You need to go back to St. Michael's with the sword."

"That's it? I mean I'd figured out that much on my own."

"Then you need to … slay Dušan with Joyeuse to make certain the Veil can't be reopened. There has to be a sacrifice. Blood has to be shed." Mary looked up before meeting her gaze again.

Jo's stomach sank. She professed to hate Dušan to just about anyone who would listen, most especially to herself. She knew it was bluster and bravado and assumed everyone else had figured that out too. There was no pretending to herself that she hadn't loved him once and that in some small way she always would. She couldn't look at her own son and not see him. Whatever Dušan was, whatever he had taken from her, he was part of Faron and she felt in some way he was also a part of her.

The snow came down harder, covering the ground and drifting against the trunks of the trees. Jo couldn't tell if she felt cold or if she was the cold.

"And Morana?"

The Blessed Virgin squeezed her hand. "It's complicated, but your body is yours."

"For good?"

"For good."

Mary walked past her, back toward wherever Dušan was waiting for them to return. Did he know? Jo remembered an ethics thought experiment one of her professors had presented to them when she was still at university in Tennessee, before she'd even known Slovenia existed. It was something about a runaway train and having to choose to divert to a track that killed one person instead of several people if the train kept on. Death was going to happen either way, but you had to choose. There was some complicating factor about the one person being a doctor who had saved lives and the others being thieves or murders. It had been a long time ago, and the thing she'd walked away with is that even when you refuse to decide you are still making a choice to let something happen without intervening. There had definitely been no discussion of any of the complications involving one of the people who could die being a god and the father of her child, whether she still loved him or not.

Jo followed Mary back to the clearing. Dušan was waiting. His white collar pressed to a knife's edge showed above the black wool of his heavy peacoat. The shadow of dark unshaven beard showed on his pale chin and jaw. He just sat there, waiting on a chair he must have conjured himself from the ethers in this cathedral, looking up at her with no reproach in the green-gold depths of his eyes. He didn't know she'd been tasked with killing a god.

He stood and straightened himself, smoothing the front of his coat, patting his pockets. "Shall we go?"

Jo closed the gap between them and cradled his stubbled jaw in the cup of her hands. She kissed him, open-mouthed and anxious. Thoughts of kissing in the cathedral pinpricked her conscience, but she wasn't answering to anyone in that moment. It was her cathedral after all. Mary murmured something about leaving them alone and disappeared.

A summer bower of slender trees and blooming vines grew around them, hiding them from the snow still falling thickly outside and from whomever could see them standing among the trees in her version of this cathedral. Jo laid them down on a bed of thick moss. Goodbye sex for a god. She'd made her decision. It would break her, again, but the whole world was standing on the other track.

———

Faron stood close to the window and watched the sky for the first signs of dawn. Their mobile phones were all dead, and who still wore a watch when they carried a computer in their pocket? The clock in Vesna's office had stopped when the electricity went out. There was only observable time left, and even to someone like him, who could feel the days that stretched out ahead of him into infinity, that night seemed to last several lifetimes.

Ivanka joined him in his vigil and slid her arm around his waist as the sky began to change in the square patch they could see framed by the terra cotta roof tiles of the building.

"I thought I'd lost you." He pulled Ivanka closer to him and kissed the top of her head.

"I saw it. Saw that Vesna and I were going to die."

"Why didn't you tell me?" He said it as much to the glass in front of them as to her.

"I didn't know how. And what was that your mother said about trying to outthink fate?" She shrugged under the weight of his arm.

"I wouldn't have let you go. Even though you said before—"

"I know what I said before. And I meant it then. But I wasn't ready for this life to be over."

He nodded. It wasn't just him she wanted to stick around for. Her sisters needed her too.

"How are we going to do this?" She pulled away enough to look him in the face.

"Do what?" He had no idea how their lives would play out from here if they all made it through closing the Veil again. Could they stay here as she aged and he didn't?

"Close the Veil. Bettine hasn't exactly been chatty about it, and Minerva and Achelous act like we all know what we're doing."

He smiled with relief. "I don't know, but I think mom and Dušan have to be there to do it."

Ivanka nodded and laid her head on his shoulder. The dark pre-dawn blue outside slowly gave way to a strange lavender-hued gold.

"It's the solstice today." Vesna came up behind them.

"Is that important?" Ivanka turned to look at her.

"Maybe? I read through my grandfather's book with Fand. She said to her people the Veil thins between the worlds at Samhain, the last harvest, until solstice when the light is reborn. I don't believe in coincidences anymore."

A heavy knock disturbed the silence after Vesna's pronouncement.

Someone else had come to them looking for shelter. At least they'd survived the night. Faron slid from Ivanka's embrace and went outside to see who it was.

They knocked again.

"Hello?" Faron called through the door. There was still the possibility that it was someone or something they didn't want to let in.

"Yes. Is that Vesna? It's Alessandro the Observer from Venice. I am with Paolo, the Venetian Witchfinder."

Faron opened the door to let the two men inside. They looked exhausted.

"How did you get here?" Faron wasn't sure which was Alessandro and which was Paolo.

The two men seemed to understand his confusion and introduced themselves more formally with handshakes.

Paolo, the younger one, answered his question. "It doesn't matter. Do you have the sword?"

The three men looked up at the sound of roof tiles cracking

above them. Silhouettes of the four dragons from the *Zmajski most* perched on the edges of the roof line, peering down into the courtyard. A couple tiles broke away and crashed onto the cobbles near them.

Faron pushed the two men ahead of him. "Let's go inside."

CHAPTER 29

"It's here. I'm sure of it." Dušan watched as Jo stood with her hands on her hips and looked down the long promenade that led to the Tivoli Castle. The park had settled back into its modern layout, but she couldn't remember which bench Morana had rested on when she'd laid down the sword.

Dušan walked a few paces away to look under a bench hidden by the bare branches of a hedge that needed to be trimmed back. He returned and presented the sword to her with an exaggerated bow.

She took it from the platter of his outstretched palms and secured it around her waist. He watched as she adjusted the scabbard's belt so it didn't ride against her hipbone and bloused up Morana's black velvet cloak over it so it didn't drag behind her.

"You seem awfully keen to undo all of this." Jo cocked her eyebrow at him and moved her hand in a circle next to her face to indicate the changed park and everything that lay beyond it.

He wasn't surprised she was skeptical. He couldn't say himself why this felt like the right course of action. He could almost hear Rebecca Wiley's voice in his head. *You know exactly why.* Jo stared up at him in his god form. Once they'd left the cathedral, he'd been unable to maintain his human disguise, but she seemed unbothered by the change.

He leaned down and kissed her again. His Jo. No. Not his. Only Jo. But so much more than that too. He saw now that it was her fire he had truly missed, what he had needed. She tasted of vanilla, the scent of carefully cultivated and cured seedpods of tropical orchids, but for him it was the scent of the bakery she had conjured with her friends as a place of safety. The world could burn for all he cared. She was returned to him, and she wouldn't stay if he didn't put things back the way she wanted them, or thought she wanted them.

"I am not keen, as you say, to return the world to its dulled state, but I will do it for you."

She still didn't believe him. He could see it in her face. He had the long life of gods to convince her. He could thank Morana for that, wherever she had gone. It was also Morana's doing that he still couldn't read Jo's thoughts beyond her expressive face.

They walked together in silence toward the Church in the Marshes. The city had not come to life with its usual morning routines. The citizens who had survived the night weren't eager to see what was left. How would they explain it to themselves when Jo closed the Veil again and righted their world? Mass delirium? Space weather? He looked forward to the mental contortions the papers would be filled with in the coming days.

They made good time and reached the church as the top slice of the sun showed above the horizon. It was the solstice.

He'd almost forgotten. Sad the few believers he had would probably not venture out that day to honor the light.

The priest who had met them in their transformed state after opening the Veil stood at the bottom of the long steps leading up to the entrance and the strange façade that had protected the thin place in the membrane between the worlds.

"Have you devils returned to finish the job?" The man looked haggard after what surely had been a night of terrors. He clutched a crucifix in one hand and his Bible in the other. Dušan was glad to see someone with so much fire in his belly. His belief had protected him and this place.

Jo approached him. "We've come to close the Veil again. To set things right."

"Witch! How dare you approach the house of God." The priest stood to his full height and blocked her way.

"I will totally cop to being a witch. But I can assure you that your God is good with what needs to be done. Let me go do what I came to do." Jo's words calmed the man, but he didn't back down or move out of her way.

Dušan stepped up to intervene, but Jo put her hand out to stop him.

"Let me show you." Jo clasped her hand over the man's that held the crucifix.

He fell to his knees in the fine gravel and turned his face to the sky, his eyes shut tightly. His lips moved in silent prayer, and he waved Jo on.

Jo walked past him and climbed the steps to stand below the small set of stairs on the façade, right above the main entrance to the church. Črnobog had helped her up there before, but she didn't need his assistance now. She looked up, and he watched as her feet left the ground, toes scraping against the stones before she was fully airborne, and floated to the landing. He was reminded of how so many of the old gods had become saints, or—in his case—demons, of the new religion. *Saint Jo.* He smiled to himself at the thought.

Taking the steps two at a time, she was to the door in an instant and held the sword aloft. The morning sun glinted on the blade as she dropped it through. He waited for the winds that would signal the Unseen returning to their secreted place, but there was nothing.

She turned to look at him, still waiting at the base of the long steps, the priest crying and praying on his knees in the dust next to him.

Why had they failed? She had the sword. The Veil had been opened here. What was missing? Was it too late? Panic, something he had only ever had the briefest understanding of when he was playing at human, crept into the edge of his thoughts. She would never forgive him if this couldn't be undone.

Jo flew to him, touching down as softly as if she had taken the last stone step down to him.

"I saw the first closing of the Veil. We need the others. Charlemagne's witches cast the shroud. They used the power held in the sword, but the sword can't seal it alone." Her eyes were dark again with Morana's power. Blackened veins snaked out from the sockets, but it was still Jo's face, still her body and her voice.

And there was more to her vision, he could sense it, but

she didn't share it. Whatever it was pained her. He couldn't lose her again. He wouldn't allow that to happen.

"We have to go to the teahouse." She pulled the priest up onto his feet. "We might need you."

He wavered and Črnobog thought he would fall again, but he steadied himself. "I can't help you."

Jo smiled mostly to herself. "It's all the same magic, just wearing different clothes."

CHAPTER 30

The city had settled mostly back to its present-day layout. There were gaps though. A few open plots lay between the tightly packed buildings closer to the central area. Other things were just gone, like landmark statues and in one case a whole block that had been broken up into separate offices and buildings had reverted to what looked like a pre-World War II warehouse. Jo looked around and wondered if it would stay like this if they closed the Veil. When we close the Veil. Humans were so good at adapting to and explaining away things that were too difficult to sort through, but how would everyone be able to move on past this? The city was changed, people had been killed. Closing the Veil wasn't going to sweep all that under the rug.

She could sense a few creatures of the darkness still lurking in shadows. They were biding their time until the sun set again. Disappointing them would be its own pleasure. Črnobog—it would be easier to complete her task if she didn't think of him as Dušan—chatted with the priest as they walked. The man's name was Peter, like the saint, though Črnobog addressed him as Father. Jo thought the three of them must have been a strange sight to anyone peeking out onto the street as the day progressed. A witch, a priest, and the devil walk into a city … she hadn't figured out the punchline yet.

They had made it to French Revolution Square. She was happy to see that the version of Križanke the city had settled on was the one with crimson Virginia creeper sweeping above the green-patinaed bronze doors to the roof line. The vines should be bare this close to Christmas, but she smiled up at the red leaves as if they were a personal welcome back to the city. The teahouse was only a couple minutes' walk from there, and the trio were soon standing in *Zajčeva ulica* staring at the arched doors of Number 2.

A bubble of fear crept up into Jo's throat. She had believed Mary and Dušan when they had told her that Vesna and Ivanka had survived Morana's wrath, but Jo couldn't help wondering what damage that resurrection had caused. Her own had conveyed immortality on her and Faron. Could either woman forgive her if she had brought the same sentence on them? And that only accounted for the damage she had personally done. There had been many other things marauding during the previous night.

Jo wrapped her fingers around the cold handle and depressed the latch with her thumb expecting resistance, but the door opened with only a stutter as the corner of the wood rubbed across the cobblestones of the courtyard. The well was still there, with its magical covering keeping the crawling things of the earth at bay. A shower of pottery dust fell between her and the door to the teahouse. She looked up to find four dragons, statutes come to life, shifting for position, their claws finding purchase in the eaves. She, Črnobog, and Father Peter were fish in a barrel for a bunch of hungry dragons, but none of the creatures made an effort.

The teahouse door opened, and Jo found herself face to face with Vesna.

"You came back." Vesna looked relieved more than angry.

Jo nodded, taking a moment to find words. There weren't words in English or Slovenian that could convey the apology needed for murdering her best friend. They would have to figure that out later. She went back to the problem at hand. "I can't close it back by myself. I tried."

None of them were capable of fixing this alone. Their lives, and their deaths, were all inextricably linked and had dragged them to this moment together—and they would continue in a tangle beyond this time, even as some of those shorter threads fell away. Jo could see the cords spinning out into the future, but she didn't want to follow them. Knowing the future couldn't interfere with what she had to do now.

The others spilled out behind Vesna into the courtyard. Gregor and Janez, Fred and Reka, Milo looking much healthier and less bruised, Achelous in his verdigris god form, Minerva in her bright robes, Faron and Ivanka holding hands, Ivanka's sisters—Veronika and Ana, and their Aunt Olga, Bettine whom Jo had seen earlier when peering through Morana's eyes, her many greats grandmother Rebecca, and a few faces she didn't know. Vesna introduced them as Otto, a member of the Board, and Paolo and Alessandro, the Witchfinder and Observer from Venice. Goran was missing, she barely had to let her senses into the surface of Gregor's thoughts to know why.

There were enough of them to close the Veil. They weren't all witches, but surely having a few gods in the mix would make up for those who couldn't do magic.

"Where did you open the Veil?" Bettine shouldered her way to the front of the gathering and planted herself in front of Jo.

"At St. Michael's in the Marshes. But I couldn't close it there." She unsheathed the sword and held it in front of her, hands wrapped around the hilt and the tip resting between two cobblestones.

Minerva gave Bettine the best side-eye dismissal Jo had ever seen. "It doesn't matter where you close it. The Council didn't close it there. They met in France." The goddess cocked her eyebrow. "You should know that, considering you were there."

Every face in the courtyard turned toward Bettine. She didn't have the good sense to back down. "We don't have to go back to that church, but it needs to be a holy place, a sacred place."

"There's nothing holier than a well." Jo indicated the new fixture of their courtyard with a tip of Joyeuse's pommel toward the granite enclosure.

Bettine sputtered something about profaning the memory of Charlemagne and blah blah blah before Minerva told her to shut up. Clearly the goddess was over Bettine's bullshit.

"What do you want us to do?" Vesna took charge again, and Jo caught a glimpse of the new steely sparkle in her eyes for the first time. She realized the price her friend and Ivanka had paid for their resurrections. Jo had reverted permanently to her human, demigod form because after she had taken full control she had splintered the divinities within her among the three of them. She had made them the three sisters, a triple goddess. How the hell was she going to explain that?

Jo looked to Minerva and Achelous for guidance, but both gods deferred to her as if she had suddenly become the authority on ancient cloaking rituals. Bettine probably knew exactly what to do, but Jo wouldn't even consider asking for her assistance in that way. She was an unrepentant murderer and had Gustaf's and Vesna's mother's blood on her hands. Črnobog hadn't spoken since they'd entered the courtyard. He walked up next to her, his robes billowing out as he towered over everyone but the other two deities present.

"You have the sword, and you now have enough beings to back up your will." He started to step back again, but she clutched his hand. She wanted him close as much as she needed him close for the end. She'd be joining Bettine officially in that family of murderers soon enough.

As she'd done several times since learning she was a Voice and Portal, and apparently more, she quieted her thoughts long enough to know what needed to be done. There was a distinct difference between thinking and knowing, and right then she needed to know. With Črnobog's hand held tightly in hers she went to that quiet place, the walled garden at the center of her understanding, and waited for the answer.

———

"Circle around the well. We need to concentrate on this point." Jo was dealing with several folks who had no clue about magic but were all smart, capable people. "Imagine a stage and the curtains closing at the end." *And then for an encore, I'm going to have to sacrifice Dušan to keep them closed.* A ring of barbed wire tightened itself around her heart. She would carry his death on her conscience until the last implosion of the universe finally took her thoughts away.

Even when she tried to blame him fully for this situation and therefore his own coming death, she remembered that he had planned it all with Morana, some earlier version of her.

Their circle of gods and humans, and several beings in between, pushed out to the edges of the courtyard. Vesna stood on Jo's right with Ivanka next to her. Ivanka's eyes carried the same glinting flecks of silver, and Morana's power flowed through the three of them when they joined hands to step out and organize the circle. Jo could see the golden thread connecting the three sisters. Morana's prophetic words rang in Jo's thoughts, another piece she had carried this whole time sliding into place. They were uniting the witches, but they would still have to be hidden.

Minerva stood across from Jo. Fred had taken up the spot next to the goddess and held Reka's hand. A fleeting thought of what a strange family that made flitted through Jo's thoughts. The others fanned out around the well, though Jo noticed Minerva had made sure to have Bettine on her other side and held the woman's hand whether she wanted it held or not. By the sour expression on her face, Jo guessed not. She looked up at the dragons waiting quietly above them. Either they had a part to play or they were waiting to pick the bones of the dead if this backfired or failed. She couldn't imagine them sticking around when the folks below them had every intention of returning them to statues on the bridge otherwise.

Jo dropped Vesna's and Črnobog's hands and unsheathed Joyeuse again. In the circle, the blade glowed with the blue light of magic. Vesna raised her arms, the palms of her hands facing the well. The others followed. No one spoke, but everyone seemed to be following a script. A low hum started in Jo's chest and was picked up by the others, and she watched as a gossamer column of the same blue light flickered and climbed toward the dragons' perch and into the sky above the courtyard.

She raised Joyeuse aloft, the pommel pointed up, and felt it pulse with power as the column stabilized and strengthened. The tone of the hum changed, and the magic tightened in her chest. The pitch continued to crescendo, and as it reached its peak, Jo thrust the blade of the sword down through the membrane over the well. The gauzy layer of magic crystalized and exploded outward, knocking everyone back and down except Jo. The column began to rotate and quickly swirled into an azure tornado of light sucking everything down into the depths of the well. The wind roared in Jo's ears and tried to pull her in with the demons and ghouls and tattered bits of buildings and bodies swirling into the darkness below them. The roar filled her head and she felt as if her eardrums would burst as the whirlwind continued.

The four dragons lifted off and flew around above the whirlwind before lighting off to return to their watches on the bridge. As protectors of the city, they had been waiting to make certain Jo did her job. After what seemed like hours but had been only minutes, the funnel collapsed into the well, and a new cover of shimmering magic ringed with glyphs and symbols Jo knew only from some ancient part of herself sealed the opening. The slightest exertion was like moving underwater, but she had to find Črnobog. She had to complete the spell.

Turning to look for him, she found it was Dušan waiting and looking all too human in his usual black suit and crisp, white shirt. Jo stopped cold. She couldn't do it. All those people, the whole world waiting on the other set of tracks while she hesitated. Not making a decision was still making a decision. She didn't have time to stop to figure everything out. She had to know.

Morana's voice rose up inside her. *Are you the Queen of the fucking witches or not?*

Jo pulled the blade of the sword across her own palm, reddening the steel from midway to the point. Making her own small sacrifice was a Hail Mary in the truest sense. She reached out for Dušan's shoulder with her bloodied hand and drove the sword through his gut. She held his gaze unbroken, attempting to communicate everything that she felt and wanted in those moments before the light went out of his eyes and he slid to the ground at her feet. She stood over him and pulled the blade free. The others were forgotten around her as she dragged his body to the well and watched it slip into the In-between with a ripple across the glowing seal. She sank to her knees, the sword Joyeuse forgotten on the cobblestones where she'd run Dušan through.

She caught movement toward her in her periphery and heard Ivanka's voice yell "Bettine" in her head. Before she could fully react, Vesna picked up the sword and held it out, catching Bettine under the ribcage as the woman ran toward them with the blue lightning of magic crackling between her palms. Ivanka had seen Bettine's intent to kill them all in her own sacrifice, starting with Jo. Ivanka had shared her vision with her sisters with a thought. Vesna stumbled back with the pressure of Bettine impaling herself on Joyeuse. Jo couldn't see Vesna's face, but Bettine's visage quickly shifted from murderous intent to relief and even happiness before she crumpled next to the well.

Vesna sat down hard on the cobblestones and reached out for Jo's hand, the other still gripping the sword trapped under Bettine's body. "I didn't mean to … she was going to kill you."

Jo nodded and squeezed Vesna's fingers. Telling Vesna then that Bettine's magic couldn't touch the three of them would have only fed her friend's guilt over taking a life. And if nothing else, she had saved Jo from having someone else's blood on her hands and Bettine's rage would have turned to the others less able to protect themselves.

Morana's presence made herself known again in Jo's thoughts. There wasn't a voice but the feeling that Morana was at peace, her revenge delivered appropriately on the one person there who had made it her business to persecute witches.

CHAPTER 31

There were bodies to bury. Not just in their enclave but across Ljubljana. The power came on, and lights and appliances and clocks jangled back to life—giving the city back the modern hum of power and vehicles. The storm and the deaths had to be explained by governments. The churches, mosques, and synagogues of Europe swelled with new attendees, as did the ranks of believers in the old Gods of this continent and in the traditions of places beyond in the months that followed. The world hadn't been reenchanted as Dušan had wanted, but for every single person who brushed aside the Solstice Storm—as it had been named in the press—as some bizarre natural disaster, there were a score who had seen deep into the In-Between and knew the world wasn't comprised only of what could be touched. The resurgent interest in the spiritual and supernatural was heralded as a worldwide Great Awakening.

For the people who had been at the center of the storm, things righted themselves slowly. Goran's ashes were scattered in the forest where he had taken Ivanka and her sisters to teach them about herbs and the spirits of the land. Bettine's body was returned to Paris to be buried in the secret graveyard of the Board, established when it was still the Council led by Charlemagne himself. There had been arguments about not allowing her to be interred in sacred ground, but Jo and Vesna were clear that too many witches had suffered that last indignity. Bettine had been a murderer and more and had earned retribution, but it wouldn't come in the form of any of the old punishments used against witches or heretics.

Alessandro assumed control of the Board and offered Otto the choice of execution or exile for his role as Bettine's accomplice. He chose exile, perhaps to his own surprise, and flew off to somewhere in North America to disappear into the wilderness, his demons still on his heels. After that order of business, Alessandro dissolved the Board and turned over the archive of the order to Vesna.

Vesna had expected chaos as the old school Witchfinders and Observers across Europe jockeyed for position and power without the stranglehold of the Board. Some secrets were hard to keep even for those again tasked with keeping the supernatural hidden, and word that witches had closed the Veil spread quickly through the networks. There were a few holdouts, but with Vesna's leadership and Alessandro and Paolo's assistance, almost all of the former ghost sheriffs—as Jo had once imagined them—rallied around Vesna's new program of protection rather than persecution to form the combined Guild of former Observers and Witchfinders. Jo would have liked to believe it was the beginning of some halcyon era, but humans were still involved so schisms and bullshit were still bound to occur.

While those big pieces were shifting into place, the smaller tectonics of the lives of those humans, gods, and shades who had closed the Veil again caused their own upheavals and eruptions.

Though Fred, Reka, Gregor, and Janez had come to the teahouse to shelter from the supernatural, they'd had had no part in it previously aside from knowing it was real. They learned quickly afterward that no mundane could be that close to as much magic as they had raised to save the world and not be affected. Janez took it the hardest and left Ljubljana to ponder on an existence where ghosts were real and he could accidentally light a fire with the snap of his fingers or a stray angry thought. Gregor let him go, as gracefully as Gregor could, but Janez's absence left Jo's friend with a heaviness only masked by busyness. His busyness also kept his new visions at bay.

Jo's own heartbreak at having sacrificed Dušan strengthened her connection to Gregor. He was by her side handling the everyday logistics as she set about hiding them all fully from the mundane world. The well was now a place of power and a vulnerable point of the newly laid Veil. It had to be protected, which meant *Zajčeva ulica* needed to disappear from the city's and the world's maps.

While Jo worked with Minerva and Achelous to ward the entire street so no mundane could see or find it, Gregor quietly bought up the buildings and made sure there were no records or deeds to trace them. It wasn't that hard to make a whole street disappear in a city that had been permanently altered while the Veil was open. Julija never returned to her window frame to be gazed upon creepily by Prešeren's statute in the square, and as far as anyone knew, Renegade Tea and *Zajčeva ulica* had disappeared the same night.

Gregor moved into a flat in the building next door and set up an office on the ground floor for a holding company that would handle any legalities their new sanctuary might encounter. One of the first things Jo had him do was transfer ownership of Renegade Tea to Fred and Reka. They had both decided to stay, and Vesna and Jo, along with Gregor and his silent partner share, had decided the business should go to them.

Thankfully neither of them had the misfortune of becoming a fire starter or a seer, but they were both still getting used to the aftereffects—Fred called it the backwash—of magic. So far Reka had learned she could see auras, and Fred had developed a very strong sense of psychoscopy. It was strong enough that he had to wear gloves except when he was cooking, or he would accidentally learn things about people they didn't want to share.

Minerva, or Minnie as she preferred to be called, decided to relocate to Ljubljana, so an apartment was set up for her as well. Fred was smitten and happier than he'd been in all the time Jo had known him.

Olga moved into another flat next door with Veronika and Ana. Minnie took it upon herself to sort their educations, since returning to school wasn't the best option. Everyone could come and go as they pleased, but a child with a nonexistent address registering for school would be difficult. Milo offered to be Ana's spirit guide since she had lost hers when Breda crossed over into the next with Goran, but Olga had balked at a grown man stepping into that role. That left Milo, a shade now clearly visible while in the vicinity of the well, with not much to occupy his time.

Reka, as the new manager and owner, hired him to work at the teahouse, which had gotten much busier much faster than any of them had expected. Renegade Tea couldn't be found in any tourist guides or located on a map, but word spread to those who lived with the secret of the Veil, and their punk rock teahouse quickly became a gathering place for shades and magic users, members of Vesna's Guild, and even the occasional well-behaved lycanthrope. Ivanka and Faron opened the Renegade Inn in the building across the street, and soon *Zajčeva ulica* was a coveted address for the supernaturally inclined of Europe and a vacation spot or waypoint for the truly odd traveler.

Rok took off again to roam the world as he had done before. He and Jo would most likely end up as friends with benefits again, but rebuilding trust between them would take time, something they both had a lot of.

That new abundance of time was more difficult for others to cope with.

CHAPTER 32

Jo pulled an apron off the peg next to Reka's office. Reka and Fred were already at work prepping for the day. Fridays were always busy. They didn't have an open mic anymore, but Reka always managed to book a band for the night. Jo hadn't been that surprised at the number of supernatural beings and magic users who moonlighted as musicians.

The prep list was taped to the reach-in cooler door, and Fred had marked the items with the initial of who was responsible. His neatly printed J was next to "brownies" and "set tea specials." Jo's thoughts drifted briefly to Milo, whom she had left in her bed upstairs since he didn't have to be at work until noon. Neither of them slept much, but he did like to linger. A sated smile found its way to her lips.

"You look happy this morning." Fred teased her. She could have easily pointed out that he had his own happy sex glow these days, but she just shrugged and tied her apron on.

Was she happy? Momentarily yes. She could enjoy a romp with Milo and was enjoying the flirty game she and Achelous were playing. They were too much alike to ever make a real go of it though. Besides, he had actually known her since she was a kid, and she found that a little weird if she thought about it too long. There was a witch who kept visiting from Dubrovnik and asking if Jo was in when she came to the teahouse for breakfast. Jo was open to seeing where that would go. It was all just sex, though she and Milo had good conversations and could enjoy each other's company. Funny how death takes the pressure off of figuring out what you are to each other.

She and Gregor were thick as thieves as they figured out the day to day of Renegade Holdings, but it was much harder to navigate her relationship with Faron and, by extension, Ivanka. No amount of tearful apologies changed the fact that Morana's actions through her embodiment in Jo had forever altered Vesna and Ivanka's lives and tied the three of them together. Rebecca, with her Death hat on, had confirmed their new statuses as what she described as semi-immortal. They had each taken on aspects of Morana or the Goddess Vesna when Jo resurrected them.

"Don't go there with that triple goddess, maiden, mother, and crone bullshit with me." Minnie had been quick to squash Jo's modern interpretation of what had happened. "Women, and goddesses especially, are not defined by some patriarchal assessment of their proximity to a dick. The triple goddess are sisters. Morana knew what the hell she was talking about." And that had put paid to any further discussion about their new roles in Minerva's presence. "You'll figure out how it all works eventually" had been Minnie's final comment on it.

Jo pulled the *mise* for brownies and started weighing out flour. And that "eventually" part was the problem. Faron was contending with having watched his mother murder his father—surprise! family trauma visits the second generation—and the fact that the struggle he'd been having with his girlfriend's mortality had now been replaced with the fact that she could live as long as he would. Faron wasn't ignoring his mother, but he wasn't exactly coming to her for advice. The distance was palpable and painful.

Ivanka seemed almost relieved but didn't exactly gush about it. She instead followed Faron's lead in interacting with Jo, though the occasional stray thought filtered through. For the past couple of weeks, their exchanges had been almost entirely about the inn and rooms for patients at Dr. Struna's clinic, which had moved onto *Zajčeva ulica*. Vesna had convinced her that Faron would come around. He had a lot to process.

There was a lot to process for everyone, but she missed her son. *Time.* They all had a lot of it, and, as Minnie had said, they'd figure it out. Jo had to keep reminding herself. Not everything could sort itself out over a couple of bottles of very good wine and an ugly cry.

That conversation had taken her weeks to get to, but Vesna had waited quietly until Jo was ready to stop tiptoeing around her and crawl up into the corner of that leather monstrosity of a couch and spill her guts. It had taken over an hour for Jo to retell everything that had happened in the Nav and while her body had been hijacked by Morana. Jo had held it together right up to the part where she'd put a sword through her ex-lover's belly. Vesna had bridged the chasm Jo had imagined opening between them and had forgiven her immediately. They uncorked a second bottle of wine, and Vesna filled her in on what she had learned from Fand on the Isle of Man. Vesna understood things about what had happened that Jo hadn't even realized. The elasticity of friendship wasn't something she would ever take for granted again.

The last of the chocolate chunks and walnuts disappeared into the thick batter, and Jo scraped it out onto a floured sheet pan to bake. She set the timer and washed her hands before drawing a line through her first task on the list. Now to the tea specials.

"Who's playing tonight?" Not that she matched the tea to the musicians, but she wanted to make sure whatever she picked they had a good stock of.

"Theremin guy." Reka shrugged. "Liar's Knot and Hat Pin Panic aren't back from their tour until the end of the month."

Jo nodded and untied her apron, which now bore a huge smear of chocolate across the front. She balled it up and tossed it into the hamper inside the office door. Before poking through the tea canisters on the shelf, she prodded the shop iPod to life and spun through the playlists. Milo had given her shit for the never-ending loop of Leonard Cohen she'd been filling her flat with, but his bard sensibilities helped her mourn and figure things out, like why her Hail Mary with Dusan had failed. Nick Cave. Brooding but not dirge-y. She hit shuffle on the playlist, and "Nobody's Baby Now" flooded the shop with a layer of her externalized feelings.

After jotting down some teas and setting up a few pots so they'd be ready when they opened, she propped herself against the prep station bar and surveyed the teahouse. Reka and Fred had updated the furniture. It had been looking pretty shabby. Igor's ship mural was still emblazoned along the wall they shared with Dušan's gallery. Jo bit her lip. She was going to have to deal with that eventually. Their real estate had become too precious to leave it as some kind of shrine to a dead god.

No time like the present.

"Can you take the brownies out when the timer goes off?" She stuck her head back into the kitchen. "I'm going to go next door and—"

Fred waved her off. "Go do what you need to do." He caught her eye before she turned and nodded at her, acknowledging that he understood exactly where she was going and why.

She had to run upstairs to get the key. Milo was gone and the bed was made. A quick rummage in the kitchen drawer produced a tarnished bronze-colored key tied on a red ribbon.

Back in the courtyard, Jo paused in front of the door. No one had been in since Zala, the assistant Dušan had apparently hired to look after the gallery in his absence the previous year, had tracked Gregor down to check on a mold problem. Leave it to Dušan to hire a rusalka with a penchant for photography and cleanliness to run his gallery. Jo slid the key in, thinking of the conversation she'd had with Dušan when he'd showed her the space the first time. He'd kissed her, and she'd pushed him away. He'd rented it not long after she and Faron had moved into the flat upstairs, just to keep an eye on them, or so he'd said.

Inside, the gallery smelled slightly antiseptic, a holdover from the mold treatment, but it also smelled like petrichor and woodsmoke, like the scent of Dušan's magic had woven its way into the walls and floorboards. The photographs that had lined the ledges were stacked in a wooden crate on the desk at the back. She left the key in the lock but pushed the door closed behind her. Someone, probably Zala, had tied a string of bells onto the handle, and they chimed against each other as the door latched.

The box held mostly landscapes and a few photographs of buildings that were hard to place. The black and white images of steel and sheets of glass could have been New York or Hong Kong for all she knew. The last picture looked like a landscape, but the print was fuzzy like it had been made from a damaged negative. She started to put it back in the box but pulled it out again when she saw the smudge in the corner. The smudge was a tattoo. It wasn't a landscape. It was her, and the blurry mark was the shitty rose tattoo she had done on her hip before she'd left Chattanooga to find her fortune in India.

She sat on the edge of the desk and stared at the image. *When did he take this?*

The bells on the front door rang. She continued to look at the photograph, thinking it was Fred or Reka to let her know they needed her back in the kitchen. They could wait another minute or two.

"I like that one."

Dušan Črnigad stood in front of her looking entirely too pleased with himself.

"Does this make us even?" He reached out for her free hand and brushed his thumb over the scar on her palm where she'd sliced herself with the sword.

Jo smirked at him and laid the photograph on the desk next to her. "We've known each other too long to keep score."

LOOKING FOR MORE FROM VICTORIA?

The complete *Voices of the Dead* series is available now from 1000 Volt Press.

Who by Water - Voices of the Dead: Book One

Our Lady of the Various Sorrows - Voices of the Dead: Book Two

Like A Pale Moon - Voices of the Dead: Book Three

Sign up for the Notes from the Dead Letter Office at victoriaraschke.com for information about upcoming book releases, author events, and an exclusive *Voices of the Dead* short.

ABOUT THE AUTHOR

Victoria Raschke writes books that start with questions like "what if you didn't find out you were the chosen one until you were in your forties?" When she isn't holed up in her favorite coffee house to write, she can be found at the nearest farmers' market checking out the weird vegetables or at her home where she lives with a changing number of cats and her family who supports both her writing and her culinary experimentation — for the most part. Her first book, *Who by Water*, was published in 2017.